$\mathcal{V}$OICES OF THE $\mathcal{S}$OUTH

Almost Innocent

ALSO BY SHEILA BOSWORTH

Slow Poison

Almost Innocent

by Sheila Bosworth

Louisiana State University Press   Baton Rouge and London

Library of Congress Cataloging-in-Publication Data
Bosworth, Shelia
   Almost Innocent.
   I. Title.
PS3552.O815A5   1984   813´.54   84-14164
ISBN 0-8071-2066-9 (pbk.)

I gratefully acknowledge permission from the Times Picayune
Publishing Corporation, New Orleans, to excerpt from the
article by Meigs O. Frost on the Sacred Heart Convent in
St. James Parish, Louisiana; and permission to reprint lines
from "It's Raining" by Naomi Neville, © 1962 UNART
MUSIC CORPORATION, rights assigned to CBS
CATALOGUE PARTNERSHIP, all rights controlled and
administered by CBS UNART CATALOG INC. All rights
reserved. International copyright secured. Used by permission.

For A. E. Hotchner, and for Constance

AUTHOR'S NOTE

My thanks to my editor, Morgan Entrekin, for his talent, his dedication, and his unfailing gift for sustaining a writer's courage.

Sheila Bosworth
New Orleans, Summer 1984

ONE

He who is penitent is almost innocent.

—Seneca

1

I saw my father yesterday. He was downtown in a short-sleeved shirt and khaki pants, coming from a new dentist probably. My father dresses down for the dentist, to keep his bill at a poor man's level. It usually works for two or three appointments, then he slips and says something like "I wrecked that back filling on a deep-fried ball bearing the Louisiana Club was passing off as an oyster." And the next bill he gets, sure enough, that particular dentist has upped his fee considerably. The funny part is, my father probably makes less a year than the waiters at the Louisiana Club. All he can really count on is the closetful of expensive, wrong-size suits my Great-Uncle Baby Brother left to him, along with a lifetime, dues-and-fees-paid membership to that club, which is an old-line Mardi Gras organization. He also has his meager dividends from some La Dolce Vita sugar stock. Uncle Baby Brother—who was his mother's change-of-life child and bad luck from the word go—willed everything else, his entire self-made sugar fortune, to the Home for the Incurables on Henry Clay Avenue, where his wife Ida Marie had died in the 1950s of a progressive genetic disease. The rumor was, she was strapped into an indoor hammock at the time, watching *The Big Payoff* on Channel 6, just as happy as if she'd had her right senses.

My father shouted "Clay-Lee!" and caught up with me on the Canal Street neutral ground, after nearly sacrificing his life, he said, sidestepping a turning St. Charles streetcar. My mind was elsewhere, I told him. "I've just been over to that real-estate office, that Latter and Blum, for the hundred and tenth time. Another buyer for the Bogue Falaya property fell through. Nobody's got the money for a summer house right now."

"Rosehue could be a year-round house," said Daddy, looking hurt, although he knows as well as I do the place is ready to fall in on itself. I only said "summer house" instead of "wreck" to spare his feelings. He was proud of Rosehue; he painted the inside of it almost single-handedly, one summer many years ago. The house is in the town of Covington, on the Bogue Falaya River, just across Lake Pontchartrain from New Orleans. Once it was my favorite place to be, but my father never set foot in it again after he moved his clothes and things out, several months after my mother died.

"This house belongs to you, Clay-Lee. It's entirely yours," he told me then, dragging a loaded clothes tree across the porch. He was crying at the time, and had apparently forgotten I was only eleven years old.

"Mama would have wanted us to stay!" I begged him, not so sure of that; I'd never known exactly what my mother wanted, but what was the alternative? Spending all year round in our alleyway-shrouded, half-a-double house on Camp Street in New Orleans, where most of the sunlight shone through the windows on the rented-out side? It wasn't until after I finished Sophie Newcomb College of Tulane University, B.A., scholarship, in English literature, that I moved to Covington again by myself. That was years ago, and the daily drive across the lake to teach an eight o'clock class and then back home, seems, at times, to be too much for me. I put the house on the market again, late last spring.

Standing on the darkening neutral ground, my father asked

me to have dinner with him; I knew by that it must be dividend day.

"I'm driving back to Covington tonight," I said. "So why don't we just go around the corner to Felix's and eat some oysters?" A pneumonia-weather wind was coming up and when I looked at my father's thin, half-covered arms, my knees shook.

"I can do better than that!" said Daddy. "We'll stop by St. Peter Street for my coat and tie, and then walk up for an early dinner at Galatoire's."

So we went down Bourbon Street together, past Galatoire's near the dust-blowing corner of Iberville Street, all the way to St. Peter and back again to Galatoire's. By then I wasn't even hungry. My father's little wooden house always saddens me, with its river damp, and unfinished canvases, and all the unopened mail. The unopened mail frightens me. I wish I had some good news to write to him.

At Galatoire's we were taken right away—it was still early for the dinner crowd—to a table near the little bar where the waiters mix the patrons' drinks. "Mr. Rand, Miss Clay-Lee," said Vallon, his thin face smiling at us atop the black tie of his waiter's tuxedo. "What can I bring you?" Vallon is old now, almost eighty. He used to give my father's father red beans and rice in one of the upstairs rooms, generations ago.

As I leaned back in my chair I saw several women looking at Daddy and at me, wondering, I guess, what our connection was. Because our coloring's so different, strangers never take us for parent and child. I have brown hair, like my mother had, but none of her beauty, and my father has the kind of blond good looks that don't betray his age unless the room is lit from overhead. I'd have settled for looking like either of them. Sis Honorine, who still cooks for me in Covington, told me I had the promise of becoming a beauty till about the time my mother passed away. I remember feeling beautiful just once, when I was about ten years old. My father was angry with my mother, a rare state for him, over a little sailboat, a Rainbow, that she had committed herself to buy and that he couldn't pay for. Uncle Baby Brother had to bail him out, of course, and then my uncle made my mother a present of the boat. I was delighted, and kept running my hands over the glossy colored photograph of it that Mama had placed on her little oak lady's desk. Daddy took the photograph away from me and put it on the top shelf of the bookcase. "Clay-Lee," he said, his gentle hand on my head, "on the night you graduate from Sacred Heart, I'm going to buy you a white convertible to match your dress, and we'll drive up St. Charles Avenue, the two of us. We'll leave your mother standing at the curb." To my knowledge, she didn't hear him tell me that. It didn't matter, as things turned out, if she had heard. My father spent my graduation night "not himself" in a bar on Napoleon Avenue, a block from the ceremony, and my mother had by then been dead a long time, past caring who left whom at the curb.

At our corner table with its good white cloth and heavy silver, I had a Ramos gin fizz and my father a Jack Daniel's. While I drank, I looked into the mirrored wall opposite my chair and picked out familiar faces in the early dinner crowd. Just behind us was the only son, middle-aged now, of a prominent coffee-importing family. He's in the process of dying from anorexia nervosa, that self-starvation ailment supposedly restricted to affluent young girls, but I guess nobody's passed the word along to Roger Addison, Jr., that he doesn't qualify for the disease. There he sat, enjoying his entrée, a double portion of cracked ice. At another table I saw the sad, olive-toned face of a woman who is the second wife of a third-generation heart surgeon. She met her future husband one night five years ago, while handing out menus at Brennan's, and as of two years ago she holds the current title of first woman to survive a leap from the Huey P. Long Bridge. ("Not crazy enough, you see, to leap with her coat on," Sis Honorine told me when it happened. Sis's brother Orville was a member of the bridge police. "Folded it up on the front seat of the car. Sealskin. Wouldn't wrap herself up in nothin' less, that one." Sis had been baby nurse to the first Mrs. Heart Surgeon's infants, and remained bitterly loyal.)

At a table for four with his elegantly dressed sister-in-law was a noncrazy, a famous writer who lived in Covington. I suddenly remembered that when we were twelve years old the writer's older daughter and I had planned to petition the pope for early entrance to the Carmelites, a religious order famous for its romantic iron grilles and nervous breakdowns among the novices. I caught myself smiling at nobody in the mirrored wall, and stopped.

"You can smile. I'll let you," said my father. "How do matters stand among the nontenured at Sophie Newcomb College?" He was already on his second Jack Daniel's and was saying a few words just to be polite. Daddy is a painter, a good one, and has always faded away during dinners; I like to think he retreats to some intricate new canvas in his mind. When I was a child and there was a noisy group at the table, my Uncle Baby Brother and my mother's cousins and aunts, all talking at once, he never had any idea what the conversation was about. If my mother tried to pull him in with a "What do you think about that, Rand?" he was likely to look up and answer, "Well, yes and no."

I looked at him now and saw the yellowness in the whites of his eyes. The sight of it gave me a sick, startling rush, like being retold without warning bad news I had managed to forget. I thought of Uncle Baby Brother on his deathbed, many years past, his face yellow as an old squash. Daddy had coerced me into visiting him, no doubt in the expectation I'd be remembered in Uncle Baby's will. I could've set him straight on that score, all right, and spared him one more terrible surprise. I didn't, though. The setting straight would've cost us both too much. . . .

Uncle Baby's bedroom. The perpetual gloom, ceiling fan noises, and the mahogany four-poster with a sunburst canopy in eggshell damask, the tucked and swirling design that made me sick to look at the time I broke my ankle skating on the hilly sidewalk in front of Uncle Baby's house. It made me sick to look at Uncle Baby, too.

"Your father's getting to be a drunk, same as me," he was saying. Tremendous revelation. "Lucky for you. In a few years he won't be able to find his way home to his turpentine-stinking hole in the Quarter, much less haul himself across the lake to bother you."

"What do I have in Covington to be bothered, Uncle Baby? Easy-crying infants and a husband who needs his peace?" Shutters banging someplace, and a smell of boiled brisket and vegetable soup.

"Don't try to stop him drinking," continued Uncle Baby. Who are you to warn me? I was thinking. "If you stop and consider, he's entitled. Then again, I don't have to tell you not to interfere. You've always known how to let nature take its course." I pretended not to hear, not to hear, not to hear.

"I declare, but Rand's impossible, at that," came Aunt Mathilde's unconcerned drawl from some gloomy corner of the bedroom. She apparently felt compelled to sit there all the time, as if it had been she instead of my mother who was related to my uncle by marriage. "Was he drinking last New Year's Open House when he referred to your poor little step-cousin as the whore of Mount Holyoke?"

Uncle Baby gave a rattling gasp intended to be a laugh.

"Couldn't forgive Cousin Megan, goddamn him, for wearing that gold ankle-bracelet and going on so proud about her Yankee women's college. Goddamn it, she is a Yankee woman! What was she supposed to've done, gone and pledged Kappa Delta at Ole Miss?"

Another terrible gasp-laugh; this one brought Leatrice, the Negro factotum, in from the kitchen with a forbidden cigarette still in her lips and brisket grease on her apron. He laughed a lot, my Uncle Baby. Laughed the whole time he was writing out his will that made life sweet for the Incurables. You don't

have to be strapped into a hammock to be an Incurable, was Sis
Honorine's remark. Bitterly loyal. . . .

"Cousin Courtenay was in town; she telephoned me yesterday," I said to Daddy. "She told me she looked in on you at St.
Peter Street last Sunday afternoon, but you were sleeping like a
little log." "Passed out" floated overhead, unspoken, on the scents
of Trout Marguery and a more distant rum sauce. He looked up,
back for a moment from the invisible canvas. "Don't hold it
against me," he said, and smiled. He's got no right anymore to
a smile like that. It's the smile of a young man, a man with his
life ahead of him still, full of pleasure and expectation. The way
he was when he first knew my mother, Constance, when the beginning of their life together must have seemed to him un-
matched for reckless sentiment, and for love.

She was Constance Blaise Alexander, Queen of Comus, the
most magnificent of the Carnival balls, on the night they fell in
love. Just eighteen years old, her debut pushed ahead one year so
that her father, Louisiana State Supreme Court Justice Thomas
Alexander, whose health was failing (and whose wife had failed
altogether and was buried in St. Louis Cemetery No. One),
could be there to see his baby on her night. The photographs
show a fine-boned beauty, her brown hair shoulder-length, dark
against the silver collar of her robe. James Rand Calvert was a
Comus duke that night, one of the privileged horsemen, masked
and velvet-cloaked, who rode in the flambeaux-lit street parade
before the ball. The floats stopped as always in front of the
draped and purple-billowing balcony of the Pickwick Club, so
that Comus could toast his Queen where she awaited him. As
Constance leaned forward to greet her consort, Rand Calvert, far
below, defied tradition by throwing aside his mask to see her face
more clearly.

Unfortunately, it was apparent almost from the start that Judge Alexander didn't think much of the match.

"What's his future?" he shouted repeatedly to Constance.

Daddy says he can see him yet, propped up stiff as a corpse in an old leather wing chair in his study, clenching his fists and flinging off the restraining arm of Skinner, his manservant. "What's his future, I asked you? The whole goddamned bunch of 'em's either an artist or a cellist! A cellist, for Christ's sake!" (The Calverts, with the exception of Uncle Baby, were long on name but short on money, a condition common among certain New Orleanians since General "Beast" Butler came to town and confiscated the household silver of the Confederate aristocracy. Worse yet, to the Judge's way of thinking, the Calverts were politically liberal, and they were "artistic.") And so Mama's daddy continued to cry out and go on till his face darkened, and Skinner had to half-carry him to bed. The Judge was worried, as Mama told it, that no one could take care of her like he had. She was small, delicate, her lungs unsuited to the Louisiana dampness. Why, her father had taken one look at her, when she was just three hours old, and called her "Lamb."

When she married Rand Calvert, Constance brought with her to her new husband's house only a few of the Alexander treasures. The old, elaborately carved cypress four-poster that had belonged to her mother, Solange Mallard, a bed so high on its legs you needed a footstool to climb onto it, its headboard scarred with hairpin scratches where generations of Mallard ladies had rested against it. The circa 1780 rosewood secretary with the scent of an exotic, persistent perfume in its secret drawer. The Woodward oil portrait of Constance's father, its canvas cracked from decades of exposure to New Orleans heat and damp.

Tommy Alexander's last birthday present to his daughter had been a purebred, Russian wolfhound puppy, which she named Mishka; Mishka, too, went with Constance to the new place of residence on Camp Street. (Mishka would eventually become Constance's close companion, her protector. I see Constance so often in my memory now with Mishka at her side, Mishka's watchful eyes following her mistress's every movement, as if my mother were a child left in her care. I envied Mishka; I longed to learn the secret ways that would make my mother's white fingers touch my hair in conspiratorial affection, as they did that regal dog's.)

With Mishka in Constance's arms, the newlyweds went to live in Rand Calvert's half of the two-story, two-family, frame house he owned on Camp Street, a shabby old house on a shabby block, the place that would become my first home.

The waiter, Vallon, had brought our appetizers. I could see my father wasn't interested in his; he was waltzing his Crabmeat Maison around on his plate with his fork, while he gazed off in the direction of another table somewhere behind me. Suddenly he leaned forward in his chair.

"On our way out, I want you to glance at the last table near the door, and look at what's left of Phil Harris," he said in an undertone. "Remember when your cousins took you to see Phil Harris perform at the Blueroom, for your birthday? What were you then, nine? God Jesus, baby, then how old does that make Phil Harris now?"

"I would guess about two years younger than you."

"Very funny. I don't believe you're even concerned about poor old Phil Harris. You've got that 'don't bother me' look you were fortunate enough to have inherited from your father."

"I was thinking about Mama, about how she was before I was born."

He sat back again in his chair.

"It's too bad you couldn't have known her, Clay-Lee, the way she was then."

"But, Daddy, I feel as if I do, I do know her the way she was then. The way she was even before that, before she married you."

"How can that be? Don't tell me they're finally paying you

something over at Tulane, and you've gone to the expense of hiring yourself a medium." He shook his head sadly. "The next thing I know, you'll be riding around in taxicabs."

"I didn't need to hire a medium, I just asked Felicity to talk with me about Mama. You're forgetting all those Friday-night dinners I had with Felicity."

"You're right. I forgot about Felicity for a minute." He added gallantly, "Possibly the only man in the State of Louisiana who knew Felicity and ever forgot her, even for a minute. . . . Felicity, God bless her."

He picked up his glass, saw that it was empty, and signaled again to Vallon, with his eyes.

TWO

You ain't born in the South unless you're a fool.
—Lillian Hellman, *The Little Foxes*

1

Long before I was born, my mother had a friend she had known since childhood: her cousin, Felicity Léger.

A white-blond, olive-skinned beauty with the great, dark eyes of her maternal great-grandmother, who was descended from Spanish royalty, Felicity was a dangerous combination of guts and guile. Tales of her bewitching magnetism, her pitiless heart, ran rife among a certain segment of New Orleans' population. Felicity Léger had trifled with the affections of a brilliant Jewish medical student, wrecked his studies, and robbed him of his future; she had worn underpants fashioned from a Rebel flag to a childhood friend's coming-out party, lifted her skirt, and shown them to the orchestra leader, whose band then burst into the most rousing rendition of "I Wish I Was in Dixie" ever heard at the Southern Yacht Club; she had promised to marry Caffery Scott, a Virginia millionaire, in a ceremony under the dueling oak at the New Orleans Country Club, and then announced her engagement to his widowed father, Edward, instead; Edward dropped dead on the train from Roanoke to New Orleans, with a five-carat diamond ring engraved "EC to FL" in his waistcoat pocket.

Just when everybody had turned their backs on her, Felicity did possibly the only thing in the world that could make them forgive her: one sleety New Year's Eve, she got into a near-fatal automobile accident with a Tulane law senior from Shreveport who couldn't hold his liquor. The story ran that she had begged him to let her drive, and he refused; that the speedometer was frozen at 95 when the little Triumph finally cut a lamppost in two at Calliope and St. Charles; that the son of a bitch from Shreveport had walked away with barely a scratch; that Felicity herself had been so badly cut, lost so much blood, that the first witnesses on the scene thought she was wearing a scarlet gown.

She came out of it with a pronounced limp and an ethereal look in her eyes, a combination that made the most hardhearted bachelors in New Orleans (and several married men) want to protect her from further harm. Then, one autumn, an unscheduled event occurred, which would prevent her from reigning as Queen of Carnival. On the October night of her formal presentation at the Pickwick Club, she discovered she was unable to fasten the waist of her ballgown. Within three weeks, Miss Léger got herself married to a young doctor from the Mississippi delta, named Airey de la Corde, and seven months after her wedding day, she gave birth to a daughter, christened Courtenay, who, luckily, had the savoir vivre to grow up resembling nobody but her mother.

During the last months of Felicity's life, I spent a great many hours with her. By then, her husband was dead, her daughters had married and moved far away from New Orleans, and Felicity, chronically ill and prematurely old, was as thankful for my company as I was for the kind of emotional exorcism which her talk of my mother effected in me. On the first Friday evening of each month, I would go to Felicity's elegant little house on Harmony Street, at the edge of the Garden District, and we would have dinner together: artichokes and oysters when they were in season, or pompano en papillote, baked with crabmeat and white wine, and we would talk about Constance Calvert till Felicity had drunk all of the Calvados in one of her crystal decanters.

Then I would call to her old servant, Viola, and together Viola and I would help Felicity to bed.

Because my mother had never been inclined to reminisce with me, and my father only rarely, it was through listening to Felicity that I was finally able to conjure up certain visions of the past, of events that had preceded—and ultimately resulted in—the beginning of my own life.

"You knew, Clay-Lee, that I was half in love with Constance for most of her life?" Felicity began at the first of those Friday dinners.

The soup course that night was crab bisque with sherry; I remember spilling some of it on the tablecloth as I answered no to Felicity's question.

Felicity went on: "I recall my heart going like a jackhammer one night as I watched her walk into a dinner party, late and unescorted, the summer she was seventeen. The lamplight in the room brought out the gold streaks in her hair, and she was wearing pleated, white linen trousers and a wine-colored silk waistcoat she'd found in a boys' clothing store on Magazine Street. Nothing under the waistcoat but her suntan. Every other woman in the room suddenly looked like they'd been dressed in pastel rompers by their mamas. As stunning as she was, though, she was frail; she made people want to take her in their arms.

"It wasn't just the way she looked that was appealing, although, God knows, it was a pleasure to look at her, wasn't it? The deep-set blue eyes, the small, square chin, and there must have been an Irishman somewhere in her father's family—remember her long Irish upper lip, her fair Celtic skin?

"She looked as easy to love as a docile child, but she wasn't. When you loved Constance, you paid heavily, because the desire to care for her became almost a compulsion. You see, Clay-Lee, a great part of Constance's strength lay in others' presumption of her weakness; it was their presumption that allowed Constance to command them, the way a beloved child will command an entire family through its needs and expectations."

Felicity reached out, tilted one of the silver candlesticks toward her, and lit a cigarette with the candle's sputtering flame. "I don't know exactly what went wrong in the end, though. Maybe, toward the end, Constance's expectations got out of hand, and then—"

"You're getting ahead of the story," I pointed out, as Viola brought in the main course. "Go back to the beginning, Felicity."

2

Felicity said:

The beginning was the Twelfth Night of Christmas, the night Constance was born during a rare Louisiana snowfall. That also happened to be the opening date of the Mardi Gras season, and the obstetrician, who'd been called to the hospital from Municipal Auditorium, where he was taking part in a Carnival ball, performed a drunken Cesarean delivery with his satin costume showing beneath his surgical gown. That part of the story was a family legend, and so was Solange Alexander's hospital bed vow to dress her daughter in only blue or white till she was five years old, as a sign of thanksgiving to the Mother of God for the child's existence.

Constance's father was sixty years old at the time of her birth, and Solange, her mother, was thirty and had a history of heart trouble; three miscarriages and one full-term pregnancy followed by a surgical delivery didn't do her any good, but the family consensus was that she never could say no to Thomas Alexander, and he had his sights set on a baby.

Solange's crippled heart finally gave out the summer Constance was six months old. She died at home, sitting up in bed, nursing her child. Sis Honorine found them a few minutes after it happened—poor little Constance rooting at the breast of her mother's corpse.

With Solange gone and the Judge half out of his mind for quite a while after it happened, Constance spent a lot of time with her Léger relatives—which partially explains why she became as close to her cousin as she might have been to a sister.

Constance had a peculiar childhood in some respects.

When she was about four years old, for example, her daddy began to take her around with him to his favorite bars on Friday afternoons. One of the places they were partial to was the old, no-women-allowed Sazerac bar, on Carondelet and Gravier, down in the central business district.

Dressed to kill in one of her handmade, lace-trimmed, blue-for-the-Mother-of-God dresses, Constance would be lifted by her father onto the bar, where the bartender would station two old-fashioned glasses within her reach. One glass was filled with Maraschino cherries, the other with pimento-stuffed green olives; the barman liked to boast that the baby had never been known to get sick on the combination.

Among the bar's regulars was a worldly old Dutch priest who was locally notorious as "the Sazerac Chaplain." While the Sazerac Chaplain told tales of World War I, or of the life stories of the sad, lovely show girls at a Berlin nightclub called the Chez Paree, Constance would nod over her ginger beer and eventually collapse against her father's shirt front, like a wilted, blue and white boutonniere.

Felicity smiled as she uncorked the wine, and went on:

My own mother used to give Uncle Tommy hell for taking Constance to a "barroom," as she called it. I remembered being in the front hall one night when Tommy came to deposit his only daughter at our house for another long weekend.

"What's the latest draw for the baby down at the Sazerac? A mug full of pistachio nuts?" said Mother.

"No, but what have you got against pistachio nuts?" said Uncle Tommy. "I've never known a child to get into trouble eating pistachio nuts."

"Me, neither," said my father. "Not if you discount the possibility of a series of mild convulsions."

"Now you're wrong there, Frank," said Uncle Tommy. "You're contradicting your wife. Your wife tells me convulsions in children are a direct result of ice-cream cones mixed with Ferris wheel rides."

"I don't need you to help me go crazy, Tommy," said Mother. "I'm doing fine at it on my own. Now give me Constance, and go on home." Then she looked more closely at her brother. "Was it raining downtown? Have you had this baby out in a rainstorm? You've got water all over your hat!" She took Constance and felt the top of her head for dampness.

"It was only raining in the men's room at the Sazerac," said Uncle Tommy. "A drunk splashed water on my hat while he was reviving himself at a washbasin."

"I don't believe you," said Mother, narrowing her eyes at him. "You had her out in the rain, and she's prone to bronchitis! You know what's the matter with you, Tommy?"

"Is this multiple-choice?"

"You think you're Jesus Christ when you're with this little girl, and you take all sorts of chances with her, because nothing can possibly happen to her as long as you're around. Why, you'd break my neck if *I* ever took her out in the rain!"

Uncle Tommy stood there, rainwater dripping from his hat onto the hardwood floor.

"Oh, go on home, Tommy," Mother sighed, "before you catch pneumonia yourself. Have Skinner help you into a hot tub."

"Skinner? Skinner is purging crawfish. Skinner is helping a hundred and ten pounds of live crawfish into a hot tub. Been at it all day. By the way, am I giving a crawfish boil tonight?"

"You'd better get Skinner to purge you, along with the crawfish," said my father. "The New Orleans Bar Association is meeting at your house at seven o'clock."

"Beedle lum bum bum, put a nickel in the drum, buy a War baby," sang out Constance.

"Listen to that," said Uncle Tommy. "Just like the Sazerac Chaplain. She's picked up a pretty good Dutch accent, too, don't you all think?"

By the time Felicity had talked long enough to get Constance up to the age of reason, seven years old or so, she was eyeing the decanter on the sideboard. That was my signal to try to keep her talking as long as possible, before she started in on the evening's more serious drinking.

I said, "Just listen to Viola, she's been calling curses at the dessert soufflé for the last twenty minutes. I can hear her right through the swinging door. You want me to ring for her to bring it?"

"Ain't going to be no soufflé now, not unless you two want to suck it up through a straw," yelled Viola, from way out in the kitchen.

"Long ears," complained Felicity. "Now where was I? I was still telling, wasn't I?"

"Go on and keep telling, Felicity. 'Years went by,' " I suggested.

Felicity continued:

Years went by, and Uncle Tommy Alexander continued to indulge in eccentric behavior.

He took as his mistress a chinless redhead from Tangipahoa Parish, and kept her in a permanent suite at the Monteleone Hotel. He got into the habit of betting heavily on several entries in each race out at the Fairgrounds. And he was creating in Constance a dangerously dependent attachment to himself, the way he spent most of his free time with her, catering to her childish desires.

A good example of that went on every February 14 for several years running, when he'd put Constance and her favorite cousin in the backseat of his big black Packard and drive us all over the city of New Orleans on a hunt for the perfect Valentine.

Constance would wait in the car while the Judge went into each candy store and selected the biggest, most elaborately wrapped heart-shaped box in the place, which he then brought out and presented for her approval.

"This one's big enough, Daddy, but it's purple instead of red," Constance would say. Or, "Doesn't this box of candy smell like violets to you, Cousin Felicity? I'll bet there are violet perfume candies in this box, the same kind that made the barman at the Sazerac sick last Valentine's."

"We'll drive down to Russell Stover's, where I know all the salesgirls," Tommy would promise. "The salesgirls there will let me tear open the cellophane wrapping, and you can give the candy the once-over before you say yes or no."

Everyone who knew Tommy Alexander criticized him for his indulgent behavior; they were so busy criticizing him, they seemed unaware that he had finally grown old. One Valentine's Day, while the Packard was parked in front of Refferty's Candies on Carrollton Avenue, Constance appeared to notice for the first time that when he spoke, the Judge's voice trembled, and there was a blind blue glaze over one of his eyes. With that year's winning candy box on her lap, she suddenly reached up to hug her daddy, and the smells of Tommy's pipe tobacco, and his rye whiskey, and the slightly sickening aroma of chocolate were all mixed up together inside the car.

Constance had a weak stomach as well as weak lungs, and she pressed her face against her father's sagging neck and asked him, "Am I going to vomit, Daddy?"

And the Judge—the oracle, the comforter—he never missed a beat.

"Not necessarily, sweetheart," he ruled.

•   •

The day after Felicity told me that Valentine story, she slid through the glass door of her bathroom shower and severed a tendon in one arm, and had to stay in bed for two weeks to recover from the loss of blood. The two weeks coincided with the Christmas holidays, and with Tulane closed I was able to spend several days and nights at Felicity's house, relieving Viola a little, and keeping Felicity from becoming too fretful. She seemed to forget the pain while she was telling stories, and it was during that time of Felicity's recuperation that I heard the dramatic account of my parents' courtship and marriage.

3

Sitting up in bed, one arm heavily bandaged, Felicity said:

One night during Christmas week of the year Constance was seventeen, she saw Rand Calvert for the first time. I was a guest at the Alexanders' house in the Garden District that December, because I had been recently injured in a freak accident—the overly muscled young starboard winch grinder on my father's racing sloop had jammed his elbow into my eye while engaging me in some carnal gymnastics. It became necessary to wear a black eyepatch for a while, and in order to avoid making awkward explanations to the general public, I went into seclusion at Constance's house.

Under any circumstances, it was a treat to visit the Alexanders. The house had been built in 1850 by the famous New Orleans architect, James Gallier, Sr., and it was all big square rooms with polished heart pine floors, beautifully furnished with English antiques. There were landscapes by George Inness in the dining room, several watercolors by Charles Alexandre Lesueur in the solarium, and a Degas in the first parlor. All through the rooms were the blending, alternating aromas of sachet-scented bed linens, hand-embroidered by French nuns at a convent in Vermilion Parish; of magnolias and camellias, floating in silver bowls in every room, each spring and summer; of pine logs

33

burning in the wide fireplaces in winter; of freshly baked biscuits and of French-drip coffee in the mornings, gumbos and baked hams and honey-basted plantains at dinnertime. The house had been run for years by Skinner, the Judge's manservant, and by Sis Honorine. Both French-blooded Negroes from upriver, near Pointe Coupée.

Felicity paused for a minute, to swallow what looked like a Percodan, then went on:

A few nights before Christmas, that season of my self-imposed exile, I went down the back stairs to the Alexanders' kitchen and put together a supper for myself, out of the party food that I found out on the counters. The Judge was hosting a small holiday gathering, and when Skinner and Sis, carrying trays of food, pushed open the swinging door between the kitchen and the dining room, Constance could be seen standing near the buffet table. She was talking to a brown-haired, brown-gowned woman whose lower face appeared to have caved in, as if she'd lost her teeth. "Smelled a rat in April," the woman said to Constance, in a loud, languid voice, and then the door swung shut again.

A little while later, Constance came into the kitchen. She had her dress on backward.

"Your dress is on backward," I said. "Oh, I see, you prefer the way the back of the dress is cut. Décolleté. Lucky for you your bosom is so small, you'd be scandalizing your father's guests."

"You're not supposed to drink whiskey on top of all that codeine you've been taking for your eye," said Constance.

"I haven't taken any codeine since this afternoon. Who was that brown lady you were talking to, the one who looks as if she's lost all her teeth? She seems familiar to me."

"That's Mimi Arden's mother. You were in Mimi's class at Sacred Heart, weren't you? And she hasn't lost her teeth, she's lost her husband. He left her."

"What happened?"

"I don't really know. I stopped listening after the part where she smelled a rat in April."

"I think I remember the rat. Mimi's fat-assed father, sure, I remember him. He used to wear Tyrolean hats in the winter time. God. Imagine having *him* bolt on you; no wonder her face fell in."

"Constance walked over and sat down at the table. Her eyes were startlingly blue against the white of her complexion.

"Somebody out there has on perfume that smells like a funeral arrangement," she said, closing her eyes for a few seconds. "I feel . . . greenish."

"You look greenish. You want some bourbon?"

"Not now. What if Daddy walks in and catches me? Daddy doesn't allow me to drink unless he pours."

"What would he say if he knew I'd taken you with me to all those places down in the Quarter last summer? I mean, now that you're too big to sit up on the bar and eat cherries."

Constance smiled. She had a lovely smile, but people rarely saw it. A formidable old nun had warned her at an impressionable age that only street peddlers and whores walked around grinning all the time.

"He'd probably tell me that if I don't stop drinking, I'll never be able to have a baby. That's what he told me last fall, when he wanted me to stop riding."

A few seconds of silence followed that remark. Then:

"Oh, come on, Constance, you know your daddy, he was just scared you'd break your neck, jumping the goddamn animals all the time, like you were doing."

"Sis thinks Daddy's had a stroke. Maybe more than one."

Another few seconds of silence.

"Well, shit, what does Sis know?"

"Everything," said Constance.

"Does Sis know he's still got a mistress, that chinless redhead? He can't be failing if he's still seeing the chinless redhead!"

"The toothless redhead is more like it. How old is she by now, a hundred and ten? Don't answer that. Because if she's a hundred and ten, then Daddy's a hundred and twenty. And I might as well tell you, Sis thinks he's been giving money, a lot of money, to that girl from Boston, that law student, who comes here to type his letters and his legal research papers. I don't mean her salary."

"What else makes you think he's had a stroke?"

"He undergoes snap personality changes, Felicity. Last Saturday, for one. He took me out to the Fairgrounds Club House for lunch because Willie Shoemaker was riding. We had a lovely afternoon together, but then by ten minutes after midnight the same night, I found him galloping up and down the front gallery like he was hearing polka music, just because I came home late from a party I'd been to with Walter Cheney. Daddy called Walter a degenerate."

"Don't worry, then, your father's definitely got all his buttons. There's an excellent chance Walter Cheney *is* a degenerate. Listen to this: I once saw him hanging around the Airline Highway Drive-In, all by himself."

"Felicity. Walter Cheney had a summer job at the Airline Highway Drive-In. He was hanging around by himself, all right, taking tickets at the entrance."

The swinging door pushed open and Sis Honorine walked into the kitchen.

In one movement she slid a tray of dirty glasses down her arm and onto the counter near the sink; with her other hand she untied her apron.

"I ain't said I'm quitting this family, Trouble, I said I'm quitting this here party," she said to Skinner, who was right behind her.

"Miss Sis, watch you don't say nothing you won't feel up to remembering you said later on," said Skinner. "My own rule always been, don't say nothing when anger got hold of you, or misery take over soon as the anger let up."

Sis looked at him.

"Now you can't be as big a fool as you make out to be, can you, Skinner? You just testing me, ain't that it?"

Skinner went over to the sink and began to chop up a block of ice.

"Going over the wall, Sis?" I said. "I wish you'd take me with you. I'm sick of sitting around here, half-blind."

Sis jerked her chin in the direction of the bottle of Jack Daniel's on the kitchen table.

"Keep on doing what you doing, the whiskey on top the codeine, and you not going to be going over no wall, nor no place else." She took a deep wicker basket from a shelf and threw some Irish potatoes into it from the potato bin under the sink.

"What are you doing with all those potatoes?" said Constance.

When Sis was upset, her eyelids moved rapidly up and down as if a cloud of irritating dust had blown over her face. "Cousin Julia Sawyer got some bad trouble by her house," she said. "I got to leave here now and take her these groceries. Judge Alexander say I'm to take whatever I want to take." Sis threw in some onions and apples and collard greens to jostle with the potatoes. "I ain't got time to cook those chickens," she said to Skinner. "Quit fooling with that pile of ice and get the chickens out the icebox for me! Put them in the basket, raw. I got to go find the Judge and get my carfare."

As soon as Sis was out of the kitchen, Skinner started talking. Skinner's record for keeping his mouth shut always had been poor.

"One of Judge Alex's party guests, Lawyer Harvey Whitehall, Jr.," Skinner said, talking fast, "he just got finished telling Sis that Julia's husband, James, got himself drag back of a sheriff truck, down the old Shell Road in Caritas Parish. Same sheriff got ahold of James's brother Sam. Sam up in the jail there now, and Mr. Whitehall, Jr., said Sam just sitting there, waiting for his turn to die."

"You got that basket fixed for me, Flap-Jaw?" said Sis, coming up from behind.

"Yes, indeed, here it is, ready to go," said Skinner loudly.

"Sis, let Felicity and me come with you?" said Constance, who must have sensed adventure somewhere in all this. "Wait for me to get our coats!"

"You not going with me. You got your chest all open in that dress; it's too cold out tonight for you."

"Yes, forty-six degrees," remarked Skinner pleasantly, heading toward the dining room with a bowl of cracked ice. "I expect Mr. Harvey Whitehall, Jr., going to come looking for the young ladies to go for a drive with him, in a short while. He already been asking me, where is Miss Lamb?"

Skinner knew as well as Sis did that Harvey Whitehall, Jr., had an open sports car, a drinking problem, and a yen for Constance Alexander.

Sis stood looking at the swinging door for a minute after it shut behind Skinner. Then she sighed and put the basket down on the counter.

"You two wait right here in this kitchen for me to get your coats. Julia Sawyer's house just over here near Washington Avenue, that's not but ten minutes away on the streetcar."

Julia Sawyer's house was ten minutes away by streetcar, and another ten minutes' walk after the streetcar went on; it was a half-dozen blocks down the lake side of Washington Avenue to Claiborne, where there were no streetcar tracks, and where the radio music from Negro barrooms was louder than the sound of tin garbage cans hitting the sidewalks in a high wind.

"Up ahead there, on the end of this sidewalk," said Sis. "The house with the half a stoop. One of you hit on the door hard so Julia can hear us. She going to be at the back, in her kitchen. That's where she got her coal heater."

Julia Sawyer was an Indian Negro, and she was visibly pregnant. She led the way to her kitchen through three dark rooms, damp-smelling and one behind the other; the house was a shotgun single, so-called because if you stood at the front door and fired a shotgun, the shell would travel in a straight line with no walls to block it, and exit through the back door. Julia's kitchen was lit by an amber-colored electric bulb that hung from the middle of the ceiling, and whose light threw the edges of the room into darkness.

"Cousin Julia, I'm sorry for your trouble," Sis began. While she spoke, a small black boy darted from the shadows in a corner of the room, pulled one of the chickens out of Sis's basket and began to tear it apart with his hands, cramming the raw chicken flesh and entrails into his mouth. Constance cried out and moved toward the boy, who turned and moved blindly away from her, bumped into the table, and turned back to collide with Constance. Blood from the chicken ran all onto Constance's white wool coat.

"James! Quit your running! She ain't going to take it from you!" called out Julia Sawyer in a high, sharp voice. "Turn loose of the chicken now; Nelson going to give you a piece of it when he finish cooking it. Nelson coming here tonight to cook it for you."

The child went over to the table and laid down the mutilated chicken. Sis took an apple from the basket and gave it to him, and he wandered off into the darkness.

"Julia, where is James now?" said Sis.

"James dead now. So all I got to worry about is James's brother, Sam. Sam probably busy at this minute shooting his mouth off up in the Caritas Parish jail, in line to get himself killed next." There was a lopsided wooden cradle next to the table. Julia went over to it and lifted out a little girl, two or three years old, a little girl who was too big to be lying in a cradle. The child was wearing a white flannel nightgown and she was wide awake. The bones in her small face stood out sharply in the amber light.

"Sister Honorine, my time is come," said Julia. "I'm fixing to leave my boy here with my half brother, Nelson. But my little girl I ask you to take back home with you, for the one night only."

"Take her back home? Now where is that?" said Sis. "You know I live on by Judge Alexander."

"We can take the little girl, Sis," said Constance. "Julia doesn't have to come get her tomorrow, we can keep her as long as you want."

Before Sis could say another word, Julia Sawyer sprinted across the room to Constance and put her daughter in Constance's arms. She wasn't moving like a woman in labor then, she was moving like a desperate mother.

Then Julia sat down at the kitchen table and held her hand open, the palm flat, while Sis taped a nickel and two pennies to it. Seven cents was carfare; if Julia lost it while she was at Charity Hospital, delivering her child, she and the new baby would miss out on a streetcar ride home.

"Sister Honorine," said Julia, when Sis had finished, "I thank you for your kindness, for these chickens, and for taking Naomi. . . . James, come out from the corner there and go let Nelson in. I hear him at the door, knocking."

"I don't hear no Nelson, Mother-dear," came James's frightened voice out of the darkness.

"He scary to pass through those front rooms by himself, in the dark," said Sis. "I'll go let Nelson in."

"I'll do it," said Julia. "I feel the pains less when I move my legs."

"Sis, if this Nelson isn't reliable enough to baby-sit for the little girl as well, then maybe we ought to take both of them, take the little boy home with us, too," said Constance, after Julia left the kitchen.

"Which one of us going to break it to the Judge we opening up a orphan asylum in his house?" said Sis. "And 'reliable' don't enter into the picture. Julia ain't counting on no man to act 'reliable' who got a female child alone in the same house with him, especially during drinking season. Not one of 'em. Not so long as they got that thing on 'em."

"Amen," I said.

Julia had returned to the kitchen. "Nelson on his way back here now," she said. She was carrying a length of chenille that looked like a remnant from an old bedspread, and she gave it to Constance to wrap around the child, Naomi. "Sis, I got a car ride to the Charity Hospital. A white gentleman who been trying to help us get Sam switched to a different jail, he out in front waiting. He says he willing to drive you and the young ladies home, too."

"Who you mean?" said Sis. "Mr. Calvert, that your mama worked for?"

"That's him," said Julia. "He gone out his way to act kind to Mama, and now to me."

"Do you mean Rand Calvert?" I said.

"Mr. Rand Calvert," repeated Julia. "His daddy was Mr. Leland Calvert, used to play the big fiddle with the symphony down at the Municipal Auditorium."

I turned to Constance. "Let's get out of here," I said. "Hurry! We can run down the alleyway!"

"Run down the alleyway?" said Constance. "Why on earth would I run down the alleyway? We've got a ride home! I'll be dead with cold by the time we walk all the way from here to the St. Charles streetcar!"

"I'm dead the minute Rand Calvert sees me in this eyepatch!"

"Then take off the damn eyepatch! You won't go blind if you take it off for a few minutes!"

"What do you think my eye looks like *under* the patch? It's all swollen and smeared with that grease!"

"Oh, what do you care if this Rand Calvert sees you? He's a perfect stranger!"

"No he's not! Don't you ever listen to me when I talk to you,

Constance? I've told you about Rand Calvert a hundred times!
I've had my eye on him since last spring, and this winter he
finally took me to three parties. I don't want him to see me looking like this."

"Too late now," said Sis. "Here come somebody got the Calvert hair."

The Calvert hair was dark blond and unruly, and there was
a great deal of it. And Rand Calvert, standing there in the
kitchen of a New Orleans tenement, had the kind of broad-
shouldered body and Nordic face that set off to perfection his
romantic hair.

"Come on, Julia, hurry," Rand said; "let's not push our luck
where my car is concerned. I can't swear to you it'll still be running in another five minutes."

Constance said later that at the sound of Rand's voice, a slow,
easy voice that implied a familiarity with all kinds of agreeable
things, she suddenly became embarrassed by the bloodstains on
her coat, and, still holding the little girl, she stepped back into
the shadows.

"Is that Felicity Léger standing over there?" said Rand. "You're
about the last person on earth I expected to see here."

He came closer.

"Well, God, honey, what have you done to yourself this time?
You have an injury to your eye!"

"Something got jammed in it," I said.

"I'm sorry to hear that, I surely am," said Rand, but he was
looking toward Constance's corner, where Naomi had begun to
cry. "It's very cold for you all in here, let's go on and get into the
car. We'll take Julia over to Charity Hospital and then get the
rest of you back home."

"No, I've got my own car, it's parked just around the corner,"
I lied. "I'll take Sis and my cousin home with me."

Sis started to protest, looked over at Constance and stopped.

"All right, then," said Rand Calvert. He turned to Julia. "Julia, there's a gentleman waiting for us out in my car who's been studying the law. He thinks he may have found a way to get Sam out of the Caritas Parish jail to one over in East Feliciana, before there's any more trouble. . . ." He looked over at Sis. "This fellow Nelson is out in front on the stoop, finishing his Coca-Cola, I guess it is; he says he'll be in directly to look after the little boy." He nodded in the general direction of Constance, said, "Ladies," and was gone.

"Shit," remarked Sis Honorine.

"Amen," said Constance.

Back in the Garden District, Judge Alexander's house was quiet and dark, except for a light in one of the first-floor windows. The Judge never stayed up late, worrying about Constance, when she was out with Sis Honorine. The only one who ever took better care of Lamb then Sis does, is gone to God, the Judge liked to say, thinking of Solange.

Inside the house, the smell of Skinner's freshly brewed coffee floated up the stairwell while Sis ran bathwater and took Naomi, who was snoring, out of Constance's arms. Sis brought to Constance's bedroom a tray of little sandwiches, smoked turkey, rare roast beef, and Virginia ham, plus a thermos of hot milk laced with honey and Kentucky bourbon, and a thermos of coffee. Constance came out of the bathroom wearing an embroidered white nightgown that looked like it belonged on a bride or a corpse, took a sandwich off the tray, and slid under the covers.

"I guess I'm supposed to just stand here in my soot-covered coat and rot," I said, from the foot of the bed.

"Sis went down to her room with the little girl," said Constance, "but there's enough food on this tray for both of us. I guess she's mad at you because you made us walk halfway home."

"Rand Calvert doesn't have a house like this one to walk home to," I said. I selected a sandwich and sat on the bed. "He lives in a dump over on Camp Street that he inherited from some old aunt of his. Right now he's probably eating a bowl of grits with his gloves on, so his fingers won't freeze to the spoon."

"Come on, Felicity, I've heard of the Calverts. That's cotton money."

"Yes, cotton money, once upon a time. You know that saying, one generation makes the money and the next generation spends it? Rand's not doing either one. The only Calvert left who's got any money is Rand's uncle. 'Uncle Baby Brother.' And he didn't inherit it. I think he stole it." I took a swallow of the milk, honey, and bourbon mixture. "Goddammit, why does Skinner have to bring everything to a rolling boil? He should have served this stuff in a caldron, so I'd have gotten some *hint* I was going to have my tongue sterilized."

"He's very good-looking, Rand Calvert," said Constance. "In spite of the fact that apparently he can't afford to buy an overcoat. Did you get a good look at those corduroy pants he was wearing? Beat up. And I think I saw a hole in one sleeve of his sweater."

"I thought you were hiding in the corner, in the dark, the whole time," I said.

"Well *he* wasn't hiding in a corner, in the dark, he was highly visible," said Constance.

"You know who Rand Calvert *is*, don't you?" I said. "In addition to being a rescuer of doomed Negroes? He's one of the people who was in that house down in the Quarter last summer, with crazy Dimity Yancey, the night Hunter Bell got himself killed."

Constance became as still as a cat. She'd been overly protected for so long, by her father and by Sis, that she was naturally spellbound by danger of any kind, even danger at secondhand.

I went on: "Now the way the newspapers told it, Hunter Bell just happened to be cleaning his pistol in the middle of the night and it went off accidentally and blew a hole the size of the Pass

Manchac swamp in his skull. That's when Dimity Yancey alerted the public by running out barefoot onto Burgundy Street at midnight, covered in blood and howling like a she-wolf."

"But what *really* happened?" prompted Constance in a half-whisper. She sounded mesmerized.

"What really happened is that Rand Calvert was renting that house, and Dimity was living there with him, the whole while she'd told her family she was attending the summer session at LSU, Baton Rouge.

"So Fourth of July night, while Rand and Dimity were giving a party, Hunter Bell, drunk, naturally, comes beating on their door with a thirty-eight, offering to assassinate Rand Calvert right there unless Dimity leaves the house with him, and never returns to it. Hunter had taken it into his head that Rand was responsible for Dimity's refusing to see him anymore, and, of course, Rand *was* responsible. 'You took what was mine!' Hunter kept shouting to Rand, waving the pistol around.

"Then somebody—nobody claims to remember who, but everybody in that house at the time *had* been drinking, separately or together, since noon—suggested Rand and Hunter end the impasse with a round of Russian roulette. And that's how Hunter Bell ended up killing himself. A Khachaturian toccata was playing on the phonograph while he did it—I forgot to mention that Rand Calvert is musically inclined; he plays the piano beautifully, himself."

"Why wasn't any of this in the newspaper?" said Constance. "I don't recall Rand Calvert's name even being mentioned."

"Oh, it was mentioned, but just offhand, as one of the witnesses to the 'accident,' same as Dimity's name and some names of the other guests were mentioned. And the reason for that is, Hunter Bell was the only son of the editor of the *Tuscaloosa Journal*. His daddy once won some kind of prize for journalism, and is a personal friend of the editor of the *New Orleans Item*."

Constance's eyes had turned a deeper blue, and the blood had darkened in her face. Right then she must have begun visualizing Rand Calvert as reckless and brave and wild, all the things the other young simpletons she knew weren't. Maybe somebody should have suggested to her that Rand was just a sexually appealing gentleman who preferred to fight his duels indoors and while seated, particularly after he'd been drinking all day, but she wouldn't have listened. After all those years as Daddy's little girl, it followed that Constance was ready for risk, or for what *she* saw as risk.

"How did *you* find out the real story?" Constance asked, just before I left her room to go to my own bed.

"How do you think?" I said. "From Dimity Yancey. She's my second cousin, and I'm the only one who ever bothers to visit her up there in Jackson, not counting the doctors on the staff."

I wanted to hear the rest of the story right away, of how Constance and Rand eventually got together, but I had to wait until the following day because Viola barged in and sent me to bed, and yelled after me that if Felicity died in the night from exhaustion, it was blood on my hands. The next morning, when I brought in her breakfast tray, Felicity grumbled that her sliced-up arm was hurting her, and that she hadn't slept well.

"It was all that talking I did, Clay-Lee," she complained. "I dreamed all night about Dimity Yancey, barefoot and yelling. Even in my sleep she wore me out."

"Right after you told Constance the Russian roulette story, did she make up her mind to have Rand Calvert?" I interrupted, trying to get Felicity's mind back on the track.

Felicity was prying the raisins out of her toast before eating it.

"Maybe she did, and maybe she didn't," she answered after a while. "Nobody was ever completely sure what was in Constance's mind; that was part of her appeal. But if I had to guess, I'd say she put the thought of Rand to the back of her brain for a year or so, till after I had married Airey de la Corde and become a mother, with a second baby on the way. Remember, I'd told Constance I was quite taken with Rand Calvert, and she was too loyal to me to have gone after him behind my back.

"So, as far as I know, the next time Constance saw Rand Calvert was more than a year after my Russian roulette story. It was the Mardi Gras night she was Queen of the Comus Ball."

4

Felicity began:

Your grandfather Alexander had been deathly ill with pneumonia for three weeks before Carnival, but Dr. Villere and Skinner had pulled him through it somehow, and there sat Judge Alexander at Municipal Auditorium the night of the ball, looking pale as a shroud, his eyes shining with tears as he watched Constance and whatever old gentleman was Comus that year circling the floor together. As it turned out, of course, he had more than enough reason to weep, but all that came out only after he died.

The Queen's Supper after the ball was held at the Alexanders' house. The backyard had been tented with green-and-white-striped canvas, but it was too cold that night for anyone to want to wander around outdoors. The result of the weather was that the supper guests were crowded three deep in front of the bars in the library and the second parlor, and you couldn't get to within five feet of Constance unless you happened to be her escort. The escort was Harry Lyle, a Tulane halfback who had shoulders that could knock you down; he was sticking like cane syrup to Constance, and blocking traffic to the powder room and the buffet table while he was at it. I eventually gave up trying to reach food, drink, or Constance's company, and slipped upstairs to lie down for a while in Constance's bedroom. I was three months' pregnant at the time and suffering intermittently from morning sickness, night and day.

I must have closed my eyes for a minute and gone to sleep, because the next thing I knew, Constance was lying next to me on the four-poster, in her Queen's dress that was stitched with seed pearls and bugle beads and must have weighed twice what she weighed. That Russian wolfhound puppy her father had recently given her was on top of her, snapping at the pearls on her skirt with its sharp little teeth.

"Are you crazy, Lamb?" I said. "You're letting that puppy eat your dress, at around five hundred dollars a bead."

"So what?" said Constance. "Daddy's giving the dress and mantle to the Cabildo museum tomorrow anyway, for a tax write-off. Felicity? Guess who's downstairs?"

"Harry Lyle, for one. How did you ever extricate yourself and get up here?"

"Rand Calvert's here, Felicity! Did you know he smokes a pipe? He said he recognized me tonight during the street parade, when he saw me on the balcony of the Pickwick Club. He told me at the ball that he's never forgotten me since that Christmastime a year ago, when we were at Julia Sawyer's house. He said, 'You're the little girl who was holding the crying child in your arms, down in the colored section. I remember thinking you have a face like Botticelli's *Madonna of the Magnificat.*' "

"He's surely got a way with words, hasn't he? Not to mention exceptional eyesight. Remember how dark it was at Julia's that night?"

"Felicity?"

"What?"

"I'm in love with him."

That announcement came as a shock. Up until then Constance had been about as impulsive as a professional chess player. "You'd better be careful," I warned her, "because he's going to want you to go to bed with him. None of this Catholic-boy reticence with the clammy hands. Remember that Rand Calvert's a good bit older than you are, and he's a Presbyterian. A Presbyterian's the next best thing, in bed, to a Jew."

Constance suddenly sat straight up, tumbling the puppy, Mishka, to the hem of her gown.

"Felicity, I don't even know him, but when I'm standing next to him, I keep hoping he'll touch me. All those stories the nuns at school told us about being good, all the guilt? It's as if I've suddenly forgotten it."

"Don't worry, it'll come back to you. Where were you with Rand? Every time I saw you downstairs, Harry Lyle had you in a half nelson."

Constance's mouth turned down suddenly at the corners.

"I'd managed to free myself from Harry for a quarter of an hour, and I was in the solarium with Rand, when Aunt Mathilde came crashing in with some wild-eyed blonde in a beat-up velvet gown. 'Here's a young lady who's been looking everywhere for Mr. Calvert,' she announces, and drags me off to find Harry while the girl in the velvet rags flies over to Rand like a vampire bat. I haven't seen Rand since, and I never saw that blonde before in my life. Who is she?"

"Did this girl have eyes that were too big for her face, and was she wearing the tiara from the night she was Queen of Proteus?"

"I guess so; she did have some rhinestone thing on her head. Why?"

"Dimity Yancey. I saw her when she came in. They must have let her out for Carnival."

Constance got off the bed and straightened her gown, looking worried and determined. She needn't have, though. Dimity Yancey was a knockout, in a scary sort of way, but she couldn't compare with Constance. Constance had the sort of beauty that would appeal to an artist like Rand Calvert, beauty that told you the first time you looked at her that her soul was as finely made as her face.

Downstairs, a string quartet played "Who's Sorry Now?" while

Harry Lyle, looking as brokenhearted as if he'd fumbled at the goal line in the last seconds of the Sugar Bowl, watched Constance maneuver Rand Calvert away from Dimity Yancey. And Rand helped her do it; he was staring at Lamb as if the two of them were alone in the house, although Dimity was commanding her own share of attention from the other guests, by attempting to engage poor Skinner in a waltz.

After that night, several months went by during which Constance would periodically report to me the progress of her love affair with Rand. By May she was spending entire nights at his house on Camp Street, telling her daddy she was staying over at my house with me and Airey. The Judge didn't like her seeing Rand—he didn't like her seeing anyone who made her look the way Rand Calvert made her look—but he didn't forbid her to do so till one awful day at the beginning of June, and by then it was too late.

I was over at the Alexanders', helping Constance with some household tasks that Sis Honorine and Skinner couldn't do. One of the tasks was polishing the Fiddle Thread flat silver, which was too much for Skinner's arthritis, and the other task was dusting the crystal chandelier in the dining room. You had to stand on the table to reach the prisms, and Sis was too heavy for the table to bear her weight. So Skinner hoisted Constance up, and she was dusting and I was polishing when Sis called Constance to the telephone.

"Your Aunt Mathilde says she wants to talk to you," called Sis from the kitchen.

"Tell her I'll call her back," said Constance. "Tell her I'm tap-dancing on the dining-room table, with the chandelier on my head." Constance had been as giddy as a bride for months, ever since she'd fallen in love with Rand.

Sis came into the dining room and stood there looking up at Constance.

"You better come on down now and talk with your auntie.

Your Aunt Mathilde's so upset she sound like she's fixing to fall out. She says your daddy ready to call the state police after Mr. Rand Calvert and have him thrown in the jail."

"Call the state police," repeated Constance, going completely white in the face, and clutching her dustrag to her bosom. Sis swung her down off the table.

I put the Fiddle Thread aside and went up to Constance's room to wait for the bad news. A few minutes later, Constance came in and began nervously rearranging some valuable old toys in the play cupboard, a corner cabinet that was set against one wall.

"Miss Marianne de Bardeleben's maid saw me outside Rand's house, picking up the newspaper, at seven o'clock in the morning one day last week, and Mrs. de Bardeleben rang up Aunt Mathilde and told her so," Constance began.

"So what?" I said. "Nobody can fault you for picking up a newspaper."

"But I was wearing Rand's bathrobe at the time. Mrs. de Bardeleben told Aunt Mathilde that, too."

"You just tell Aunt Mathilde that was your new spring coat. You've been known to have eccentric taste in clothes."

"Then the worst of it is, yesterday afternoon, on my way home from Rand's house, I stopped by to have tea with Aunt Mathilde while she was entertaining the Regina Coeli Mission Ladies, and I left a silk stocking case with a pair of my underwear in it, sitting on her sofa." Constance shut the door to the corner cupboard and sat down heavily in a rocker.

"It's not against the law as yet to tote your underwear around in a bag, is it?" I said.

"What about when there's a man's undershirt in the bag, too, and everything smells of either perfume or pipe tobacco?"

"Don't tell me Aunt Mathilde told all of this to your poor daddy! He's got a vascular condition!"

"Yes, well, he's not too sick to have put the puzzle pieces together. Aunt Mathilde said he's on his way home from his club now, probably to saw me in half, and you along with me."

"Me!"

"Oh, he knows you're in on it, all right. It was your house I told him I was spending the night in, remember, every time I was really over at Rand's. I told Daddy you were having marital troubles, and needed my advice."

"Jesus Christ. Look, Lamb, you go on and promise your daddy I *am* having marital troubles, if you think it'll make him feel any better. Meanwhile, though, bye-bye. Airey might be coming home early from his medical convention, and I've got to straighten up the house and bathe the baby, before he arrives."

"Felicity, if you move from this room, I'll set myself on fire! You know perfectly well Viola's in full control of your house and baby and always has been, and I need you to stay here with me and help me pacify Daddy!"

At that moment Uncle Tommy roared, "Constance!" up the stairwell in a voice that was suddenly as powerful as a man's thirty years his junior, and Lamb and I were compelled to face the music for the next thirty minutes in his library, with Skinner pretending to polish the outer knob on the French doors the whole while.

The Judge started off by saying that while the Calverts had once been a fine old family, the last two generations had gone to seed, running high to musically inclined bums, and that Rand Calvert had become a local disgrace; he had the artistic temperament, and was low on ambition, high on liberal politics.

"You want my opinion, the man's a goddamned Communist!" he yelled at one point. "In addition to that, he's an idler, with swamp gas in his blood!"

"Oh, Daddy, what's swamp gas?" said Constance, her voice trembling as if she were afraid to find out.

"It's something in the air around the city of New Orleans, like the summer heat! It gets into the blood and turns men like this Rand Calvert into people like Felicity's Uncle Max!"

"What's wrong with Uncle Max?" wept Constance, so upset now that she was losing her train of thought.

"That hasn't been determined!" shouted the Judge. "But maybe it's swamp gas in his system that's stopped him from stepping foot off his front porch for the last twenty years! Maybe it's swamp gas in young Calvert that prevents him from getting a job!"

"But he's a fine painter, Daddy, he's an artist—"

"I'll say this for Calvert," the Judge raved on: "at least he had sense enough to sneak around with you, Lamb. At least he had the brains not to come to me in his paint-splattered rags and say, 'Judge Alexander, let me take your daughter away from all this!' "

Constance went flying off up the stairs, crying, while her father yelled after her that if she ever saw Rand Calvert again, he'd take her off to live in Europe till she was an old lady. At that point, Skinner came in with a heart pill and led the Judge off to a downstairs bedroom.

When I tried to join Constance in her own bedroom, I found the door locked and the black cord from the hall telephone jammed over the threshold, so I went to one of the guest rooms and lay down till after dark, when Sis announced dinner by calling *"Madame est servie"* up the stairwell.

While this predinner lull in the storm was going on, Constance, as became clear later, was hysterically relating the events of the afternoon to Rand, over the telephone. As soon as he was able to make out what Constance was telling him, Rand took charge of the situation—for what may have been the last time in his life.

"We both know things have reached a point where we can't have your father forbidding me to come to your house," he said. "And this is not the moment for me to disregard reality and ask him for your hand."

"Are you saying we should listen to him? We shouldn't see each other anymore?" cried Constance. All she'd heard was the terrifying word "reality."

"I'm saying for you to put on a dress you wouldn't mind getting married in, and I'll pick you up on the corner of First and Prytania in twenty minutes."

Dinner that night was certainly no treat, with Constance's empty chair staring us in the face, and the Judge looking a hundred years old, his eyes drained and swollen from crying all afternoon. Aunt Mathilde had dropped by to ascertain the extent of the damage she'd done and she was the only one at the table who could swallow anything—she sat there eating *pommes frites* like she was deliberately attempting to put on several inches in the hips.

Finally, during dessert, the Judge rallied.

"Rum baba is Lamb's favorite thing on earth," he said sadly, breaking his portion into pieces with his fork.

"Felicity, you run upstairs and tell her to come join us."

So I ran up, and then I ran right back down. Constance's bedroom was empty, and all the dresser drawers and the armoire looked as if they'd been ransacked by a porch climber.

As soon as Aunt Mathilde heard that, she leaped up from her chair and cried, "What about her dog, is the dog missing too? Constance wouldn't have gone off without Hitler, she takes that dog everyplace!"

" 'Mishka,' " I said. "And Mishka's gone, too."

Aunt Mathilde clutched the edge of the table, looking melodramatic and put upon, as if Constance's departure wasn't mostly her doing. Then she said, "Lamb's run off with that Rand Calvert, of course. That innocent child!" She shook her head as if to clear it of unmaidenly visions. "Tommy, I'm going to get on the telephone right away and begin calling the hospitals and the morgue!"

"The morgue—that makes perfect sense," I said. "Rand Calvert goes to the trouble of running off with Constance, and then he kills her."

"Nobody asked you to comment!" said Aunt Mathilde. "You've got a drinking problem!"

"Sit down, Mathilde," said the Judge, sounding tired to death. "You know as well as I do that the places to call are every Wig-Wam Tourist Court from Mississippi to the Tennessee line, and I flatly forbid you to do that."

So there was nothing left to do except go to bed and wait for whatever catastrophes the following day would bring.

By the next morning, the long-distance telephone calls started coming in for Uncle Tommy, from concerned but smug-sounding justices in Louisiana, Mississippi, and Alabama, all along the tristate elopement route; men who'd recognized Constance's name and had refused to marry her to Rand, out of respect for Judge Alexander. It looked like Uncle Tommy's spirits started to pick up then; he must have thought Constance would become discouraged and return home, still as Miss Alexander.

Another night passed with no word from Lamb. By that time, the Judge looked so ill it would have been taking a chance to leave him in the house, for even a minute, by himself. Sis and Skinner were hiding out all day down at Our Lady of Guadalupe Mission Church on North Rampart Street, and Aunt Mathilde was no help; she was lying by the hour on the sofa in the front parlor with a wet rag on her head, as if *she* were the one who had a heart condition, till Uncle Tommy finally told her she was working on his nerves and to go on home.

Early the next morning, as if in a dream, I heard the Judge shouting and carrying on, but when I awoke it was quiet again, and there was Lamb. She was standing at the foot of the bed. She was dressed all in pink, a wide-brimmed, pretty hat dipping low over her forehead, and her eyes were the clear blue of aquamarines in the morning sunlight. She was too beautiful to be anything but a bride or a vision.

"Rand's downstairs," she said. "Daddy was a little upset earlier, but he's finally so glad to see us he's opening champagne, and Sis is fixing us a wedding breakfast. Get up, Felicity, and come kiss the bride and groom."

Her face was so highly colored, her voice so vibrant with restrained passion, that I must have made some wordless sound of envy and concern, because Constance came over to the bed and knelt beside it, her lovely face close to mine, and began to talk about why she'd done what she had.

"I wouldn't have hurt Daddy for the world," she said, "but when he told me I couldn't see Rand again—" She reached for my hand, and held it. "I can't live without Rand, Felicity. Ever since I've known him, even the sunlight looks different to me, brighter."

In the recent past Constance and I had done volunteer work at Hôtel Dieu hospital, and two categories of people there had confided to us they perceived the sunlight differently: the mental patients and the expectant mothers. There was a strong possibility that Rand Calvert had been playing a form of Russian roulette again. This time with Constance. Constance was saying, "Felicity, I hated leaving without telling you, but I'd involved you too much as it was, and then, too, to be honest, I didn't want you to know where I'd gone. I was afraid Daddy would work on you and get you to tell."

"But who finally married you? Uncle Tommy's phone was tied up all day yesterday, with circuit court judges calling here, swearing to your daddy they'd thrown you two out on the streets."

"Oh, we finally found a senile old justice of the peace in Selma, Alabama, who appeared to be on the verge of a mental collapse. . . ." Constance stood up and handed me my robe. "Felicity," she said, "we spent our wedding night in a country hotel, nothing but candles to light the bedroom. When I'm lying next to him, it's as if I can't get enough of him, of the way his hair smells, and the touch of his skin."

It seemed to me then that everything might turn out fine.

After all, they were so much in love, Rand and Constance—the looks on their faces that morning stilled even the Judge's tongue during the "wedding breakfast" Sis had prepared.

Constance had done her hair up in a loose knot on top of her head, and her dress was severely cut; it was from Madame Lanvin, Faubourg St. Honoré, but even so, the new Mrs. Calvert looked as frail as a child, and barely old enough to be charged the full price of admission at the movies.

Rand was dressed in a faded brown corduroy suit and a heavily starched white shirt, his hair wilder than ever, and he sat at the table next to his bride, looking at Lamb with a mixture of adoration and apprehension, as if she were a beautiful, unpredictable mirage that might suddenly disappear without telling him where she was going.

"Take more toast," he said to her at one point, and then to the Judge, "You'd never know it to look at her, but Lamb's a good little eater." He spoke as if it were Rand Calvert who'd cared for Constance all her life, and Thomas Alexander who was the interloper.

As for the Judge, he had to sit there at the breakfast table and take it, and without even having known the satisfaction of standing up in a church and answering "I do" to "who giveth this woman?"

Felicity's own breakfast had grown cold while she spoke, and her face was white with pain from her injured arm. I took away the tray and settled the comforter over her, and when I next looked in on her, at lunchtime, she was still asleep.

That afternoon I left for Covington, and almost a month went by before Felicity was feeling well enough again to host one of our Friday dinners. As it happened, it would be our final meeting, but that winter night I had no sense of the approach of another ending in my life, and in good spirits I sat on at Felicity's table, drinking her fine Bordeaux, completely absorbed in the visions of the past that her words evoked.

With smoke circling slowly from the cigarette she held, Felicity began:

To this day Clovis Villere, M.D., won't divulge the name of the little twit of a nurse he had working for him, who made that fatal phone call to the Judge. That happened a week or so after Constance had returned to the house on First Street, as Mrs. James Rand Calvert.

It was a warm afternoon in June, and Constance and Airey and I were sitting in the solarium, with the ceiling fan going, while the Judge napped on the sofa in his library down the hall. Rand had gone off for a few hours to the house on Camp Street, to draw pictures or to fiddle with clay or something, and Constance was utilizing the time he was away to go through some real-estate listings in the newspaper. She was looking for a house that her daddy might buy for the newlyweds.

"I'm surprised your father isn't set on you and Rand living here on First Street with him," said Airey. It was his afternoon off from Ochsner Clinic, and he was drinking gin and tonic with a big wedge of lime in it.

"He's set on it, but he's not demanding it yet," said Constance, her head bent over the newspaper. "Rand's opposed to the idea, so he's suggesting we go live at *his* old place, on Camp Street." She looked up and let her eyes roll back in her head a minute.

Airey said, "You tell Rand that a doctor advised you you're too pale to spend even a single winter in his drafty shotgun house. Hell, I'll tell him myself."

"Why is it Skinner refuses to answer the telephone while he's cooking dinner?" complained Constance. "He knows it's Sis's day off, and there's no telephone in this room. All that ringing's going to wake up Daddy." The Judge at that time was truly better off asleep. Awake, he still tended to vacillate between half-hearted resignation to Constance's marriage, and sudden apoplexy over it.

"Well at last," Constance said, when the ringing stopped. She had just returned to her perusal of the real-estate listings when the commotion began.

"What the hell is that noise?" cried Airey, jumping up from the glider and spilling gin all over his shoes.

"I think it's coming from the library," said Constance, throwing down the newspaper and starting for the hall.

"Lamb, that's your daddy," I called out, following after her. It was the Judge all right, and he was howling like a Catahoula hound that had lost the scent of the hogs.

When we found him at the library desk, Tommy Alexander had become suddenly, deathly quiet. He was gripping the telephone receiver with one hand and clutching his throat with the other, his face as blue as his daughter's eyes. Still gabbling away on the other end of the line was the nitwit nurse from Dr. Villere's office, who'd seen fit to leave a message for Mrs. Rand Calvert to the effect that "Congratulations," the rabbit had just died.

Airey laid the Judge back on the sofa and loosened his necktie—who else but Judge Thomas Alexander would have been wearing a necktie in his sleep?—and yelled for Skinner to find the nitroglycerin pills. By then, the Judge could talk again, and he lay looking up at Constance, and calling her by her dead mother's name. "Solange, I don't want you to leave me," he said, "and you know this one could kill you, Solange. The Catholic Church be damned, it's not too late for us to do something about it!"

That was the first anybody knew that it had been Solange, not Tommy, who'd insisted on their having a baby. And all those years, Tommy had been quietly taking the blame for having killed his wife.

Within minutes he appeared to be in a coma; Lamb was kneeling next to him, holding onto his hand, while Skinner, cry-

ing like a child, tried to force a nitroglycerin capsule under the
Judge's tongue.

"Daddy, it's Lamb," Constance was saying, "I'm right here,
Daddy, I'm never going to leave you." And then frantically, to
Airey, "Does he hear me, does he know me?"

"I doubt it, dear," said Airey, but the Judge, as if he had
heard, rallied one last time. He drew Constance's hand closer,
and rested his head on it, the way a tired, peaceful child might
do, and then he closed his eyes.

He was dead before Rand Calvert walked into the room a few
minutes later.

During the two days preceding her father's funeral, Constance never left the house. She lay in bed, her rosary in her
hands, staring out her windows at the moss that hung from the
oak trees like mourning crepe. She said later that she felt a certain sense of unreality about the events of her recent past; it
seemed to her then that the winter of her discovery of love, and
the passionate nights of her marriage, had occurred in someone
else's life, had happened to some strange young woman who was
driven by wild desires and unfamiliar dreams.

It must have been the French blood in Constance, her heritage
of sangfroid, that made it possible for her to stand by her father's
casket, as tranquil as a nun, the morning of the services. She
greeted by name most of the hundreds of callers who moved
through the rose-scented reception rooms at the House of Bult-
man funeral home, spoke graciously to people who looked un-
sure of what to say to a bereaved bride, the sole surviving Alexander.

Next to Constance stood Rand, looking at his wife with such
love that he seemed unaware that Tommy Alexander's oldest
friends were glaring at him for having finished off the Judge by
running off with his only daughter.

"Look, Felicity," said Constance, during a break in the procession of callers, "there in the last row of chairs, near the door. That must be Daddy's famous chinless redhead." The woman who had been Tommy Alexander's mistress was in the rear of the room, her clawlike hands to her trembling lips; she seemed oblivious to the fact that she was sitting among dozens of Negroes who had come dressed in their best, dry-eyed and smiling, to pay their respects to "Judge Alex." Way in front of the chinless redhead and the Negroes stood the archbishop of New Orleans, speaking solemnly to what was left of Solange Mallard Alexander's family, the cane-wielding, French-speaking old aunts and cousins and nieces who'd journeyed from Jeanerette, Louisiana, for the sad occasion. Not a male among them; all the Mallard men died young.

Just as the funeral cars drove up to the side doors to take the coffin and the family to the church, Constance turned to Rand.

"Run get Aunt Mathilde away from that gang of river-parish politicians over there, before she insults one of them," she told him. Across the room, several red-faced men in dark blue suits were proudly pointing out to the frozen-faced Mathilde their joint sympathy offering—a tacky arrangement of white carnations shaped into a giant gavel.

Aunt Mathilde didn't like being led away like an unpredictable child, though, and she shook free of Rand's arm and marched over to Constance, to get in the last word.

"Remember this," Mathilde murmured to her, as the funeral director closed the coffin's lid, "there are millions of handsome young men in this world, but you had only one father."

Constance didn't seem to hear her. She was looking toward the porte cochère, where the hearse had just pulled up, and on her face was a look of expectation, almost of anticipation, as if she were waiting to climb into her daddy's big black Packard again, to leave on another search for the perfect Valentine.

The day after the funeral Airey took me to Rome for most of that summer. There seemed to be no reason to worry about Constance, although she was pregnant and hadn't looked especially well since her elopement. But, after all, she and Rand would now have the house on First Street to themselves, along with Constance's inheritance to pay expenses, and there were Sis and Skinner to help look after domestic matters.

It was August, then, before Airey and I returned to Louisiana; we went almost immediately to the de la Corde summer house in Covington, to finish out the hottest weeks of the season. It was in Covington one night that we saw Constance and Rand Calvert, during an outdoor party that was given by a local artist at his farmhouse on Old Landing Road.

There on the darkening, torchlit lawn, near a makeshift bar, stood Constance, her bare back suntanned, the white skirt of her dress blowing in the breeze that zigzagged across the yard. Next to her was Rand, his shaggy head bent toward hers, as if he were listening closely to whatever it was she was saying to him. They were standing a little apart from the others, holding their drinks and looking out every now and then at the party guests, and there was about them that enviable air of two people whose chief pleasure lies in one another, for whom everyone, everything else, is only a diversion. They had a look of secretive delight, of superiority, of relief in having had the good fortune to position themselves, literally, figuratively, and for all time, beside one another.

"God damn! Rand Calvert! Quit hanging around those liquor bottles, you drunken son of a bitch, and come on over here," yelled Airey, over the music being played by a Negro band.

Rand took Constance's hand, and they started across the yard, Rand smiling as proudly as if he were showing off a chest full of war medals instead of one small, pregnant wife.

"Well goddammit, Lamb, if you're not like a piece of candy in a room full of kids," Airey said. "Sweet enough to eat, but not enough of you to go around. You're liable to start a ruckus here, girl."

"Did you ever hear anything so obnoxious in your life?" said Constance, smiling at Airey with her eyes.

"Did you get Felicity's letter from Rome?" Airey asked. "If you did, hold on to it, because it's a rare item. Felicity never writes letters—she told me the last letter she wrote before the one to you was to Santa Claus, back when she was eighteen."

Constance laughed. "I thought I got a letter written on what looked like your stationery, Felicity, but it had something spilled all over it, a dark stain that smelled like bourbon. I tried to make out what the letter said, but I wasn't able to decipher it."

"You horrid witch," I said, teasing her back, but there was a disturbing weak sound to Constance's voice, as if she were worn out, and she was much too thin. I started to ask her if she were feeling well, but she cut me off by suggesting we go into the house together, to find a bathroom.

Inside, a big-boned, sunburned girl and a redhead were coming out of the powder room as Constance and I went in. "That's not dirt, that's a birthmark," the redhead was saying in a hurt tone. She was touching a brown spot on her face as Constance closed the door after them.

"Speaking of births, when's your baby due?" I said.

"Sometime next winter," Constance answered vaguely. "Felicity, have you got any paregoric in your purse? I feel like I'm going to vomit."

"All my paregoric's in New Orleans; I'm past the vomiting stage. Have you eaten anything tonight? Sometimes you'll feel better if you eat something."

"That's just the trouble, I did eat. Some of that grilled fish they were serving, that tasted like it had been marinated in Tabasco?"

" 'Trout Fireball,' " I said. "Rand must be out of his mind, letting you eat spicy food like that."

"Rand's never been pregnant, how would he know what's going to make me sick? Why didn't *you* warn me, Felicity; you've been pregnant ever since I can remember."

"What do you suppose was in that letter you didn't bother to read? 'Dear Constance,' it said, 'watch out under pain of death for something called 'Trout Fireball.' ' "

Constance's mouth wobbled a little, as if she wanted to smile but was too nauseated to complete the effort.

"I think I'm going to ask Rand to take me home," she said. I saturated a hand towel with cool tap water and gave it to her to hold against her throat. "I've never been any good at vomiting anywhere except in my own house."

"How are you at vomiting in your car? Because that's what you're going to do if you take a car ride right now. Why don't you stay over at our house tonight?"

"No," said Constance, "I just want to get back to New Orleans, Felicity. I've got some pills for this at home."

"You'll probably feel fine again, Lamb, as soon as you get back to First Street, and to Sis Honorine. Sis will know what to do. Although I must say you don't look as if Sis has been feeding you very well."

Constance didn't say anything; she just stood there pressing the cold towel to her throat and swallowing. Then she said, "Sis is gone, Felicity, and so is Skinner."

"Gone?" I said. "Where did they go to?"

"Sis went back to Pointe Coupée Parish, where she came from. She's getting married. And Skinner went to work for Mrs. Malcolm Chase."

Through the open window, we could hear the horn player in the band begin a solo of "Do You Know What It Means to Miss New Orleans?" Constance started to cry.

"I didn't want to spoil your trip to Italy, Felicity, so I didn't write to you about it," she wept, "but there's been nothing but trouble ever since Daddy died! A week after the funeral, Daddy's lawyers called me down to their offices and told me there was less than nothing in his estate. They were so exquisitely polite that it took me an hour and a half to figure out what they were telling me. Apparently Daddy had a weakness for gambling, Felicity. 'Your late father was particularly partial to flamboyant football coaches and losing streaks,' was the way one of them put it. 'And then this last year, he borrowed against everything he still owned for the pleasure of seeing you, Mrs. Calvert, as the beautiful debutante and Carnival Queen that you were.' "

"Lamb," I said, "are you telling me you've lost everything?"

"Right after I spoke with the lawyers, all the letters started coming in from Daddy's creditors. Rand said to let the attorneys handle everything, but in the end the situation got so out of hand, with people showing up at the front door, wanting their money, that I had to put the house up for sale. I even had to auction off almost everything in it, the paintings and most of the furniture." She turned her face away. "Perfect strangers," she said, "sitting in my mother's chairs, and eating with the Mallard silver."

"Constance, honey," I said, crying now along with her, "surely you were able to save *something?*"

"Very little. Some of Daddy's family's flat silver and linens, and my mother's bed. Very little else."

She looked at me, her lovely eyes filled with sorrow.

"A man from Texas, who wears a big gold buckle on his belt, bought the house. His wife told me she plans to lower all the ceilings and put in central air conditioning." She wiped her eyes with the wet cloth.

"So you and Rand are living now on Camp Street?" I said, trying to give the question a casual tone. She only nodded.

Then she went over to the washbasin and began to rinse her face with cold water.

"Constance," I said, "I want you and Rand to come out here and spend some time with us, all right? Stay as long as you want. Rand's not working, is he?"

"Yes, he's working, he's painting. He's working very well. But it's important for him to work every day, Felicity, to maintain a certain discipline and momentum. And he's taking some architectural hours at Tulane, too. I don't think he'd consent to take any time off right now."

"Oh. Well, if you ever want to come over by yourself . . . God almighty, who is that beating on the door, a fireman? We're *coming*," I said, and I slid open the bolt.

Just at that moment, poor Constance was overcome by the sudden, unstoppable rush of sickness that's peculiar to early pregnancy, and she vomited in the sink.

"You should be ashamed of yourself," suggested the young woman who had been knocking. She stood there in the doorway and watched Constance retch. "I've lived here in the South for ten years now, and I've never gotten used to seeing young girls drink like you do down here. You act like it's not a party unless everybody throws up or passes out! I don't understand Louisiana. Back in Ohio, we were perfectly happy with apple cider and charades."

I wiped Constance's face, smoothed her hair, and walked with her past the outraged lady, to the yard.

Airey was standing by himself, looking over the selection of desserts on a buffet table.

"Airey, could you come over here a minute?" I called to him. "I don't trust Constance's stomach near the smell of those pecan pies."

"What's the matter, Lamb, are you sick?" said Airey. He took an immaculate white handkerchief from his pocket and handed it to Constance. "Rand will be right down to take you home. He went up to the house to pay his respects to the old painter who owns this place. Apparently, this painter knew Rand's daddy, and his uncle, too, some guy with a crazy nickname—Baby Brother? They all used to go duck hunting together."

"That figures," I said. "Duck hunting would be right up Uncle Baby Brother's alley. I'll bet he loves the part where you get to smash the duck's brains out on the side of the pirogue."

"Uncle Baby Brother?" said Constance. "He's that crook you mentioned to me one time, isn't he, Felicity?"

"I'm not surprised Rand's never told you about him. Clement Calvert's all that's left of Rand's family now, but he's a rotter, a masher, a crook, and, naturally, a multimillionaire."

"How do you know him, Felicity?" said Airey. "Rand told me he's living over in London now."

"He was in New Orleans the year I made my so-called debut, or half a debut, as it turned out. I'm ashamed to say I found him attractive. I even went out with him a few times. He'd take me to the best restaurants in New Orleans, order just about everything on the menu, and seriously deplete the wine cellar. Then one night we ran into nephew Rand at a dinner party at Antoine's, and Rand took me aside and broke the news to me that there was an Aunt Baby Brother, shoved under the carpet, so to speak, at some elaborate flat back in London. He was married."

"Well Goddamn," said Airey, sounding horrified.

"I still remember what Rand said about him, he said, 'Felicity, don't even let Uncle Baby come near your house unless you've got a large yard to put him in.' "

"Here comes Rand," said Airey. "He's not much for crowds, is he, the poor fella? He looks like he's as sick of this party as Constance is."

That autumn my second baby was born and I was too busy to see Constance very much. Besides, she and Rand seemed to prefer to keep to themselves, and Constance wasn't in the mood, for more than one reason, to entertain guests at the tiny house on Camp Street.

Then, early one evening in January, I had a telephone call from Constance, who, from the sound of her voice, was suffering from bronchitis again. She wanted to know what "bag meat" meant.

"Bag man?" I said, misunderstanding. "I think that's some

kind of a crook. I don't know exactly what it is they bag, though. Why?"

"Not a bag man, bag *meat*."

"Use it in a sentence."

" 'Attention, shoppers. Raudemeyer's bag meat is now on sale, on aisle five.' "

"Oh. Bag meat's the fat and gristle and stuff that the butcher sweeps up off the floor after he finishes carving up a carcass of beef."

Silence from Constance's end.

"Constance? Is it absolutely necessary for you to shop at Raudemeyer's?"

Raudemeyer's Discount Food Emporium catered mostly to Negroes and blue-collar whites. According to local rumor, Herman Raudemeyer routinely instructed his butchers to hose down the hams before weighing them, and had rigged his produce scales, but the place nevertheless continued to turn a huge profit.

"I have to shop there if Rand and I want to eat and brush our teeth with toothpaste during the same week. But, Felicity, Raudemeyer's is even kind of interesting. You wouldn't believe the people out there."

"Oh, I'd believe them. The only time I ever went to Raudemeyer's, I heard a fat lady at the Café for Shoppers calling her two-year-old over to her so she could wipe the chile off his face. Guess what she said to him? 'Come on over here, you little shit.' She said it very affectionately, though, and the poor child trotted over to her just as amiably as if she'd called him Sugarplum."

Constance said, "The tiresome part about Raudemeyer's is, you have to wait so long in the checkout line. This afternoon, I was standing next to a lady who had two shopping carts full of food, and she must have become tired of waiting, so she just walked out. A man standing behind her in the line pushed her cart aside, and it was still sitting there when I left. All the raw meat and ice cream, dripping and oozing onto the floor."

"Your voice sounds like *you're* about to ooze onto the floor. Tell Rand I said you're too pregnant now for him to be taking you out to hot spots like Raudemeyer's."

"Rand didn't take me, Rand's at a gallery show up in Shreveport."

"You went out to Raudemeyer's all by yourself? This is worse than the night you ate Trout Fireball."

"I feel all right, Felicity. I have to hang up now, though. I'm making bag-meat stew."

A few hours later, close to nine o'clock, the telephone rang again, and Airey answered it in the study. He hung up almost immediately and went to the coat closet.

"Come on," he said. "Tell Viola we're taking Constance to the hospital. Her membranes have ruptured."

"Does that mean her water broke?" I cried. "Of all the times for Rand to be up in Shreveport!"

"Baby wasn't due for another month," Airey reminded me, defending Rand as usual, as we ran out the door.

The house on Camp Street was as cold and damp as the catacombs.

"Lamb, why don't you turn the heat on?" Airey scolded her, settling her coat around her shoulders and picking up her suitcase.

Constance laughed. She wasn't in enough pain yet to have lost the exhilaration that early labor brings.

"The heat *is* on," she said, "but it's just one floor furnace. That's where I was standing, over the floor furnace, trying to stay warm, when everything happened. Airey, could the heat have brought this on so early?"

Airey said, "Honey, from the looks and the sound of you, you've got a viral infection that could have thrown a *Channel* swimmer into early labor, never mind a girl of your weight and stamina. Did you call Clovis Villere?"

"He's on his way to the hospital," said Constance. "And I left a message for Rand at the Cato Hotel, in Shreveport."

"Don't worry about him not making it in time for the delivery," Airey said, helping Constance into the car. "I promise you this is going to take you a little while."

Airey and Dr. Villere arranged for me to be allowed in the labor room for a while, with Constance. There were only two other women there, a Japanese girl already in hard labor, who called for "Pete" in between yelps, and a resigned-looking, middle-aged lady in pin curls, who sat on the edge of her bed, her feet dangling, while she repeated what sounded like "oy-yoy-yoy" over and over.

"Imagine having the heart to curl your hair so you'll look nice after the baby's born," said Constance.

"What she doesn't know is that the nurses are going to yank every one of those bobby pins out of her head before they roll her into delivery," I said. "She'll end up looking just as ghastly as every other new mother."

"What a comfort you are," said Constance. Her face was drawn up with pain. "What time is it, Felicity? Has enough time gone by for Rand to have gotten here yet?"

"It's eleven o'clock. Not even an hour since he left the message with the admitting office that he's on his way."

Two beds down, the Japanese girl screamed again, and started to rip the intravenous needle out of her arm. A nursing nun, in a white habit with an elaborate headdress, rushed over to her and grabbed both the girl's hands. "Pete!" screamed the girl. "Oh, Pete!"

"I'm going to tell Airey to come in and check on you," I said to Constance. "He's going to take care of you till Dr. Villere finishes with the woman he's got in the delivery room now."

Constance nodded. Her eyes were closed and her hair was damp with sweat.

"Your precious Pete's been here and gone!" said the nursing nun in an exasperated Irish brogue, to the Japanese girl.

By two A.M. Constance's eyes were wild with pain; she looked like a doe caught in a hunter's trap.

"Tell me if I'm making any noise," she said, clutching my hand. "Tell me if I start to scream."

"You scream all you want," I told her. "We'll pin the blame on the Japanese girl."

Constance managed to smile; she was unaware that the Japanese girl had given birth to Pete, Jr., hours before. By that time, she had even given up on asking for Rand.

While Constance was in the delivery room, Rand finally appeared in the corridor, looking like he'd tied his hair to the bumper of a truck and been dragged by it all the way from Shreveport. A Negro attendant came out of the delivery room and spotted Rand right away for the father.

"What you wanted, a boy or a girl?" she said to him.

"I don't care, as long as it's all right," said Rand. "Where's the doctor? Where's my wife?"

"What you mean, you don't care?" said the attendant, staring at him. "I *said*, what you wanted, a boy or a girl?"

"It's nice to start off a family with a boy," I said, to shut her up.

"Well, that's too bad, because he got him a black-headed little girl," said the attendant, grinning with tremendous satisfaction.

Felicity and I drank the last of our wine, and the hospital corridor of three decades ago vanished as Felicity's dimly lit dining room took shape around me again.

"You were born with a wild head of hair, like your father's. And those dark eyes, gypsy's eyes." She looked at me as if to determine whether my eyes were now as they once had been. I couldn't tell what she was thinking, though; she only sighed and crushed out her cigarette.

"Love child," she said. "Right from the start it was plain that no chaste conjugal coupling had produced a child with eyes like those."

I heard a slow, silky shuffling on the stairs. Viola, in her imported Chinese kimono, was descending to fetch Felicity up to bed.

"It's gotten late," I said, pushing back my chair. "Almost midnight."

"It's gotten even later than that," said Felicity, standing with difficulty, as I offered her my hand. "Clay-Lee, maybe you'd better ring up Clovis Villere in the morning, and have him give you the prognosis on me. I haven't the time or the energy or the inclination to tell you myself."

I never did telephone Dr. Villere; I didn't need him to inform me Felicity was dying. I'd seen it myself for months.

She left me enough money to pay for some major repairs to Rosehue, and she left me some valuable, old, leather-bound editions of the classics, including one of Ovid, the love poet, with a letter folded among its pages.

"Dear Clay-Lee," the letter read, "go on without me, from where we stopped our last Friday night together. If you start at the place where you recall things firsthand—that would be your first years at the house on Camp Street—you will look well and fairly at what you know of your mother's life and your own, and eventually you will see cause and effect. Felicity."

Felicity, whom I had assumed was too preoccupied with storytelling and the Calvados decanter to have been attuned to my own feelings, had understood me well after all. Beneath her signature she had scrawled, perhaps on a brandy-inspired impulse, a single line from Ovid.

Parsque meminisse doloris, she had written; it is part of grief to remember.

THREE

What really shapes and conditions and makes us is somebody only a few of us ever have the courage to face: and that is the child you once were . . . that impatient all-demanding child who wants love and power and can't get enough of either and who goes on raging and weeping in your spirit . . .

—Robertson Davies, *The Rebel Angels*

1

I remember that Camp Street was treeless, our part of it, and dusty with windswept dirt from tiny yards where grass died in the sun. Camp Street was planted instead with telephone poles, whose black cables roped off block after block; it was as ugly a place in a morning's spring rain as on a winter afternoon. The university section of New Orleans, with three different colleges within its boundaries, was veined with neighborhoods like ours: quiet, still Caucasian, but running dangerously close to the Negro slums past Magazine Street, toward the river. Blue-collar men and women shared the narrow alleyways between double houses with blue-blooded newlyweds, the progeny of the city's oldest families: young interns, unseasoned lawyers, junior stockbrokers, who served out their lean years in thirty-six-month spans and moved on, to the deep lawns of State Street or the wrought-iron balconies of the Garden District. The porch sitters of the poorer streets, the twenty- and thirty-year residents, became accustomed to the occasional sight of the slow-moving, low-slung car, tanned young mother and pink-and-white child inside. "Look!" the mother would cry, holding Baby up to see, "that's the half-a-house we rented the year you were born! You can't remember, can you, sitting in your playpen on that upstairs porch!" Then the young man behind the steering wheel would stop the car and get out, shading his eyes with his hands, staring. "For Christ's sake. Whoever lives there now has let the place go to ruin. How much could it cost them to at least slap on a coat of paint?" A few minutes more, and they would drive on, rolling up their windows, reminiscing about their bittersweet stay in Poverty. They were like rescued shipwreck victims, returning briefly to their desolate island to ponder the happy impermanence of hardship. As for the porch sitters, they acquired, through the years, a certain working knowledge of things. They could quote the price of painting, and decide when to let things go to ruin, and identify at a glance Privilege, as in the blue-eyed child who lived above them for a time, somersaulting in his playpen on an upstairs porch.

That was the Camp Street of my childhood: soup-scented, gravel-paved, bordered at one corner by a crumbling appliance repair shop (from which, Daddy said, no appliance ever emerged alive) and at the other corner by Reva and Zee's Sweet Shoppe, a wooden structure the size of an outhouse. From behind its window two Italian women dispensed nectar syrup snowballs in the summertime, and licorice Nigger Babies and other tooth rotters year-round. Only once do I remember being escorted by my mother to Reva and Zee's. It was on a cabin-fevered winter afternoon when I was about seven; classes at Crown of Thorns parochial school had been canceled for the week, due to the lack of plumbing facilities resulting from frozen pipes. Our downstairs floor furnace, the only source of heat in the house, had proven inadequate, and such was the penetrating power of the New Orleans chill that it was colder inside our drafty Victorian than it was outside. Daddy was sculpting at his studio, an elevator-sized room he sometimes rented in the basement of a friend's house, and Mama, after being subjected for half an hour to my requests for butter mints, finally gave in. She dressed me in a fleece-lined red snowsuit and cap that were so cocoonlike only the skin of the lower two-thirds of my face was exposed as we started down to the Valmont Street corner, my mother, her big white dog, Mishka, and I.

That afternoon, Reva and Zee's had been converged upon by a swarm of Negro children, including four or five small boys who were improvising a sort of tribal dance in an effort to stay warm. I remember wondering how so many of them had managed to slip past their mothers without their coats on. Mama and I waited in line behind bowlegged black children, their hands held by stoic big sisters who wore school books strapped to their backs and who had women's faces, and behind sisterless children who consistently forgot what they wanted when their turn came at the window. These last were razzed unmercifully by the tribal dancers, none of whom had the wherewithal to place an order of his own. "What you want, a sugar teat?" Reva would finally, wearily suggest, and the speechless child would nod, hand over a penny and depart, sugar teat in fist. While my mother waited for Zee to locate a box of butter mints on the shelves, the razzers whirled around her white wool coat, touching its braided trim and tugging at the tassel on my cap. "Leave the people be," intoned a gravel-voiced girl behind us. "Oh, say, miss!" called out a shivering black boy, seizing my mittened hands in his bare, half-frozen ones, "how old he is?" "That's a little girl," Mama said without turning around. "How you can tell?" teased the child, who was about my age, and centuries older. "Where his hair is?" This brought a gust of giggles from the big sisters, one of whom collared the interrogator and told him to get himself home before she called that spotty dog over there to come chew on his leg a while. "And he don't care if you boy or girl, black or white!" she yelled after his ragged, retreating form.

Back at our house, my mother opened the box of butter mints and found a cobweb inside. My mittens were strung with chewed-up Nigger Baby and so was the braid on Mama's coat. When Daddy returned, blue-lipped, from his studio a few minutes later, he walked in on my mother rubbing an ice cube over an expanse of licorice and white wool, and crying from the cold, while I begged loudly to taste the butter mints, cobweb and all. "On the face of it," Daddy murmured to me, springing me from my fleecy straitjacket, "I'd say the expedition was a bust." He went next door, and brought back Mrs. Mococaux to baby-sit with me. Then he bundled Mama into an unlined raincoat and took her out to a lakefront restaurant for an early dinner. They were meeting some of his sculptor friends, I heard him say.

Mrs. Mococaux was a half-deaf Creole-French widow who rented the other side of our double house. She still wore black for her husband, dead since the Spanish-American War, and her only intelligible English was "You bet your life!" delivered with gusto at odd moments. I was delighted to be left with her. I reasoned it would take me roughly ten minutes to get at the mints-and-cobweb, which my mother had placed on top of the armoire in her bedroom, and Mrs. Mococaux wouldn't recall seeing me eat them, let alone remember to tell my mother on me.

The evening ended badly, despite my eventual success with the mints. Mama, her bronchial tubes in spasm from the interior damp and from the final insult of the freezing air off the lake, developed a hard cough and a high fever by midnight. Daddy was downstairs before the sun came up the next morning, telephoning Aunt Mathilde to come and stay with us. She had taken over their bedroom by nine A.M., crowding my mother's perfume bottles off her dressing table with vaporizer equipment, and fashioning out of sheets a tentlike structure designed to trap the steam near the patient. My father departed for his studio.

"Rand Calvert," Aunt Mathilde began, as soon as he was gone, "has a good heart, I guess. And I know he's supposed to be 'artistic.'" Her face held the same look of controlled revulsion that Mama's did when Mrs. Mococaux presented her with a dish of creamed figs. "But all the same, I wonder, Constance, if he ever plans on growing up? Taking you out dressed like that, in this cold and damp!" Mama's voice was gone by this time, and she made no response. "He reminds me of Fayard Cole, remember him? Gifted as Mozart at the piano, but still bringing home stray dogs and cats for poor allergic Ann to clean up after, till the day he died. Another man who 'meant well.' " She clicked her tongue against her teeth.

I slunk off to my toy box. My mother's ineffectual raincoat hung sadly on the coat rack in the hall, and my stomach ached from the last of the butter mints, which I had eaten right after breakfast. I found a musical metal carousel near the top of the toy heap, pulled it out and brought it in to Mama, placing it on the blanket near her thin, pretty hands. The bubbling vaporizer had frosted the mirrors and windowpanes with steam, and there was the feeling of being inside a gently boiling, glass teakettle. "If you stay in here with the vaporizer going, you won't be allowed to go outside again," warned Aunt Mathilde. "Your pores will all be open, and you'll be a candidate for pneumonia."

I wondered, not for the first time, exactly what a "candidate" was. Aunt Mathilde used the term so often, and always in such an ominous context. "She's a candidate for divorce, with that flirtatiousness." "That child's a candidate for lockjaw, running around over splintery floors in her bare feet" and so on. I asked Daddy once, and he said it meant the same thing as "a natural." That can't be right, I told him. You say "natural" when you mean somebody's good at something, like "he's a natural on a sailboat"; "she's a natural on the dance floor." "Maybe you and Aunt Mathilde don't talk the same," I pointed out. "Clay-Lee," he said, "that's a very delicate way of putting it."

Having no desire to become one of Aunt Mathilde's candidates for anything, I left Mama's bedroom and went to wait for Daddy, who'd told me he'd be coming home for lunch. On the right-angled turn of the stairway that was too small to be a landing, I assembled my current treasures: a red crepe paper surprise ball I had saved from Christmas; a mesh change purse containing a tiny pearl rosary my mother had given me, and half a candy cigarette; an old black enamel rouge case that shut with a click and still had traces of sweet-smelling pink cream inside. As I struggled against an urge to taste the rouge, the tinny sound of the musical carousel came from above. Mama or Aunt Mathilde had wound it too tightly, and "In the Good Old Summertime" was playing over and over again at a crazy rate of speed.

The view from our front porch (where no one except Mishka was allowed to sit; Mama had decreed front porch sitting in the city "trashy") included a shabby gray frame house across the street that had been rented since the previous Halloween by a boyish-looking, middle-aged man named Henry Kurtz. Mr. Kurtz was the only man in the neighborhood under the age of sixty-five, other than my father, who regularly came home for lunch. I asked my mother once what Mr. Kurtz's job was; she said as far as she knew he was unemployed. Daddy contradicted her. Henry Kurtz, he declared, was a poorly connected expert on horse racing, and he conducted his business affairs out of a telephone booth on Canal and Royal.

Mr. Kurtz had explained on various occasions to his stone-faced neighbors that he was forced to return each noon in order to feed his sick mother, who, he said, was confined to a bedroom at the rear of the house. "She's prone to fits," I heard him shout once to a mystified Mrs. Mococaux, "so there's no sense letting her roam around the place. The furniture might fall on top of her, when she gets to flinging herself around."

Although most of the residents of our block, for want of anything better to do, had already peeped into Henry's front window and ascertained he didn't have any furniture, nobody confronted him with the knowledge.

"Who gives a good goddamn?" as Mr. Abbot, who lived next door to the Kurtzes, put it to Daddy once. "Although I will say it's got Mrs. Abbot wondering. You want my opinion, the guy's never had no mother in there at all. Nobody's seen her, right? What he's got in there, you ask me, he's got some goddamn racehorse in there he stole from the track." Mickey Abbot was a fat, retired policeman who had what he called "a healthy respect for out-of-nowhere hurricanes," one of which had destroyed the stationhouse on Carrollton Avenue back in November 1947. I never saw him without his red Civil Defense helmet, which he wore at a deliberate tilt, as if he had just leaped from a burning building somewhere with a baby in his arms and couldn't be bothered with details like having his hat on straight.

On that endless day following the butter mints incident, I grew tired of my safe harbor on the stairs and soon after the noon Angelus rang out from some nearby church's bell tower, I went outside to wait for my father. He was across the street on Mr. Abbot's porch with Mr. Eigenbrod, a frail, ancient antique dealer who lived down the block from us. Mr. Abbot was gesturing excitedly toward a small pickup truck that was parked at the curb. The truck was badly dented on one side and was painted with yellow lightning zigzags and electric bulbs.

"So Mrs. Abbot, she found out a thing or two," Mr. Abbot was saying as I climbed the steps to his porch. "She's been at her flower beds back there the last day or so, pretty close to those windows in the rear; you know those ones Kurtz nailed some sheets up over?"

"I saw Mr. Kurtz earlier today," came the gentle voice of Mr. Eigenbrod, "and he told me Mrs. Wilkie has evicted him for having what he called a 'cheater' hooked up to his water meter. Now, what exactly is a 'cheater'?" Mrs. Wilkie was the local slumlord, a New Orleans native of good family whose head for business and thirst for revenue had finally led her down the perilous path of real-estate transactions with the likes of Henry Kurtz.

Mr. Abbot snorted. "Yeah, Wilkie was by here last night. Went blasting into Kurtz's place and told him to be out of there by this afternoon. Called him a brazen son of a bitch, too. Me and my wife could hear her yelling right over the noise from the water heater." He tipped back his metal porch chair and briefly pinched shut his nostrils with his thumb and forefinger. "I'll tell you what else. Wilkie ain't going to believe what Henry done to her bathroom. Only things I seen him throw in that truck so far, besides a skinny mattress and a bag of what looks like clothes, is the toilet and the sink from inside. Must of went into a rage and ripped 'em right up out the tiles. The only thing left in there is the shower spigot." He brought his chair forward again and landed it with a thump. "I ain't moving from right here till he drags out the so-called sick mama. Hey, Eigenbrod, you want to place your bet on whether she's two-legged or four-legged?"

The screen door of the gray house creaked open, and Henry Kurtz backed slowly out, a bundle of white sheets in his arms. When he turned around we could see the sheets were wrapped around a person, a skeleton-faced, sad-eyed young Negro woman with café au lait skin. Her arm shook where it lay curved behind Kurtz's neck. He hesitated, then nodded to us and started down the steps.

My father went out into the street and opened the door on the passenger side of the truck and helped settle the woman, still bundled in the sheets, on the front seat. As soon as he stepped back and closed the door of the truck, the woman leaned her head heavily against the window's glass, as if she couldn't sit up.

Henry Kurtz looked at Daddy a minute, then he extended both his meaty hands and clasped my father's fine-boned ones. "I want to thank you, Mr. Calvert," he said, "for looking in on her those days I was out of the city. And for the medicine that time. As soon as I can come up with the money, I'm going to pay you back for the medicine. The thing is, I had to rent this truck and all." He let go of Daddy and started around to the driver's side. Mr. Abbot's wife had come to her own screen door and was standing silently behind the mesh, watching, her mouth half-open. From across the street, Mrs. Eigenbrod walked toward us, her arms folded, her eyes full of questions.

Henry Kurtz started the truck's engine, then he rolled down the window on his side. "I'll tell you the truth," he called to my father, "I don't know where the hell I'm going to find a place to rent where I can leave her by herself in the daytime." The truck rattled down the block and turned at Dufossat Street, toward the river.

"See? You was right," Mr. Abbot said over his shoulder to his wife. He looked around at the assembled neighbors. "The son of a bitch was holed up in there with a nigger whore." He bent his forefinger and scraped it along his lower teeth for a second. "Crooked water meter and a sick mama, my ass."

"My little girl's standing right behind you," Daddy said, "and I'm not lucky enough to be moving away from here, like Kurtz. So I want you to remember to keep your mouth shut every time you see her from now on." He reached down and pulled me over to him. His hand was cold, as cold as the Negro boy's hand had been when it brushed against my cheek at Reva and Zee's. "She's his daughter," my father said, "and this is still a white neighborhood, at least on paper. Just think, Abbot: thanks to you, Mrs. Wilkie's property values have been preserved."

"Rand Calvert," rang out Aunt Mathilde's voice from above us. She was on the second-story balcony outside my parents' bedroom. "Could you quit visiting for a minute, do you think, and come up here? Your wife is having trouble breathing!"

"Son of a bitch," Mr. Abbot said again, as we crossed the street and closed the door behind us.

That night I lay in my bed, looking up at the glow-in-the-dark stars and crescent moon my father had painted on the ceiling, and listening to Aunt Mathilde dream. Whenever I was forced to share sleeping quarters with my aunt, she gave me a sporadic nocturnal commentary, as if she were a well-meaning friend who had taken a blind person to the movies. At the moment, "You can't come through that window there!" she was telling someone, a burglar perhaps, whom she had conjured up. "Watch it! Watch out! Well . . . there goes that china bowl."

She caught at the sheets, gave a loud half-scream, half-snore, and rolled onto her side, subsiding till the start of the next episode.

Down the hall, my mother coughed, a drowning sound. I reminded myself that Aunt Mathilde had announced to Daddy and me at dinner that Mama was improving, her fever was down and her cough was "breaking up." I slid lower under the blankets and pretended it was someone else coughing, Mrs. Mococaux, or that Negro girl who'd been carried off, wrapped in sheets. . . .

I closed my eyes and pictured the yellow face of Henry Kurtz's daughter. Her eyes had looked like Mishka's eyes when Aunt Mathilde ordered her out of Mama's bedroom earlier that morning: sad, reproachful eyes that said: You should know better. Shame on you, with the advantage you've got, doing this to me. Camp Street was despised by my mother, laughed at by my father, and considered by both of them a jumping-off point to better places—they must have been telling each other that since before I was born. But maybe Henry Kurtz saw it differently; maybe Mr. Kurtz saw Camp Street as a step up from the crime-in-the-daytime Negro section back along the river.

"It's all in the way you look at it," my father told me once, when I wept at being punished by my mother for mixing paints in what I had thought was a dented tin cup. "That was Mama's silver baby mug, and it's not a piece of junk to her. What you took it for, and what she considers it, are two different things. . . ."

Next to me, Aunt Mathilde stirred and began a monologue about broken jelly jars and spoiled pears. I wondered again how anyone could stand being around Aunt Mathilde for any extended length of time. The answer, of course, was that no one could. She was an emergency relative, welcome only at sickbeds and funeral homes and newborn babies' cribs. True, Aunt Mathilde had married once, quite late in life, but that ended after only a year; Uncle Howard had run off last Mardi Gras. He had been a kind-faced, puzzled-looking man, whom I remembered chiefly for his ability to make "chalices" for me out of silver foil gum wrappers, and to blow through his nose in an imitation of the sound of the train whistle on the Panama Limited. Uncle Howard's only real fault had been that he threw his clothes on the floor. That meant he failed to instantly fold, hang up, or designate for the laundry bin any piece of apparel he didn't happen to be wearing, including his pajamas and his suspenders. My aunt finally decided to discipline Howard by hiding all clothing which she found draped over the bedpost or flung across chairs; when he didn't look for the missing items, or even inquire as to their whereabouts, she began giving them away, piece by piece. One day, Uncle Howard caught Shenandoah, his yard-man, in Magazine Street Hardware wearing a red quilted smoking jacket emblazoned with Howard's monogram. By the next day, both Shenandoah and my uncle were gone, although no one supposed they had become traveling companions. "Well," remarked Aunt Mathilde, "if anybody'd told me Howard was going to turn out to be so touchy . . ." and reverted gracefully back to bullying my parents and me.

I wished I could spend as much time with Lady-Sidonie as I did with Aunt Mathilde. Lady-Sidonie wasn't really related to me; she was the mother of Felicity's husband, Airey de la Corde. She now lived with them and with my cousins, in their narrrow, three-story mansion on Philip Street, in the Garden District. Lady-Sidonie owed her double name to her short-tempered brother, Charles. When she was only a few days old, Charles, who was five at the time, overheard the family butler refer to the baby, whose French name was pronounced See-dough-nee, as "Sidney," and "he." "This baby's a lady!" he indignantly informed the butler, and "Lady-Sidonie" was newly, indelibly christened. She was past sixty now, and very beautiful; petite, with narrow shoulders and fine silver hair worn in a chignon. Her small feet had high, high arches, like dancers' feet, and blue veins showed through her delicate complexion. She told me a story once about a queen of Scots whose skin was so fair that when she drank wine, its redness darkened her throat as she swallowed it. Lady-Sidonie, with her regal bearing, her royal-sounding name, reminded me of that queen.

I heard my mother cough again, and I inched slowly out of bed to avoid awakening my aunt. Aunt Mathilde fully conscious in the middle of the night was even worse than Aunt Mathilde dreaming. There would be a suggestion of scalding milk to put us both to sleep, and perhaps an endless chapter or two from *Raggedy Ann and Andy in Candyland,* read in several different appalling voices.

My parents' bedroom was blue with light from their tiny television set, whose volume had been turned low. When my mother was sick she used the television as a sort of living night-light: its busy, murmuring figures cast comforting shadows on the wall.

The vaporizer had been shut off and there was a chill airiness to the room; from some dark corner came Mishka's gentle snoring. Mama was propped up in bed against two or three pillows, her long hair pinned up off her neck. In the dim light I could see the hollows beneath her eyes; I imagined I could hear the struggle each painful breath was costing her. Next to her sat Daddy, still in his thick green sweater and corduroy pants, his bare feet on top of the blanket. He had one arm around her shoulders, and he was leaning down, talking to her in a voice with teasing laughter just beneath its surface. He sounded as calm and happy as if they were on a Ferris wheel together, spinning slowly through a summer night.

They didn't see me at the door. She had turned her face toward his; she put her fingers up to his lips and smiled at the story he must have been telling her—my father was a wonderful all-night storyteller whenever Mama or I were sick.

"Do you have this same effect on all your women?" she asked him, in a croaking half-whisper.

"Darling," he said, taking her hand in his, "I have a stable of one hundred and fifteen such women; no, wait; a hundred fourteen—one of them I have no effect on."

Back in my room, Aunt Mathilde had fallen into a wordless, snoring sleep, and as I lay drowsily beside her, I imagined myself in Lady-Sidonie's velvet-lined lap again, breathed the scent of her jasmine sachet. It was last Thanksgiving Day on Philip Street, and there had been some swift, mysterious argument among the grown-ups. I left the crowded dinner table and wandered into a firelit parlor, where Lady-Sidonie put aside her needlework and took me in her arms. "Come sit with me," she said. "You and I aren't much for staying past an hour at the table, are we, even at Thanksgiving? . . ." Later, half-awake, I saw Airey, an amber liquid in his glass, leaning toward us in his chair.

"They're a love match, Rand and Constance," Lady-Sidonie was telling him, "and loving each other as they do is the best gift they can give this little one, better than tuition at Sacred Heart, better than all this." Her jeweled hand swept the air, emeralds streaked past my eyes.

"You're a romantic, Mother, always have been," said Airey. "Well, I was only trying to help. . . . I only hope they last."

"I think they will," said Lady-Sidonie. She smoothed my hair with her silken hand. "Although, romantic or not, I wish he'd discover some gold to go along with that silver spoon he was born with."

I didn't know what she meant then, of course, and I still didn't know, but I always enjoyed conjuring up the image her words had evoked. I closed my eyes tightly, tried to ignore the sound of my mother's rattling wheeze, and I pictured Daddy, smiling, sprinkling gold dust over Mama and me with a giant silver spoon, until I fell asleep.

2

The next morning, Daddy brought a breakfast tray up to Mama and told her he had two surprises for her. Mama wanted to know right away if the surprises were good ones or bad ones. She was looking over the contents of the tray—half an avocado, a slice of wilted toast, a bottle of Chocolate Soldier—then she looked up at Daddy and put the tray aside.

"Thank you, Warden, it's just that I'm not very hungry today," she said. Her voice sounded gravelly and loose, like Andy Devine's, on the Wild Bill Hickok television show.

"These are good surprises," Daddy promised her. "Eat your breakfast, though, or I won't tell you what they are."

"I can tell you what one is," I said. "Daddy kicked Aunt Mathilde out of the house again, while you were still asleep. Her suitcase is gone, and so is she."

"Oh, Rand," protested Mama.

"But here's the other surprise!" said Daddy, sitting on the bed and causing the tray to slide. I caught the bottle of Chocolate Soldier and set it on the floor. "I telephoned Sis Honorine over in Covington last night, and she's coming to New Orleans for a few days, to get you well. She should be here by tomorrow morning."

Sis's visits were always good surprises. I was still too young, my existence was too closely intertwined with my mother's, for me to have developed the emotional dependence upon Sis that would come a little later. I knew only that I was happy most of the time when Sis was around.

"But Sis has a new career," Mama was telling Daddy. "She does mostly baby nursing now."

I said, "You're going away again, Daddy, on a picture trip, that's why you want Sis to stay here with Mama and me."

"If that's true, then it's unnecessary, Rand," said Constance. "Clay-Lee and I aren't afraid to stay in the house by ourselves at night."

"Maybe I'm getting overprotective in my old age," said Rand, "but some of our new neighbors look like thugs to me."

"But the thugs aren't ever home at night," said Constance. "They're all out burglarizing better neighborhoods."

"It's just till Thursday, Lamb. I'm going to be in Dallas, buying for George Cather's gallery." He broke off a bit of toast and offered it to Mishka, who was standing by Constance's bed like an attending physician. Mishka sniffed at the toast and left the room, stepping around the bottle of Chocolate Soldier on her way out.

"Hey," yelled Daddy after her, "what am I, one of the burglars?"

Before dawn the following morning, I was awakened by the sound of an empty pot dropping onto the brick floor in the kitchen. Sis Honorine. Next came the drum roll of frozen orange juice cans landing, followed by a slow "Shee-it." Sis was living it up before my mother awakened; she could walk into our house and tell you right away whether or not my mother was around. I asked her once how she knew. "Silent signs," said Sis. "House looks different, smells different, when your mama's up and about. You think she'd stand around, sharin' quarters with a sponge somebody used to wipe up egg yellow, like that one over there?

Don't even get me goin' on that evil-smellin' bucket of stuff with little paintbrushes floatin' around in it, that your daddy drag out every time she step foot off the porch."

Sis Honorine loved my mother, and she deferred to her. Before I learned the rules of rank according to skin color, that submission seemed strange to me—in the hierarchy of childhood, older and bigger called the shots, and Sis looked much older and bigger than Constance. Besides, I sometimes thought Sis Honorine was smarter than my mother, though it was plain that Sis's mind did have certain limitations. For one, she couldn't comprehend that Constance Calvert had ever learned how to make a mistake. If I came crying to Sis, complaining that my mother had lost her temper with me, Sis would tell me I had goaded her into it. "Why you feel like you have to aggravate your mama?" she would say. "The poor thing is sick with her lungs most of the time anyhow, she don't need no trouble from you."

A day came, though, when I cried to Sis and saw compassion in her eyes, and then I realized that though she loved me about half as much as she loved Constance Calvert, she understood me twice as well. That day was memorable to me for other reasons, too: it was the day I made my First Communion, and it was the day I consigned my immortal soul to hell.

The spring that followed Sis's January visit to us was a cold one in New Orleans; on the April morning I was to make my First Holy Communion, the temperature in my bedroom was low enough to cause the windowpanes to frost over, and my teeth to chatter. Mama awakened me before the sun came up, to be sure that I was dressed in time for the 7:30 o'clock Mass at Crown of Thorns Church, just around the corner from our house. She was taking no chances on my being late; the day before, I had come home from school with a threatening letter pinned to my uniform. "Dear Mrs. Calvert," wrote Sister Benigna, "any child who for any reason whatsoever reports to my classroom later than 6:45 A.M. the morning of the First Communion Mass will be refused admittance to the building. Yours in Christ's love, O. Benigna, Religious of the Sisters of Mercy."

("Why would the Sister have singled out Clay-Lee this way?" said Daddy after he had read the note. "Because Clay-Lee's been late every morning you've taken her to school since last September, that's why," said Mama. "What do you two do, stop in at the zoo along the way?")

"Put your socks and shoes on, Clay-Lee, this floor is cold as ice," said Mama. She was wearing bedroom slippers and one of her embroidered, white cotton nightgowns that reminded me of the guardian angels' dresses on holy cards. I stood shivering in my batiste slip, my patent leather shoes cold and heavy on my feet. "Did Daddy remember to pick up the wreath that goes on my veil?"

"He brought it home from the florist last night, but you'd already fallen asleep and I wouldn't let him wake you to show it to you. You weren't feeling sick last night, were you?"

"No, ma'am," I lied.

(I was afraid Constance would keep me home in bed if I admitted I'd vomited in the church vestibule the previous afternoon, shortly after making my First Confession—receiving the Sacrament of Penance, Sister Benigna had called it—while a thunderstorm howled like a banshee outside. The church was full of shadows, and as I knelt in the pitch-dark confessional I also knelt in the puddle of urine left by the terrified child who had confessed just before me.

"I didn't do it," I said to the priest in a panicky whisper.

" 'Bless me, Father, for I have sinned, this is my First Confession,' " coached Father Gardina. "You are here, my child, to tell our Lord what it is you *have* done."

On our way out of the church, the second-graders passed a line of eighth-graders waiting to make their confessions. Next to me, an olive-skinned child who was in my class poked me in the ribs with her elbow. "My big brother's an altar boy," she whispered. "He told me Father Gardina's going to expel all the eighth-graders who confess they went to see *Baby Doll!*"

I whispered, "What's *Baby Doll?*"

"A sex picture. You know, a dirty movie! It's been condemned by the Legion of Decency!"

That was when I vomited.)

Mama was saying "Where did you put your veil, Clay-Lee? Honey, you act like you're in a trance; are you half asleep?"

"Oh, no, ma'am," I said. "My veil's right over there on the dresser. I put a book on top of it so it wouldn't slide onto the floor."

"I hope you didn't wrinkle it," said Mama. "Now you wait right here while I go get the dress out of the armoire in the hall."

I was so excited I couldn't keep my knees from twitching; "The Dress" was all my mother had talked about for weeks, the fine, handmade white silk dress she had worn the day of her own First Communion. She and Aunt Mathilde had made a great fuss over finding just the right place in town to "do it up," and had finally taken it to the most expensive dry cleaner in New Orleans. The dress had been hanging solemnly in a plastic bag, in the armoire, for three days now.

Fine silk rustled as Mama slipped the dress over my head, the blue silk sash fluttered gaily as Mama tied it into a big bow at the back. She straightened the skirt, backed off to look at me, slid my hands into my white cotton gloves, and then backed off to look at me again.

Mama's face is so white, I thought. Maybe she's been vomiting, too. Then suddenly Mama began to cry, her hands up to her mouth.

I felt a certain giddy triumph, the first-time excitement of possessing a loveliness so overwhelming that it had made my mother cry, my serene mother who, up to now, I had seen cry only when Mishka was sick or injured.

"Don't cry, Mama," I said, benevolent in my glory. "You want me to ask Daddy to draw a picture of me in this dress? Then you'll always remember how I looked in it." I would have hugged her, but that might have wrinkled the silk.

"But it's all wrong on you, sweetheart," said Constance, tears running down her cheeks. "Why didn't I see that until now? The silk has turned yellow, and the blue sash is frayed at the ends."

I stood there, holding onto my crystal rosary and my mother-of-pearl prayer book, gifts that Felicity had given me. Felicity was my godmother; she would be there at the church to see me march up the aisle in this awful dress.

My mother was crying, "Did the cleaner shrink it? Because it's way too short on you, baby. Look at your knees sticking out. . . . You know what, Clay-Lee? My father had that dress made especially for *my* First Communion by a dressmaker in Paris. Or did I already tell you that? I think I must have been a smaller child than you are. You're taller, but you're every bit as pretty, honey, it's just that you're a different type. That dress was specially made for the type of child I was."

Downstairs, the clock in the parlor chimed once, for the half hour. It was six-thirty; another few minutes and Sister Benigna would be refusing me admittance to the building. Mama had heard the chime, too. She started to pin my veil onto my head and then one of her hands slipped and she jabbed the end of a bobby pin into my scalp. The sudden physical pain had the effect of releasing another kind of pain and I shouted, "What did you have to tell me that for, Mama? Why couldn't you have just let me have the dress?" My own words made no sense to me, and in frustration I stamped my foot, but my mother was standing close to me and my shoe came down on her bare instep. As Constance cried out with pain, Sis Honorine, an unexpected, fast-moving presence, suddenly bore down on me from the doorway, and swatted me across the behind. (I found out later that

Mama had saved up the money to pay for Sis's bus fare from Covington; she had arranged for Sis to attend my First Communion, as a surprise for me.)

"Jesus forgive me on a day like today," said Sis, straightening my sash, which she had knocked crooked. "But don't never expect me to stand by and watch you do your mama that way, Clay-Lee."

"Clay-Lee, it's six-thirty!" called Daddy up the stairs. "Come on down, and let's see you in your outfit! Your flower thing for your hair's down here, too."

"I'll get Sister Benigna to pin my wreath on at school," I promised Mama wildly; I would have said anything to get out of that bedroom. "I have to go now."

Mama knelt down and hugged me. "The day you make your First Communion, that day will always be the happiest day of your life. Remember the nuns at Sacred Heart telling me that, Sis?"

"Yes, indeed," said Sis. "You go on downstairs, now, Clay-Lee, and tell your daddy your mama and I going to walk over and meet you all at the church."

In the kitchen, Daddy was taking my wreath of white sweetheart roses out of the refrigerator. The smell of it made my throat fill with nausea. He said, "What was going on up there? It sounded like a cattle roundup."

"Nothing," I said, "I stepped on Mama's foot, I think." Then the sobs I had been holding back exploded; unfortunately they exploded through my nose.

Daddy wiped my face with a wet cloth and made me sit down at the table and drink a glass of Mississippi River tap water that tasted like I imagined iodine would taste. I looked at Daddy, as handsome and kind-eyed in his dark suit as the young neighborhood mailman with whom I was currently in love, and I began to cry again.

"Good old Sister Torquemada, friend of children and other helpless creatures everywhere," said Daddy. "You calm down, honey, I'm going to get you over to the school in plenty of time."

"Sister *Benigna,* not Torquemada," I corrected him. " 'Benigna' doesn't even sound like 'Torquemada.' "

"You'd be surprised," said Daddy.

The corridor at school looked dark and altered in the gray, morning sunlight, like a familiar place viewed through the distorting lenses of a dream. As we walked along, we passed a curly-haired child, in her white dress and veil, who was to have been my partner in the ranks. She was heading toward the exit, accompanied by her mother, and both mother and child were crying.

"Uh-oh," said Daddy. "What do you suppose could have happened to those two? They couldn't have been refused admittance to the building, it's only twenty minutes to seven."

Then we came to the row of porcelain water fountains that were set low along one wall; each of the metal spigots had been bound up with rope. All of a sudden I knew what had happened to the curly-haired little girl.

"Remind me to tie up the kitchen sink tonight," Daddy was saying to me. "It's been threatening to tear loose from its moorings and run off with the school water fountain." He shook his head. "Jesus Christ, what a strange place *this* is."

I didn't say anything; my tongue felt frozen with fear. Besides, what could I say? Daddy would never understand, he wasn't even Catholic.

"Here you are," said Daddy, installing me in my classroom. Under the fluorescent ceiling lights, my aging silk dress looked almost gold next to the store-bought white organza and dotted swiss worn by the other little girls.

"Watch for Mama and Felicity and Sis, and good old Aunt Mathilde and me, in the first pew near the side door," Daddy told me. "Lady-Sidonie's been over at the church since six-fifteen, saving us a front-row seat." He bent and kissed my cheek, said, "You're the prettiest one here," and was gone.

"Clay-Lee Calvert, take your place in the ranks," shouted

Sister Benigna, seizing me by one shoulder and shoving me into the double line. "You'll have to march into church without a partner, your partner's been sent home!"

"What happened to her, Sister?" called out some stouthearted child from the back of the ranks.

"Some people just can't learn!" announced Sister Benigna. "How long has this class been studying the rules for the fast before Holy Communion? How many times have I told you little people: you may not take a morsel of food, a drop of water, and then receive the Holy Eucharist, under pain of mortal sin! Nothing to eat or drink from midnight, till the moment Father Gardina places the host upon your tongue! How many times have I told you?"

Nobody cared to guess how many times.

Sister Benigna went on: "I even thought to have the handyman tie up the water fountains! And then to have that child's mother come up and tell me the child had taken a drink of water without thinking, before she left her house this morning!" Sister Benigna rolled her eyes back into her head, like my prayer book picture of Jesus undergoing the Agony in the Garden. "It's too bad she'll miss making her communion with her class, but thank the Holy Ghost, anyway, for sending her the courage to speak up. Imagine committing a mortal sin of sacrilege the same day you receive the sacrament of the Holy Eucharist!"

Imagine telling Sister Benigna that my father, the Presbyterian, had made me drink water after my mother made me cry.

Imagine my whole family looking for me at the church when all the time I'd been refused admittance to the building for breaking the fast.

Without further hesitation, I sold my soul to the devil to avoid disgracing myself in front of the second grade at Crown of Thorns parochial school. I marched into church without a partner, with my knees bent to make my dress look longer, while the olive-skinned child behind me whispered that you weren't supposed to have a *blue* sash on your dress, and while my unsuspecting family watched proudly as I knelt at the communion rail and committed my first mortal sin.

Felicity gave a breakfast after the Mass at her house, and I spent the morning eating rich wine cakes from a patisserie on Dauphine Street and thinking about living in hell after I was dead. (Never mind receiving absolution; I knew I would never have the courage to confess to a priest what I had done.)

I considered sharing my burden with my second cousin once removed, Courtenay de la Corde—Courtenay was usually in a lot of trouble herself, and she seemed to like me—but Courtenay was at her school, the Academy of the Sacred Heart. Constance and Rand had gone out to the porch to drink coffee together, Mama looking very pretty and content, as if the scene she'd participated in earlier had completely slipped her mind. She'd been right, though; my dress was a terrible mistake. None of the grown-ups in the room had even mentioned my dress; instead they'd all told me how pretty I looked in my wreath and veil, as if they were blind to the disappointment in my face, the worry in my eyes. Only Lady-Sidonie seemed aware that I was upset about several different things, but she was too kind, too well-bred, to pry into the secret sorrows of a child. She only patted my hand with tenderness and affection, while I sat beside her on a yellow damask love seat, and dripped jelly from my pastry onto the cushions.

After a while, I wandered out to the kitchen and coaxed Sis into giving me some coffee.

"Where did Viola go?" I said, glancing around the room, while I waited for my coffee to cool.

"Up to Langenstein's grocery to scare a cut of meat out the butcher," said Sis. "Watch, now, that you don't spill coffee on your good dress." She looked at me as if she were dazzled by me. "You're a vision to my eyes in that beautiful dress."

I put my coffee cup down then, and began to cry, tears flying one after another out of my eyes, my chin wobbling. I told myself I was crying because I felt sorry for Sis, who loved me blindly, who couldn't see the difference between a beautiful vision and a nightmare, as long as I was playing the central role.

After a while I stopped crying, and with Sis's arms around me I told her the events of the morning, the scene with my mother which Sis had interrupted, the drinking of the water, my decision to make my communion after drinking it—the decision which was going to cost me my soul, and so much pain.

"That's all right, now, you all right; you not going no place where nobody going to burn you," promised Sis, holding me tight against her. Then she said, "Clay-Lee, you know that wasn't your mama spoke those things to you."

I looked at Sis, astonished. That old, desperate child's lie, told now *to* a child, by an adult? ("Clay-Lee, I saw you set your glass down on this table, and now there's a water mark on the wood!" "But that wasn't me, Mama, I didn't do it!").

Sis said, "Everybody sooner or later got something in their life that when they think about it, it bring them to what I call their vanishing point. For your mama, it's thinking about her daddy, who's passed on."

"Is 'vanish' the same thing as 'disappear'? Because Mama didn't disappear, she was standing right there in my bedroom, going on about—"

"But she wasn't herself; that wasn't your mama you heard, that was a grieving child. When your mother saw you standing there in that dress her daddy bought her, that set her off to thinking certain things, and she went off a ways. That's all right, though, you understand? The whole thing didn't have nothing to do with you. It was between your mama and her daddy."

I didn't know if it was all right or not, but it would have to do. It was the closest Sis had ever come to apologizing for Constance Calvert.

3

For a long time I tried to tell myself that things wouldn't have ended so badly for Mama and Daddy and me if Mrs. Mococaux, our tenant-neighbor, hadn't died when she did. If she hadn't died at that particular time, I reasoned, my father wouldn't have rented out the other side of our house, Mrs. Mococaux's side, to the McCalebs, and so he would never have become involved in John McCaleb's risky scheme that eventually cost him so much trouble.

But the truth is that the most dangerous, far-reaching event in our lives—Constance's, Rand's, and mine—occurred the Mardi Gras day that my mother first met Clement "Baby Brother" Calvert, my great-uncle. In order to understand why that was so, I had to go back in my mind to the events preceding that meeting—events which took place during the first months after Mrs. Mococaux's death, when I was nine years old.

Mrs. Mococaux spent the afternoon of the day she died in our backyard on Camp Street, drinking iced coffee with Mama and me, looking no worse than she usually did.

But a few hours later, she was gone. Mrs. Mococaux's pelican-faced bachelor son came to our door at dusk, to tell us calmly that he had found her in her bedroom, slumped over her prie-dieu, the endless murmur of her prayers for the dead silenced by her own death. He had come as always, he said, from Esplanade Avenue by bus for his Saturday visit with her. But no, he answered my father's offer of a ride back in our Volkswagen; the car from the funeral parlor would be arriving presently. Its driver had promised him on the telephone to let him out at home.

A week passed. Mrs. Mococaux's son removed the last of her belongings, and my father telephoned Emmay Waldman to tell her the other side of our house was for rent. Mrs. Waldman was a retired real-estate broker who acted as a liaison between uptown New Orleans' well-connected prospective tenants and landlords. For a reasonable commission and psychological satisfaction, she would consult her waiting list and place wild-streak bachelors with long-suffering widows; insolvent divorcées with gallant old attorneys ("Now don't concern yourself about paying exactly on the minute, dear. This rental property is chiefly a tax shelter."); child-blessed women with landladies who had wall-scribbling broods of their own. One afternoon while I was at school, Emmay Waldman brought a young married couple through the vacant side of our house. They signed a two-year lease that same afternoon, and the following Wednesday moved in.

The first time I saw Honey McCaleb, I mistook her for my mother. She was looking out our kitchen window, her back to me, when I returned from school. Her hair was the same color and length as Mama's; like my mother, she was small, and had a way of standing with one hip jutted slightly upward, one foot turned out like a ballerina.

"Mama," I called to let her know I was there—Constance disliked having people run up on her from behind. Honey turned and looked at me out of my mother's eyes, deep-set eyes so blue I imagined everything they saw must be washed with that same aqua hue.

"I'm Honey McCaleb," she said. "Your mother went down to the grocery store for a minute, and she asked me to wait here for you. You're Clay-Lee, aren't you? She'll be right back, Clay-Lee; she just went to pick up some rice."

I stood there, struck dumb by the resemblance, even to the way she spoke: the drawn-out vowels, the discarding of final r's, that are the verbal concessions of New Orleans' well-born natives to their Southern origins. As I looked at her and listened, I noticed some differences, too. Honey McCaleb's lips were fuller than Constance's, her voice was slightly higher; and there was a quiescence in her lookalike eyes that was missing from my mother's. Constance's eyes were alight at times with some feverish, half-hidden emotion which I couldn't identify by name.

I saw that Honey differed from my mother in another respect; she was pregnant, just noticeably so. "There you are, petite," came my mother's voice behind us. "I'm sorry I didn't get over to school this afternoon to pick you up. Have you said hello to Honey? She and her husband are going to rent 5213."

Although it was clear to me even as a child, it is difficult to describe what my mother's friendship with Honey McCaleb came to mean to her. They were not strangers. Honey, two years younger than Mama, was familiar to her from dancing classes, from parties and weddings, and volunteer charity groups. But until they lived in the same wall-divided house on Camp Street, they had never had a real conversation; until Honey, no woman since the days of her girlhood attachment to Felicity Léger had been entrusted with the outpourings of my mother's enigmatic heart.

Honey was from a large, fiery Gallic family, none of whose members ever seemed to be on amiable terms with one another at the same time. My mother, compared to a Robilliard, was a serene angel from some distant planet. "You've no idea how difficult they all are," Honey, whose real name was M'Adele told us once. "My brother, Buddy, for instance. Buddy married a St. John—one of the Cotton Exchange St. Johns—who, it turns out, had a late calling to the religious life. Too bad about that: she also has four wild-Indian children under the age of eight, who swing their rosaries around like lariats all during Mass. She and Buddy have taken to going on separate vacations now. He goes to Sea Island, Georgia, and makes a fool of himself on the beach, while Margaret drags the children to visit poor Cousin LeClair in that monastery he's shut up in, outside of Atlanta. One thing, though, the children have all learned how to bake bread beautifully and to age brandy."

I never tired of listening to Honey describe the morass of broken-down communications and hurt feelings that ensnared the Robilliards and their spouses. She was the only woman, other than my mother, who could ever entice Rand Calvert to linger at a dinner table. "Give us the history of the demise of David Robilliard," he would say to Honey at one of the McCaleb-Calvert Sunday brunches.

Our house took on a certain richness during those warm, coffee-flavored hours, when Mishka and I were silent spectators at our end of the dining room. The table, laid with Alexander linen and china and dully gleaming silver, was as fine as the de la Cordes'; the scents of sherry and my mother's perfume blended in the sunlight that slipped through the loosely shuttered windows.

Down the long expanse of white linen from my chair, my mother and Honey McCaleb sat beside one another, their lovely twin faces pink with wine and laughter, their heads together, whispering for a minute behind their manicured hands, while Daddy and John, Honey's handsome, moody-as-a-cat husband, told stories of soft-spoken beauties with a passion for tearing apart men's souls, of ancient duels and fascinating family secrets in Virginia, where John was born, and of hushed-up New Orleans suicides.

"This city must be the suicide capital of the nation," John said. "I've never known a soul in Charlottesville who even attempted it, and then I came down here, and I find that half of Honey's friends are dead by their own hand."

The suicide stories upset Honey, particularly when John would tease her about what he called the strain of morbid sensibility that ran through the Robilliard family, and ask her when she planned to haul out the champagne and cyanide for her farewell appearance.

"It would be funny if it weren't so tragic," murmured Honey.

"There it is!" John McCaleb slapped his palm against the table. "A little of that Honey Island Swamp logic you were christened for." The Honey Island Swamp was a marshy spot in the Bogue Chitto–Pearl River stream system in St. Tammany Parish, where the mosquitoes were said to drive men mad.

"Now hush, John," said Constance. "Your father-in-law just called her that because with four other daughters he couldn't remember a name as complicated as M'Adele."

David Robilliard, Honey's father, had been a man of considerable wealth ("Lake Charles oil, two generations of it, on his mother's side," Daddy told my mother). His main diversion in life had been his job as crime reporter for the *New Orleans Item,* a position he inexplicably coveted and won while in his forties.

"Poor Mother," said Honey, "Papa always *was* in trouble, even before she met him, and he just never got the wildness out of his system. Throughout their marriage, every time they had a social engagement, he kept her out so late she says she's fallen asleep in the powder room of every bar in the French Quarter."

"Why didn't she just stay home?" asked Mama.

"Constance would sooner give birth in a taxicab as nap in a public rest room," explained Daddy.

Honey hesitated for a minute; Rand's humor seemed to confuse her at times. "In any case, Mother didn't get much sleep at home either: if she wasn't out with Papa, she was waiting up for him. The morning of the day she went into labor with my brother Buddy, my father came home lying down, at four A.M., in the coroner's ambulance, with the siren going and the red light spinning around. The Orleans Parish district attorney was at the wheel. They'd been playing five-card stud at the Bienville Club, and Papa was dead drunk, with four thousand dollars in cash hanging out his back pocket."

"Two days later," said John, "a grand jury indicted the DA for public bribery, and Mr. Robilliard was asked to resign from the Bienville Club. He'd sneaked the coroner and the crooked district attorney into a game with some half-blind old gentlemen who'd thought they were playing with Robilliard and two out-of-town members of the Securities and Exchange Commission."

When Honey was fourteen, Mr. Robilliard died under cloudy circumstances in a flash fire at an epicurean *maison de plaisir* on the fringes of the French Quarter, where the girls were reputed to be the beautiful, runaway daughters of some of the finest families in the South, and who would, upon request and for a considerable fee, dress in elaborate bridal gowns and veils.

"Well, David, where are you now?" sighed Barbara Robilliard when her husband telephoned at 10:00 P.M. to say he wouldn't be home for dinner after all.

"I'm down at a whorehouse on Basin Street and Dumaine," explained Robilliard.

"Oh, ha-ha," Barbara said, and hung up, picturing him in the cigarette-littered newsroom at the *Item,* surrounded by his bad-egg but harmless reporter pals.

"To this day," Honey said, "Mother swears he was just covering a story for the *Item* when that boiler blew up."

"Goddamn it, I wish I'd known him," said John McCaleb. "A man like that, who sired seven Robilliards and still had strength left over for the faux brides."

"Look," said Daddy, "I think we've almost put our smallest component to sleep."

"Thank God," my mother said. "She's so quiet I forget, sometimes, that she's even there. No, don't worry about helping me clear, Honey, run home and take a nap. I hope your baby will be as little trouble as Clay-Lee's been."

. .

Many Saturdays of my childhood I spent with Constance, and with Honey McCaleb, running the streets. "Running the streets" was John McCaleb's description of our trips downtown to buy Easter dresses and the thin, sugary pralines made by a Canal Street department store; running the streets was going to lower St. Charles Avenue for lunch at a German restaurant, dark and wood-paneled, where mechanical dummies dressed in lederhosen turned the cranks that turned the ceiling fans. Some Saturdays we went to movies, at the Joy or the Loewe's State on Canal Street, or the Orpheum on University Place.

The Orpheum was my favorite theater because it was easy to take a wrong turn on the way to the Orpheum's ornate, second-floor ladies' room and end up in the Colored Only section. Colored Only wasn't air-conditioned; it smelled of talcum-powdered sweat and contraband homemade lunches, and the Colored Only audience talked back to and commented upon the characters on the screen. ("If he don't act just like Vernon," I once heard a Negro woman say, referring to The Man with the Atomic Brain.)

I have no clear memory of why I was included in so many of these outings; I do have some recollection of repeatedly appearing, dressed for downtown, on our front porch, just as Mama and Honey were starting off for the streetcar stop. I knew my mother wouldn't have the heart to leave me home with Daddy, who spent most Saturdays sculpting in the kitchen, with chunks of plaster sticking to his hair.

Like most only children, I had developed a certain talent for making myself so unobtrusive that grown-ups often forgot I was around; thus I overheard some interesting lady talk, running the streets.

One hot Saturday, Constance and Honey announced they were taking me downtown to the Loewe's State, to see a revival of *Gone With the Wind.*

"Why don't you all ask Mrs. Poirier to go with you?" suggested Daddy. "Carmen Poirier told me last week she'd never seen *Gone With the Wind.*"

Carmen was the flashy Brazilian wife of René Poirier, one of Rand's painter friends.

"Carmen Poirier. That tramp," remarked Constance, looking at herself in the hall mirror while she straightened the big white collar on her navy-blue dress.

"All she needs are a few grapes on her hat and she'd be Carmen *Miranda,*" put in Honey, who'd never met Mrs. Poirier, but who usually went along with Constance's opinions of people.

"What have you two got against this Carmen Poirier?" said John McCaleb.

"Carmen Poirier sits naked in front of the open refrigerator in her kitchen to keep cool in the summertime," said Constance. "She told me so herself, and she sounded like she was proud of it."

"You want a nickel for a Sugar-Daddy?" Rand interrupted loudly, addressing me.

"Sugar Daddies cost a quarter now, Rip Van Winkle," said John, pressing a coin into my palm. "Go in peace, my children, and if you happen to run into Carmen Miranda, let me know. She sounds like a very interesting lady, although I admit I wouldn't want to eat anything perishable from her kitchen."

As it happened, we did run into Carmen Poirier; Constance spotted her jaywalking provocatively across Canal Street, as the three of us waited in a block-long line in front of the Loewe's State.

"My kingdom for a horse," Constance said, clutching Honey's arm. "There comes Carmen Poirier."

Honey and Constance immediately took their pressed-powder compacts out of their purses and pretended to be looking at whatever quarter-inch of their faces was reflected in the tiny mirrors.

"These is a lucky, lucky day!" shouted Carmen, swaying over to Constance, the false petunias on her hat shaking.

"Lucky? Who for, lady?" said a big-nosed old gentleman standing behind us, whose foot Carmen had just stepped on with one of her daggerlike high heels.

" 'Just look at these line,' I was say to myself," said Carmen. "Never in my life will I wait in such a line!"

"You won't? Well, 'bye, then, Carmen, it's been nice seeing you," said Mama.

Carmen laughed gaily, throwing her head back, showing us lots of gold fillings in her teeth. "You are so lucky to be almost by the door," cried Carmen, "and I am so lucky to be seeing you!" She wriggled into the line in front of Mama, the choking scent of her perfume swirling through the air around us like an invisible lasso. "Pray to Saint Anthony we will find the places all together!"

Saint Anthony managed to locate four empty connecting seats in the last row. While we waited for the movie to begin, Carmen Poirier described to the dumbstruck Honey McCaleb a recent evening the Poiriers had spent with the Calverts, at a French Quarter restaurant, where Carmen had drunk a lot of something called sidecars, and where Rand Calvert had come up short for his half of the check.

"René, he is my husband, René said to me, 'Carmen, you naughty girl, why you drink so many of a rich man's drinks while you are out on the town with the poor artists like Mr. Calvert and like me?' My husband, he can talk, he marry a rich wife!" More raucous laughter, more gold fillings. Mama was looking at Carmen as if Carmen's neck were dirty. My throat felt suddenly dry and I took a drink of lemonade from the little ceramic cup in the shape of a lemon that Mama had gotten for me at the candy counter.

"How much you pay for that little lemon?" said Carmen, pointing. "Maybe I will take one home for to give to my little Eduardo, if they cost not so much as the sidecars for the grown-ups cost." She flashed her white front teeth at us.

"I didn't pay anything for it," said Mama. "My husband gave

me only enough money for two tickets and one box of popcorn. He's a poor artist. You know how it is."

"Yes, yes, *I* know, but the movie place, it knows how it is, too? They give away free these cute cup to the poor artist wife?"

Mama smiled wearily.

"No, Carmen, I got a cup because the box of popcorn I bought for my little girl happened to have a picture of a mermaid on the front of it. Only *some* of the boxes have mermaids on them. If you're lucky enough to get one of them, then you present the box to the lady behind the candy counter, and she gives you a free lemon cup."

As the lights went down, Carmen spotted an empty popcorn box that had been discarded under the seat in front of her, and picked it up. "Look what Saint Anthony has find for me now!" she hissed to Constance as a shot of a Georgia dogwood tree flashed onto the screen. "Some fool is throw away the box with the picture of the mermaid on it!" She got up from her seat as quickly as the seams of her skirt allowed, and disappeared in the direction of the candy counter.

As Mammy was scolding Scarlett about sitting outside in the evening damp without her shawl, angry voices could be heard coming from the theater lobby. Then Carmen Poirier's voice rang out clearly, demanding to see the manager, her South American accent clashing with the professional drawls coming from the sound system. Somebody in the audience yelled for the South American voice to shut up.

"Constance," Honey whispered, *"all* the popcorn boxes have pictures of mermaids on them."

"I know they do," said Mama, her eyes on the screen.

Carmen Poirier never came back.

4

I wonder sometimes why it is that children, the most sensitive and perceptive of creatures, haven't the ability to recognize endings as they happen, or to remember exactly when those endings took place.

The last time I played with a certain beloved doll, when was it? Which was the final incident of dressing up in my mother's clothes, her hats, her high-heeled shoes? When did it happen, that concluding episode of skipping along the midway at an amusement park to take the last ride on the Flying Horses? When was the last time I skipped anywhere; did I suddenly, consciously, decide that the day had come to move in a more sedate fashion?

I cannot now recall the exact circumstances that accompanied another important ending in my childhood—the ending of the love affair between my mother and father. Perhaps "altering" would be a fairer word to use, but, after all, when a thing is altered, it changes, and once a thing changes, an ending has occurred. How did it happen that Constance stopped looking at Rand as if she couldn't look at him hard enough, when was it that she was done with sitting contentedly in his arms for hours on winter nights, or long summer afternoons? Why did she cease to stand watching for him at our window when darkness came and he was not yet home?

I recall a new, distracted emptiness in Constance's eyes, and an unfamiliar sadness in Rand's.

To simplify things in my memory, I date the change in my mother as taking place after a certain horrifying event at the house on Camp Street, the first year the McCalebs moved in.

The second story of the Camp Street house had an iron-railinged, undivided balcony running across its front. Two floor-to-ceiling windows opened onto this balcony; one window led into my parents' bedroom, the other into the room used by the McCalebs as a small study, with their bedroom behind it.

Constance and Honey used the balcony as a passageway into each other's houses. Most mornings, after Rand and John had left the house, there was a tap at the glass and Honey was at our window, wearing one of her elegant, sashed robes, a glass of iced coffee in her hand. "Run open the window for her, Clay-Lee," Mama would say. "She'll take a chill, standing out there dressed like that."

John McCaleb and Rand Calvert were early risers. By seven-thirty they were gone, John to his office on Common Street, where he was a junior partner in a maritime law firm; my father to whatever studio he had managed to borrow or rent, where some exhibit of major importance was forever in the works. He had spent one summer following his graduation from Tulane's School of Architecture working as what he called a "glorified draftsman" for a large firm, drawing plans for a shopping center across the river. It almost set him crazy, and after that he painted and sculpted on his own, having decided not to take the Architectural Licensing Board exam after all. Routinely, he sold work to several good galleries on Royal Street, and when prodded by absolute financial necessity, he did oil portraits of children. On portrait days, he came home looking like a man whose shoes were pinching him. ("This child, a six-year-old boy, appears for his sitting with makeup on! Lipstick and rouge, some sort of black stuff on his eyes. 'Did big sister paint your face again?' says the mother. 'Oh, God, I'm too worn out to wash you off. Just go ahead and paint him as you would imagine him without the makeup, Mr. Calvert.' ") Sometimes Honey would visit with us till eight-thirty, when Mama and I departed on our block-long journey to my school.

One cold morning a few weeks before Mardi Gras, Honey arrived with dark circles beneath her eyes; there was a pallor to her skin that faded the rosiness along her cheekbones.

"I was awake most of the night, imagining I heard noises," she told my mother. "Then this morning, when I went out to get the newspaper, I noticed my geranium plants had been pulled under the kitchen window, as if someone had used them to stand on. The window was unlocked, too, although I can't remember whether I locked it or not last night."

"It was probably just some children," my mother told her. "We've never had any real trouble on this street."

"What kind of children walk the streets at midnight, looking in people's houses? Mrs. Eigenbrod, down at the corner, told me when we first moved in that there had been some disturbance a while back, involving a Negro woman and a white man." Images clicked rapidly in my head: a coatless, sweet-toothed black boy, the child at Reva and Zee's, grown taller now, his hands working at a window latch; a hollow-eyed mulatto girl, Henry Kurtz's daughter, pulling at locked doors, looking for a place to die.

"That was a misunderstanding, a family thing," said Mama vaguely. "Come on, Honey, drink your coffee and hush. You're frightening Clay-Lee."

"The little time I spent sleeping, I dreamed of muddy water," Honey said.

Dreams and their implications fascinated my mother, and Honey, too; often, one of them would begin to describe her dream, and the other would interrupt with a remark such as, "I had the same dream. Was the water you saw muddy or clear?" Clear water signified happy change, muddy water, trouble coming. A house being built or added onto presaged pregnancy; teeth falling out, or a vision of a wedding, meant a death in the family.

"Oh, I see," Honey said now, "you dreamed of it, too." She stood up and tapped her fingernails against her half-full glass of coffee. "It's past eight-thirty. Clay-Lee will be copying out the entire catechism after school if you don't leave in a few minutes."

"Honey," Mama called after her, "take Mishka over to your side tonight. She's a gentle dog, but she'll bark like a Doberman if she hears a strange sound in the dark."

My bedroom at the rear of the house was being repainted. Daddy was more than halfway through the job—only one sunset-colored wall and the stars and moon remained to be completed. The bed had been moved out into the center of the floor, and the ladder my father stood on while painting the ceiling was down, leaning against the baseboards. I lay on my side, unable to sleep, the smell of the newly painted walls oozing down my throat like an oily, poisonous mist.

I heard, from the direction of my parents' room, the music that signaled the beginning of the late-night television news. The telephone rang, and Daddy picked it up from the little table halfway down the hall. "Honey, you're a mind reader," he said. "She hates the smell of paint, and we've been listening to her toss around for two nights now. . . . If you're sure she won't be any trouble, I'll walk her across the balcony. No, keep Mishka there with you, Lamb insists on it. Just tell her not to bark when Clay-Lee hops through the window—the Abbots across the street would love to have an excuse to call up here and complain."

I tucked a limp, stuffed calico cat under one arm and was through the McCalebs' study window within three minutes.

Honey's house was fragrant with the smells of the thick new rug in the future nursery, and with lemon-oil polish and the old wood of fine antiques, gifts from Mrs. Robilliard. The walls held silver-framed watercolors and Honey's wedding portrait—whenever I saw the photograph of Honey in her bridal veil, I remembered that Mama's only souvenir of her own wedding day was her thin, platinum ring. The most intriguing feature of this "other side," though, was the fact that it was the mirror image of our own. No matter how often I visited it, I never got used to turning left, instead of right, at the top of the stairs, if I wanted to go toward the front of the house.

That night was no exception—when John and I returned from a trip to the kitchen for chocolate milk, I stumbled into Honey, who was standing at the door to her bedroom. "Excuse me," I said, "I keep thinking I turn this way to get to the back room."

"This is 5213, and this isn't your bedroom, it's mine. By the way, I'm not your mother, either. Can't you tell? I'm fatter than your mother," Honey said. She took my hand and we walked down the hall to the nursery, organdy-curtained, its daybed scattered with ruffled pillows. Along one wall stood a baby's crib, white-sheeted and blue-blanketed; above it swung a rainbow-and-sun hanging toy, a mobile, with a music box as its base. I slid between the cool sheets of the daybed and watched Honey wind up the mobile. "How many days is it till you have your baby?" "Several months yet," she said. She leaned down and picked up my hand, kissed the inside of my palm. "Do you think you could arrange for my baby to have lovely dark eyes like yours?"

I loved Honey for thinking I was beautiful, when in fact I often prayed that my eyes would turn, as if by magic, into eyes as blue as Mama's were; I loved Honey for seeing me as I couldn't see myself. The rainbow crib toy revolved slowly in the near-dark, to the strain of an unfamiliar lullaby.

My father said later it was a poor sense of direction, plus an inability to tell right from left, that prevented complete disaster.

What he said was only partially true. A while later, when Courtenay found the police report of the incident in Daddy's desk, it was clear that my mother's good memory, her coordination and courage had saved both their lives.

That night of my stay on the McCalebs' side was a windy one. Gusts shook the windows' thin glass with a muffled rattle, like the sound of the breeze that whipped at Honey's taffeta robe when she crossed our balcony seconds before a storm. From behind the wall where the empty crib stood, I heard, within some technicolor dream, the shuffle of footsteps across the stone hearth of the fireplace in my bedroom. Then silence, followed by the noise of something colliding with the ladder that lay on the floor. I was suddenly awake, listening as intently as Mishka did when she heard a stranger's footfall on our porch.

In her bedroom on the other side of the wall, at the opposite end of the house, Constance was shaken awake by the same rattling thud. She told us later she felt like a passenger she had once read about on the *Titanic:* well aware that something was wrong, but too sleepy and warm to get up and investigate. A second tinny thump reverberated along the black hallway. This time, like a militant wraith, Constance strode off to confront the source of the disturbance while Rand dreamed on, unaware, in their windshaken bedroom.

The man was on his hands and knees, crawling toward her as she crossed the threshold of my room. He was carrying a flashlight in one hand, and in its incandescent circle a curved blade glittered, disappeared into darkness as the light clicked off. Constance stood perfectly still, afraid to turn and run, fearful of the death grip that would surely tighten around her retreating form, of the sharp steel that would plunge between her shoulder blades.

"Whore," breathed a voice. Its owner was on his feet now, the sound of him came from somewhere above Constance's head. "Whore, I want to cut you. . . . I'm going to cut out your eyes, and your tongue, and your whoring heart, and then I want to fuck you. . . . I want to feel you dead under me, you whore, I want to feel you cold under a man for once in your fucking life. . . ."

As gracefully as a ballerina's, my mother's hand moved toward the top of my chest of drawers to her left. She wrapped her fingers around the handle of the hammer she had used that afternoon to remove picture nails from my wall. In a swift, sure movement she swung the blunt steel end of it up and across, missing once, then connecting with the frontal bones of the whispering man's skull.

The black stillness on the other side of the wall was shattered then by screams, high-pitched, animal screams accompanied by the pounding of bare feet running, running the depth of the house, and by the sound of a heavy object falling against wood. Up at the front of the McCalebs' side, Mishka was barking frantically, and glass was rattling: the dog was throwing her full weight against the long window that led out to the balcony. I ran along the hall toward Honey's bedroom, panic so tight around my throat that I couldn't swallow; saliva ran out of the corners of my mouth. A knocking sound began; someone was beating on the study window with both fists.

In the McCalebs' bedroom, the bedside lamp was on, its shade knocked crooked by a hurried hand. I saw my mother, a dark stain down the front of her white cotton nightgown, step through the study window that John had flung up. With her was Daddy in his underwear, one hand gripping Mama's arm so tightly her feet were not completely on the floor. He looked like a man who'd been dynamited out of bed, with a wild-eyed sleepwalker in tow.

"There's somebody in our house," said Constance. John brought the window clattering down, locked it. Behind us, Honey was already on the telephone to the police.

A gray-haired Louisiana state trooper, whose car radio had picked up the call from Camp Street in the middle of a slow night, strutted through the McCalebs' front door a few steps ahead of two young Second District policemen. The trooper was bulbous-nosed, popeyed; veins bulged in his temples and along his neck. His entire body appeared about to explode at the slightest provocation, and I stepped half behind my mother to avoid bumping into him.

When the three investigators returned from their perusal of the Calvert side of the house, the state trooper elbowed past the rookies and descended upon the McCalebs' settee, whose springs yelped in protest. "That's the last anybody will ever hear out of the sofa," murmured Daddy to me.

I'm not frightened anymore, I wanted to tell him. You don't have to try to make me laugh. He was wearing a too-short trench coat of John's, he was barefoot, and he was smoking a cigarette down to its filter. Mama, one of Honey's robes over her ruined nightgown, sat next to one of the young policemen; someone had dragged two of Honey's Queen Anne dining chairs into the parlor.

The state trooper held up five of his overstuffed fingers and, with a sixth, began to tick off points of interest.

"For openers, your perpetrator liked to live dangerous—he'd set a small fire in a basket of cleaning rags on the kitchen table. Most likely thought he could do his job and get out of there before the flames spread, which they was fixing to do when we walked in. Two, this guy was no burglar, he was out to get somebody. Cut up the bed pretty good in that back room before he caught on he was knifing a couple of pillows and some big, cloth doll."

"Raggedy Andy," I said.

The state trooper was looking over at Mama. "And three, the next time you hit a nigger over the head with a hammer, lady, hit to kill." He tapped the side of his own head with a beefy forefinger. "Go for the temple. Because your particular nigger went out the same downstairs window he crawled in through."

"I can't be sure it was a Negro," my mother said quietly. "It was too dark."

The shorter of the policemen looked up from his report sheet and smiled uncertainly at her. He wasn't sure she was kidding.

"Lady," said the state trooper wearily, "that's nigger blood all over your nice wood floors. Take my word for it."

The "perpetrator" was arrested later that night in the emergency room of Touro Infirmary, a hospital a few miles away, on Prytania Street; the young intern on duty had called the police just before he painstakingly put thirty or so stitches in the suspect's forehead.

"I'm from Fayetteville, Arkansas," he told the arresting officers, according to police reports. "I've seen a lot of hopped-up Negroes, but I've never seen one with a head wound this bad from 'falling face-first off a barstool,' as our friend here put it."

The Negro was three weeks out of Angola Penitentiary on parole, after serving ten years on a sentence for double manslaughter. He had found his common-law wife in bed with a young boy, and stabbed them to death where they lay; the woman's body had been badly mutilated. Several pieces of the puzzle later, my parents learned the murder had taken place in the fifty-two hundred block of Annunciation, four blocks from Camp Street, toward the river, in a house remarkably similar to ours.

The man with the knife, his brain seared by amphetamines, had gotten as far as our house in his quest for reenactment, and had mistaken it two nights running for the scene of his long-ago betrayal. (Honey had not imagined the noises she heard: the man's fingerprints were found on the McCalebs' kitchen window, and on the heavy silver hand mirror on a vanity table in their bedroom.)

"I guess we'll never know for sure why he decided to wait and come back the second night; maybe he had to go out and find himself a knife," a police detective told Rand. "Of course, when he did return, he again had the wrong house and this time he had the opposite side of the wrong house. That's why he turned to the left instead of to the right to get to where he thought the lady's bedroom was. Thank God for that, and for the little girl being gone, and for his stumbling against the ladder. That was after he'd thrown himself on top of the bed and slashed the sheets to ribbons."

"Sangfroid," John McCaleb complimented Constance a few days later, trying to make her smile. He picked up both of Mama's hands and looked at them, turning them palms up. "Loosely translated as 'cool blood in a crisis.' The French are noted for it and the British are loaded with it, so never try to rout a lady with French and British blood, like our Lamb. Especially not when she's managed to get hold of a hammer."

"You all must've thought I was crazy," said Honey, "asking you to drag Clay-Lee out of bed and over to our side at that hour. But the feeling of danger was so strong . . . finally, I came up with the excuse of the paint smell keeping her awake."

"I misunderstood," said Mama; "I thought you were afraid for yourselves. That's why I insisted on sending Mishka to you." There was a distracted note in her voice; I had noticed it for several days. It was as if she were no longer attuned to people around her, but to some inner voice that told of her astonishing, hidden resources, of the newly discovered power of her hands when her neck was at stake.

Constance had seen the two most important men in her life— her father and then her husband—as her protectors. But her father had constructed the castle in the air of her girlhood so haphazardly that its eventual collapse nearly destroyed her, and Rand, her romantic defender against the terrors of hard-breathing, fevered nights, Rand who often carried her up to bed as if she were a treasured child, had nevertheless brought her here, . . . to a death-house's twin, kept her here, in a place that was being slowly engulfed by the black river beyond Magazine Street.

The incipient phase of Constance's marriage ended, I think, the night her fragile hands broke open a man's skull. A man had defiled her house with his blood, used that house as if it were a setting for fornication and carnage, among a people whose black hands she had known not as malevolent, but in terms of Skinner's hands—Skinner, who had readied her father's body for its grave—and Sis Honorine's hands, that had held Constance's newborn daughter to her breast.

During those blighted days following the break-in, after John McCaleb and my father bolted ugly iron bars over all our windows, I watched my mother go to him, put her arms around his neck . . . "Rand," she would say, "it's time. It's time now to think about moving on."

He looked down at her, his hands in his pockets, not even troubling to shake his head. Why does she keep saying it? I wondered. The expression in his eyes was telling both of us there was no place else to go.

5

That winter, Mardi Gras week was early, falling during the first days of February. The night parades my father took me to were set against a stark, chill backdrop; within the crowds that lined St. Charles Avenue, children cried to be taken home; from atop the floats, shivering maskers, waxen-faced, dead holes for eyes, scattered glass necklaces over the onlookers. Only the flambeaux carriers, bare-chested, white-turbaned, their black faces lit from above like oil paintings, seemed impervious to the cold.

Those nights, my mother remained at home. She was being paid by John McCaleb's law firm to translate from the French a nineteenth-century legal treatise on something called riparian rights; each night, when my father and I left the house, she was deep in her work, her head bent over the big *Harrap's French-English Dictionary* that was open on the dining-room table. Each night, by the time we returned, toward nine o'clock, the dictionary was closed, the dining room empty. Mama was in her bedroom, relentlessly brushing Mishka's shining coat as the dog lay half-asleep, endlessly patient, at her feet.

"Don't you want to see any of the parades, Lamb?" Daddy asked her one night. He turned to me. "I love to watch your mother at a parade; she's the only person in the crowd who stands there trembling, with her hands over her eyes, while all around her the crazed proletariat are begging the float riders to throw something at them."

"I don't like the parades anymore," said Mama. "I used to like them when I lived in the Garden District. Then I only had to walk a few blocks to get to the parade route, and there was always a lot of people and food back at the house. It's no fun when you don't have a house you can have a parade party in."

"We must get ten invitations every Carnival season to parade parties at places in the Garden District! You want me to take you to one of those?"

"Not ten invitations any longer, Rand; we only got one this year, and that one was canceled because of rain. People stop inviting you when you can't reciprocate."

"We can reciprocate! It might not be a seated dinner for fifty with an orchestra, but we can give—"

Mama said, "I don't want to have the kind of party we can give, and I don't want to go to a parade. Felicity's party on Mardi Gras day is about as much Carnival as I can stand, anyway."

"What about the balls, Mama?" I said. "I wish you'd go to a ball again. You know that blue velvet ball gown you wear, with the sleeves that look like butterfly wings? I like to see that dress; I wish you'd wear it to a ball again."

"And again, and again, the same old dress," said Constance. She smiled at me, the tolerant smile she gave to clumsy, apologetic strangers who bumped against her during a streetcar ride. "You have a nice way of putting things, Clay-Lee, you really do."

"If you won't wear the dress anymore, then give it to the child to play in," said my father. Something in his mild voice silenced Constance; she went on brushing Mishka, her head bent, but I noticed her hands were shaking. "Maybe next year," she said finally, looking up at us. "Next year, I'll go to the balls again."

• •

The de la Cordes had three houses: the galleried mansion in the Garden District; Summerhill, their white-painted country place on fifty acres in Covington; and an eight-room apartment in the Pontalba building, overlooking Jackson Square, in the Vieux Carré.

Of the three, my favorite was Summerhill. It was the setting for Easter egg hunts and Fourth of July barbecue suppers and, if the weather was fine, outdoor Thanksgiving dinners, the long table's white cloth stirring in an Indian-summer breeze that cooled the veranda. The place that most intrigued me, though, was the Pontalba, a century old the year I was born; it flanked the formal French garden of the square like twin brick fortresses. Each of its two buildings, one owned by the State of Louisiana, the other by the City of New Orleans, was three-storied and a block long, its cast-iron balconies scrolled and monogrammed with an intertwined AP, for its builder, Micaela, Baroness de Pontalba and her father, Don Andrés Almonester y Roxas. The dusky splendor of the Pontalba's St. Peter Street side was the setting every Mardi Gras for Felicity and Airey de la Corde's twelve-hour open house.

On Mardi Gras morning, I was startled, as usual, at the suddenness with which we reached our destination, surprised again by the unexpected nearness of my cousins' apartment, there among a row of what looked to me like little shops. One moment, my parents and I, costumed, respectively, as Robin Hood, Maid Marian, and Friar Tuck, were walking along the perimeter of Jackson Square, watching the other maskers, looking into shop windows, enjoying the aroma of coffee that floated from the Café du Monde; the next moment, the heavy street door of the de la Cordes' apartment swung open before us, and we were standing on the stone-floored *rez-de-chaussée* of the Pontalba. A wide staircase curved upward into dimness; from above us as we climbed came the sounds of people laughing, of the de la Corde children sassing their nurse, of Airey's voice calling out a greeting as the tops of our heads came into his line of vision. He stood near the railing, just outside the door that led into his elegant rooms.

The double parlor was bright with tulle-collared clowns and French royalty in pastel satins and white-powdered wigs. I saw several Lafittes the Pirate and one good sport in a gorilla suit. Against the far wall, a trumpet-dominant jazz quartet played ragtime; in a nearby corner, beside Courtenay's splendid old rocking horse, Sassy Patricia, a bevy of toddlers roamed across their nurses' laps, the nurses looking sharply to be sure they had the right baby in hand. Down three stone steps and to the right was the bottle-green, mirrored dining room. On an oval table were silver trays lined with cracked ice and heaped with pink, boiled shrimp, with oysters on the half shell, and tiny crab claws. From two big chafing dishes, the de la Corde servants dispensed hot shrimp Creole and red beans and rice, its gravy thick with nuggets of andouille, a pepper-studded sausage from La Place, Louisiana. Felicity had not forgotten the light eaters and pregnant ladies, either (and it seemed to me then there were always dozens of the latter, in this city of Catholic wealth and dynasty): waiters circulated with trays of watercress or Virginia ham finger sandwiches, offered iced tea to the mothers-to-be, and poured champagne for their husbands.

I saw Felicity near the dessert cart, cutting recklessly into a chocolate custard cake. She slid a piece of it onto a plate and gave it to a man who was either an elderly priest or was masquerading as an elderly priest.

"Hey, Courtenay," I said to my cousin, who had swept up suddenly in a long white nightgown, her feet bare, with some sort of gray dust on her cheeks.

"Hello, Clay-Lee," said Courtenay, whose face, at the age of eleven, held the promise that she would soon be a breathtaking replica of her mother. She looked closely at me. "What on earth are you? A mole?"

"A monk. Daddy says I'm Friar Tuck."

"Oh. Well, as you can see, I'm Joan of Arc." She held up her hands, which were twisted together with a rusted bicycle chain.

"What's Minette," I asked, "the same thing as you?" Minette, Courtenay's younger sister, was a shameless copycat.

"She's Pinky Lee."

"Here comes Viola," I said as an evil-looking, coal-black woman headed toward us from across the room. Viola, at the time, was serving as the de la Corde children's nurse. "Why does she always look so scary? What do you all do to her?"

"We don't do anything to her, that's just her natural face," said Courtenay. "She says anything she wants to, to my mother. I think Mummy's afraid of her."

"What you doin' with that dirty piece of chain all over your hands?" snarled Viola to Courtenay. She glanced over at me. "What you is, a squirrel?" I opened my mouth to reply, but she was already back to Courtenay. "Get in that bedroom and undo yourself before I tell your mama what you done to old Mrs. de la Corde's flag."

Lady-Sidonie, as a past Queen of Carnival, was entitled to fly from her place of residence the tricolored flag that signified the presence of Mardi Gras royalty within. It was fluttering now from the balcony of the Pontalba, or it should have been fluttering.

"What happened to the flag?" I whispered to Courtenay, following her into her bedroom.

"I had nothing to do with it. Minette ripped it in half. She was leaning way over the balcony railing, trying to see into a car across the street that had a gold-painted man in it lying across the backseat. Naturally, she lost her balance and grabbed onto the stupid flag to save herself. If it wasn't such an ancient piece of rag, it wouldn't have ripped." While Courtenay was wiping the dirt from her hands with one corner of the bedspread, Lady-Sidonie came into the room, carrying on her hip two-year-old Julie de la Corde.

"Good morning, Clay-Lee," said Lady-Sidonie. One of Julie's

rabbit ears was partially obstructing my view of Lady-Sidonie's face. "What a fine little Friar Tuck you are! I believe the servants and I are practically the only ones here not in costume. Your father says he can't remember a year when everyone was so much in the Carnival spirit." Lady-Sidonie was wearing a soft, white-collared dress the color of a cornflower.

"Minette, darling," she called, "if those are your checkered trouser-legs I see protruding from under the bed, please don't impale yourself on a splinter on my account. I assure you it doesn't matter a bit about the Carnival flag; it was only a matter of time before your mother put out one of her cigarettes on it anyway." Lady-Sidonie adored Felicity; it was a family joke, their being at odds about the flag, because Felicity should have been a Queen of Carnival, too, and had her own flag, instead of marrying Airey.

"Can I hold the baby?" said Courtenay. She put out her arms and Julie came to her.

"I suppose I should make you wash off the mud from that chain before you touch her, but since I found her under the dining-room table kissing Constance's dog, I guess a little more dirt won't make any difference." Lady-Sidonie sat down on one of the beds and motioned for us to come closer. "I have something to tell you," she said. Her voice had a serious tone I had heard her use only a few times before: the day she caught Courtenay getting set to pierce my ears with a staple gun, for one; the night she caught Courtenay filling me in on the facts of conception and childbirth (using illustrations from Airey's obstetrics text as documentation), for another.

"One of Clay-Lee's relatives has arrived here unexpectedly; he's just back in New Orleans from a vacation in the South Sea Islands after living for years and years in London, England. Clay-Lee, I don't believe you've ever even seen him—he's been away since before your mama and daddy were married. His name is Clement Calvert, and he's your father's uncle, and your great-uncle."

"Great-uncle?" said Minette. "How old is he? A hundred and two?"

"No, he's less than twenty years older than Clay-Lee's daddy, which makes him young for a title like 'great-uncle,'" said Lady-Sidonie. "You see, Rand's late father, Leland, had a brother who was only eighteen or so when Rand was born. That brother, Clement, was so much younger than Leland and his older brother, Clayton, that the Calvert family took to calling him 'Baby Brother,' and the name stuck. Surely you've heard your daddy speak of his 'Uncle Baby,' Clay-Lee?"

"'Uncle Baby?'" said Courtenay. "Is he the one Mummy can't stand? Let's see: he quit speaking to his wife the day he found out she'd never be able to have a baby, and finally shipped her home from London to die all by herself in that loony bin on Henry Clay Avenue."

"That's right," said Lady-Sidonie. "Although it wasn't a 'loony bin,' dear, it was the Home for Incurables. Poor Ida Marie was a victim of something called 'presenile dementia,' that may be passed on from mother to child. So you see it was a blessing, after all, that she never gave her husband any sons or daughters."

"He sounds terrible," I said. "Do I have to talk to him?"

"Of course you do," said Lady-Sidonie. "You'll probably be seeing quite a lot of him. He has a big sugarcane plantation in the country, right outside Houma."

"He sounds mentally retarded," Courtenay said. "'Uncle Baby.'"

Lady-Sidonie said, "I assure you he's not mentally retarded. I explained to you that he was the youngest of his mama's three sons, the only one of them, by the way, who's still living."

"What happened to the other two?" said Minette.

"My father's father, Leland, drowned in a boat accident when Daddy was eleven," I recited. "They had to drag Bayou Teche for him. Then the other one, Clayton, he choked on a bay leaf one night a few years later and died right there at the dinner table."

"Accident-prone, like poor Felicity," remarked Lady-Sidonie. "Now you girls be on good behavior. Baby can be a charming man when he wants to, but I doubt if he takes much to sassy children." She had the kindness not to look over at Courtenay.

The door banged open and party noises flowed into the room, accompanied by the dual mournful notes of "St. James Infirmary" on the trumpet, and Viola on the threshold.

"Mrs. de la Corde, we going to feed the babies out in the kitchen now," she announced, and took Julie out of Courtenay's arms.

"Remember, she has a narrow throat passage," called Lady-Sidonie after them. "See that you don't give her too much at one time."

"Yes, ma'am," sighed Viola. She had long ago resigned herself to Lady-Sidonie's one fall into excess, her passionate attachment to the youngest de la Corde. "The whole thing's mashed up, anyhow."

In the parlor, there was a general movement toward the door. Some of the guests were leaving temporarily, to walk through the Quarter and see the other maskers, and to watch the Rex parade, with its float bearing Rex, the King of Carnival. A woman dressed as a chef, with tiny measuring spoons dangling from her earlobes, came over to me and asked if I were looking for Rand and Constance. When I said I was, she told me they had left about half an hour before to walk along the riverfront. "Your mama took it into her head to see that Russian steamer that's in port," she said, gesturing toward the Mississippi with a deviled egg, the contents of which flew out and tumbled onto the rug. "Oh, now what!" said the woman, looking at the empty half an egg white she still held as if it were a cantankerous child. "I suppose now I'll have to go find one of the Negroes to clean the rug." She moved toward the dining room. "They'll be back, though. Your parents, I mean," she shouted to me. A red-faced man costumed as Napoleon waltzed past me into the fallen egg salad, grinding it into the carpet with the heel of his boot.

I stood still for a minute, trying not to appear lost or anxious, distress signals that might prompt some well-meaning adult to take me in hand, to offer to escort me through the crowded, dizzying streets. Felicity walked up to me.

"Sweet Jesus," she said conversationally, "this is the last year I'm hosting this circus, no matter what Airey says. Look at that mullet over there in the Napoleon suit, blind drunk before noon, strewing wreckage in his wake. . . . Speaking of wakes, there's a lovely one going on out on the balcony, with your Uncle Baby Brother's companion standing in for the corpse. Come meet them. I've never seen two people provoke such frozen stares."

Out on the balcony, a half-dozen guests were locked into the half-cocked posture of individuals who are waiting for the person next to them to be the first to get up and leave.

My first impression of Uncle Baby was of a huge piece of hazardous machinery, a locomotive engine perhaps, idling temporarily, dangerously, amidst a wary crowd. He bore some resemblance to my father—he had the wild, thick, dark-blond Calvert hair, though Baby's was threaded liberally with gray—but where Rand's nose was straight, this man's nose was slightly dented, and so were his cheekbones. Perhaps it was its irregularity that gave the face a reckless, arrogant look. (I found out much later that Clement Calvert had, quite literally, fought for his appearance; he had a penchant for straight bourbon, forthright remarks, and making love to married ladies, so long as they weren't married to him.)

He was standing with his back against the cast-iron railing, and his dark eyes, impatient in his sunburnt face, looked into mine for an instant, registered disinterest, and moved on. My own gaze shifted to the woman next to him: a beautiful creature with black hair that hung to the middle of her back. Her full lips were pushed out and partly open by her gleaming, protuberant teeth, and she was wearing a skimpy, banana-colored dress; as she half-sat upon the balcony railing, her narrow skirt rode high above her brown, well-muscled calves. Uncle Baby had brought an octoroon to the de la Cordes' Open House.

As Felicity and I came nearer, a worn-out-looking lady in a satin gypsy outfit was telling Uncle Baby that her brother, whom she referred to as "Lawyer Bartlett," was back in the hospital.

"Nothing trivial this time, I hope," said Baby. " 'Lawyer Bart-lett,' yes indeed; he cost me a half-million dollars one summer afternoon, in a court case here in Louisiana. My consolation, of course, was that Edgar Bartlett, Esquire, had to split the judgment with his client *and* with His Honor presiding on the bench."

The gypsy lady backed away, muttering "Of all the rudeness" to the onlookers. Then Baby Brother spotted Felicity.

"Felicity. Could I trouble one of your servants for a bourbon and water?" he said. He smelled of whiskey and of some exotic spice. "Apparently they all ran for cover when they spotted Thais here." The octoroon stared straight ahead, as unaffected as a deaf person would be by Uncle Baby's words. "By the way, I thought I recognized old Chick, the Léger family retainer, carving ham back there in the kitchen. What's he doing out of Parish Prison during Carnival season?"

"I suppose you asked him that, too," said Felicity. "Why don't you wait till the party's over before you run off my help?"

"Party's over now, as far as I'm concerned," said Uncle Baby. He pushed away from the railing and took a pack of Picayunes out of the pocket of his beautifully cut tweed jacket; he slid a cigarette into his mouth and lit it. "Lucky for me I brought my own matches, right, Felicity?" His eyes lifted from Felicity's face to a spot somewhere above her head. "Now wait a minute, wait a minute," he said. "Here comes some of my own help, Felicity, sugar. Nephew Rand, who, speaking of sugar, would understandably be anxious to get his hands into some of mine." He looked down at Felicity again. "I guess one of your boyfriends has told you by now I need somebody to run that damn sugar mill for me, in Terrebonne Parish?" He picked up a strand of Felicity's blond hair and wound it idly around two of his big fingers. "Who better for the job than poor old Leland's sole surviving son?" he asked. "By the way, word is the sole surviving son is politely starving to death, is that correct?"

"Get your hand out of my hair, and I'll introduce you to another survivor," said Felicity, pulling me in front of her. "This is Clay-Lee, Rand's child." She tapped me on the head and turned to go.

"Hello, son," said Uncle Baby indifferently. "Now, Felicity, don't get uppity with me, girl," he called after her, "an old friend like me! Why, I was there, remember? The night you split your dress open at that other costume party, that one at the Pickwick Club where you were masquerading as the Celibate Debutante." A collective gasp from the glacial gathering on the balcony.

"What a sense of humor you still have," Felicity called back. "I'd forgotten all about your sense of humor, thank God."

Courtenay was tugging at my sleeve. "Viola has plates ready for you and Minette and me," she said. "The best of the ham, and more shrimp than you can count. Come on, we're having a picnic in the butler's pantry." She lowered her voice. "Chick is drunk as a monkey. He promised to show us how to jimmy a lock as soon as Viola goes to put the baby down for her nap."

I said, "I'll be there in a minute." Constance and Rand had returned from their walk, and Rand was introducing his wife to his uncle. Uncle Baby Brother Calvert, looking at Constance Alexander Calvert, had the same expression on his face that the little boys at Reva and Zee's Camp Street Sweet Shoppe got on theirs when they were handed a sugar teat.

"Rand, my congratulations to you, many years overdue. I missed the wedding, but I still get to kiss the bride, don't I?"

I braced myself. For some reason I expected Uncle Baby to grab my mother by the blue satin lacings on the bodice of her Maid Marian dress and haul her off, the way big cats in zoot suits did to lady mice on the Saturday-morning television cartoons.

Uncle Baby drew Constance close to him, held her lovely little face in his huge hands, and kissed her cheek as gently as if she were made of eggshells. She barely came to the middle of his chest.

"Hermés," said Constance, smiling up at him. "You have on the same scent my father always wore; he used to send all the way to Paris for it."

"That means you like it, then?"

"I love it, it reminds me of when I was a little girl."

Uncle Baby said, "Airey tells me you're Judge Thomas Alexander's little girl. A long time ago my father heard your daddy argue, as an attorney, before the Louisiana Supreme Court, and he never forgot it. The Judge was the sort of gentleman the South is crying out for right now."

Rand said, "Constance, can I get you something, darling? A glass of wine, or maybe you want to have your lunch now. Uncle Baby, will you join us?"

But Uncle Baby had already joined; he had begun to reminisce to Constance about the impressive funeral cortege Judge Alexander, deceased, had commanded, reports of which had traveled clear over to London, where Baby had been living at the time.

Mama looked over at my father, smiled at him briefly, then continued listening.

"Lamb, guess who's here," said Felicity, reappearing unexpectedly and pulling Constance away from Uncle Baby's side. "Julia Sawyer. Remember Julia, Sis Honorine's cousin? She works now for the caterer I'm using. Come on out to the kitchen with me for a minute and tell her hello."

Uncle Baby said to Constance, " 'Lamb?' What is that, your baby name?"

"That's right, Lamb's her baby name," snapped Felicity. "What's yours? 'Wolf?' "

"Let's all walk out to the dining room and have some lunch," said Rand. "Uncle Baby, you've been away from New Orleans so long, I bet you've forgotten how to eat boiled crab."

Felicity said, "Baby hasn't forgotten how to do anything he used to do in New Orleans. Didn't you see him a few minutes ago, grinding his hips like a nigger second-liner in a Mardi Gras parade, while he was greeting your wife?"

"Clay-Lee, run eat your lunch," said Mama, turning so suddenly to me that the low-cut neckline of her dress pulled away from her bosom, exposing the tops of her small, curved breasts.

"Mama, your dress!" I whispered loudly, feeling a wave of heat creep up my neck to my face.

"Courtenay and Minette are both in the butler's pantry, honey; go on now, and have your lunch with them," Felicity told me.

As I was going, Uncle Baby said to Rand, "Did you know Felicity's mama and daddy always wanted her to be a nun? Convent wouldn't keep her, though. The nuns couldn't retrain her to say 'Superior' after she said the word 'Mother.'"

Daddy wasn't listening. He was looking with sympathetic eyes at Thais, who continued to sit there against the balcony railing, and to stare straight ahead. It occurred to me that she couldn't understand English. For reasons I didn't completely understand, I hoped she couldn't.

By nightfall, Mardi Gras had had its usual black-magic-like effect on me. In the de la Cordes' burgundy-colored study, lamplit now and quiet, with its consoling smells of leather and books and freshly made coffee, I sat in a soft old armchair, frightening myself by conjuring up scenes from the day just past.

There was the half-naked man, gold-painted, leaping on the hood of a stalled car on Royal Street, denting the car's metal, cracking its windshield with his gilded fist. And the silky laughter of a lady in taffeta ruffles, the slash of her mouth bright red behind the black veil of her hat. "That's a man," Courtenay, beside me, had whispered. "Look, Clay-Lee! His hips are shaped all wrong, and see how funny he's walking in those pretty silver shoes?" The spilled, sweet-smelling wine that dampened and stained the edges of my monk's robe; the danger just beneath the high spirits of the Wild Tchoupitoulas Indians, a locally famous band of Negroes whose exquisite headdresses fanned out high above the crowd, like the exotic plumage of strutting, white-feathered peacocks.

Most of the de la Cordes' guests had departed by now, gone home to dress for the Comus or Rex balls or to collapse, exhausted, onto their beds.

Uncle Baby Brother had hung around all afternoon, speaking to no one except Airey, once or twice, and annoying the ladies by taking Thais on his lap and feeding her finger sandwiches. I didn't see him speak to Constance again, or even look in her direction, although at one point he appeared at her side and took away the empty coffee cup she was holding. Constance, looking startled, told him thank you, and then after he had nodded to her and turned away again, I saw her look down at her hands and smile.

She said to me, "I'll bet that's the first time he's ever performed that particular service. He picked up that saucer as carelessly as if he expected the cup to be glued to it."

"Maybe he didn't care if he broke it," I said. I didn't like Uncle Baby, even before he and the octoroon vanished from the party without bothering to tell anybody good-bye.

"Comus parade coming!" called out Chick from near the French doors to the balcony. Mysteriously, he sounded sober again.

"Let's all go watch it!" said Felicity. My mother and father were already on their feet; Mama was looking behind the sofa cushions for her white wool muffler. "Come on, Airey," Felicity begged. "Don't sit there like Methuselah. Roland Finch said if we wanted to watch the parade from the balcony of his apartment over on Royal Street, he'd have hot chocolate for the children."

"Roland, roll me home," said Courtenay.

"Why not let Viola drive our girls, and Clay-Lee, home to Philip Street—if they're tired?" said Airey, allowing Felicity to pull him out of his chair. "Rand, did you remind your friend John McCaleb to join us for White Lunch tomorrow?"

"White Lunch" was a pleasant ritual Rand and Airey carried out every year, to mark the beginning of the forty days of Lent.

Even though my father was Presbyterian, he was intrigued by the Catholic ritual of the Distribution of Ashes, and each Ash Wednesday, he and Airey attended noon Mass together at St. Louis Cathedral, where their foreheads were crossed with ashes by a black-thumbed priest who murmured over them, *"Memento, homo, quia pulveris es, et in pulverem reveteris"* (Remember, man, thou art dust, and unto dust thou shalt return). Then they walked to Antoine's, five minutes away, on St. Louis Street, where Raymond, their black-coated waiter, had ready for them the first course of their annual White Lunch: Vichyssoise, accompanied by vodka martinis, followed by filet de truite au vin blanc, pommes de terre soufflés, a bottle of Pouilly-Fuissé, and for dessert, Baked Alaska. No green salad, or coffee, or cigars, in keeping with the Tout Blanc dictum.

"John said he'd be there," my father said to Airey. "Although I wouldn't count on his elbowing past us in the ashes line at the cathedral; he's a practicing atheist. I told him to meet us at one o'clock at Antoine's."

"Are you sure you've had enough Mardi Gras?" Felicity was asking me. "These spoilsports of mine can go on home; you come along with us." I think she felt sorry for having told off Uncle Baby in front of me.

"No, really," I said. "I'm a spoilsport, too; I'd better go with Courtenay and Minette."

"Then let Clay-Lee spend the night at Philip Street; Lady-Sidonie is already there," Felicity told Constance. "My girls have school tomorrow, but if Clay-Lee has a holiday, she can play with the baby till after lunch, and then Viola will drive her home."

"All right," said Mama absentmindedly. She was daubing with a white handkerchief at a corner of my father's mouth. "You've either been into the jam pots again," she complained, "or a lady with blackberry lipstick has been nibbling at your face." He bent down and kissed her on the neck. "I should have come as a vampire," he said. "Forward behavior is de rigueur for a vampire." Constance laughed for the first time I could remember since before the break-in.

On the drive home, while we were two blocks from Philip Street, Viola almost ran over a frail, gray-haired Negro who was slowly crossing Prytania.

"Get out the street, road hog," she yelled at him. "You going to be dead, if you isn't already, old Tom." Looking more puzzled than frightened, he stood there, squinting at us through the glare of the headlights. In the back seat, the baby awakened in Courtenay's arms and began to cry. Poor Julie. She didn't like Mardi Gras any better than I did.

6

Morning at the Philip Street house: Viola's gray-brown hands, wrinkled as an elephant's skin, slamming down a plate of fried grits on the tabletop in front of me. She seized a milk bottle by its neck and poured out my glassful with ruthless precision. "You seven yet?" she asked me. "I'm nine," I told her, with as much indignation as I could reasonably display, given the situation. I was, after all, barefoot, dressed in a robe my cousin had outgrown, and temporarily dependent for my breakfast on Viola's erratic sense of bounty.

"Nine, huh?" said Viola. "Well, you going to hell, then, sure as shootin': I ran out of butter, so I fried your grits in bacon grease." Ash Wednesday was an occasion for fast and for abstinence from meat under pain of mortal sin, for Catholics past the age of seven and under the age of sixty. All over New Orleans, housewives and cooks were calling church rectories, annoying priests with the same questions: "Does bacon grease count as meat, Father, if I just fry something meatless in it? What about a can of vegetable soup that has 'beef extract' listed among the ingredients?" Viola, of course, would never have troubled to consult Father Faber, the de la Corde "family priest," on a matter relating to the ultimate destination of a white person's soul. With the exception of Lady-Sidonie, we were all damned anyway, as far as Viola was concerned; we were having our heaven right here on earth, laughing it up in the present life, and largely at the expense of the black man, too.

"Where is everybody, Viola?" I asked, swallowing the last of my golden-brown ticket to hell. I had been resigned to the idea of personal damnation since the day of my First Communion. "Felicity and old Mrs. de la Corde over at the church, getting ashes. Your two cousins *been* gone; their papa dropped them off at school." Viola cackled grimly. "You should of seen 'em: Coatney with big bags near her eyes, cursing under her breath—where she picks up all them words?—and Minette, with her jacket all rurnt and wrinkled up like a old drunk's." She shook her head. "The nuns sure must dislike those children, making them wear what they do, ugly old brown getups. Must have something against them."

"Mama told me there are Sacred Heart schools all over the world," I said. "She told me Felicity boarded at Villa Duchesne, the one in St. Louis, the year she was fourteen. There's even one in Paris, called Sacré Coeur. I wonder what kind of uniforms the girls at Sacré Coeur wear?"

"Something with feathers and beads stuck on it, is my bet," said Viola. "French people! They all a disgrace."

"What about Lady-Sidonie, then? She's French."

"No, she ain't. She American, same as you and me. She maybe got some French mixed in, but not in no amount to make her crazy." She removed my empty plate and glass and began to wash them at the sink. "You going to be called upon to entertain the baby this morning," she said, her back to me. "I got ironing to do."

"Is Julie still asleep?"

"Asleep? She at the church already. Felicity hauled her off in all this cold, saying she want Father Faber to bless her. She said he just back from Europe and he dying to see the baby again."

From the direction of the driveway came the sound of car doors slamming. "There they is," announced Viola. She opened the kitchen door and looked out. "Who's that big, mop-headed gentleman? Ain't he the same one brought the mixed girl to the Mardi Gras party?" I walked over and stood near Viola. There was a dark green, foreign-looking car parked behind Felicity's yellow convertible. Across the lawn came Lady-Sidonie, her black mantilla still on her head. She was carrying the baby, who was crying. Walking several feet back of Lady-Sidonie were Felicity and my newfound, Great-Uncle Baby Brother. Uncle Baby looked as dignified as a cardsharp this morning; he was wearing a dark blue three-piece suit and carrying a tan topcoat over one arm. With his other arm he guided Felicity gallantly across the frosty grass.

"Viola, did Julie eat all her breakfast this morning?" asked Lady-Sidonie. "She cried through most of the services, and that's not like her. I think she might be hungry." Julie stopped crying when she realized where she was; she looked toward the sunny corner where her high chair stood and sniffed at the telltale aroma of bacon grease in the warm kitchen air. "Give her here," said Viola, "and let me change her out of her coat and her church clothes." She unbuttoned the baby's black velvet dress and reached into a nearby basket of clean clothes for a pair of corduroy coveralls and a sweater. "She left half her cereal in her bowl awhile earlier; looked like she was scared you all would leave for the church without her." Julie was in her high chair by the time Felicity and Uncle Baby walked in.

"Look who followed us home. I found him over at Our Mother of Perpetual Help, slithering out of one of the confessionals," Felicity said to no one in particular. "Let's see, now: Father Faber told you you'd have to petition the pope for absolution, is that right, Baby?"

"Felicity, dear, don't make light of the sacraments. It frightens me to hear you talk that way," said Lady-Sidonie, unpinning her veil.

"It frightens you?" yelled Uncle Baby. "Well it scares the

sh— it scares me, too, Mrs. de la Corde. When Felicity here starts turning judgmental, it's time for all of us to put it in reverse and back off, wouldn't you say?"

"Viola, would you heat up a little coffee and a brioche for Mrs. de la Corde and our guest and me? We'll have it in the dining room." Felicity pushed through the swinging door that led through the butler's pantry, saying over her shoulder to my uncle, "It's Lent, remember. No eggs and bacon for you."

"I didn't come here for bacon, I came for business," Uncle Baby said as he followed her. "Maybe I can talk you into investing with me. Airey's just like every other doctor I've run across. Got about as much of a head for commerce as one of those sidewalk artists out at Jackson Square. . . ."

Lady-Sidonie watched the swinging door fall shut, then she went to the oak sideboard and took a cup and saucer from the shelves. "If I won't be in your way, I'd just as soon have my coffee out here with the children," she told Viola.

"Yes, ma'am," said Viola. She poured the cup full of the black-French-drip coffee that Lady-Sidonie loved. "No brioche this morning," said Lady-Sidonie, when Viola slid a puffy roll onto her plate.

"Mrs. de la Corde, you too up in age and too underweight to be fasting," scolded Viola. "If you don't take care, you going to do just like my poor mama done; hit the floor one of these mornings and never come up." She disappeared into the butler's pantry, carrying Felicity's and Uncle Baby's breakfast on a white wooden tray. I reflected for a minute on the case of Viola's recently departed mama. According to Sis Honorine, the cause of the deceased's final crash had been not a fast, but sloe gin, self-administered in a steadily increased dosage throughout her career as baby caretaker in the overcrowded nursery of a family named Mouton.

"Look, there's the hot water ready for the baby's cereal," said Lady-Sidonie, as Viola returned to the kitchen. Steam was rising from the spout of the copper teakettle; halfheartedly, Julie began to bang her spoon against her high chair. "It's coming, sweetheart," Lady-Sidonie told her.

I had long since finished my own breakfast, but I sat on, watching Lady-Sidonie drink her coffee. Frankly, the idea of walking barefoot through the dining room, past Uncle Baby Brother, while dressed in Minette's beat-up chenille robe, seemed as out of the question as, say, appearing in Viola's kitchen wearing blackface.

Suddenly, I heard a sound like the one made by the old bathtub drain in our Camp Street house, when the last of the water was spiraling down into it: a sucking, choking noise, as if liquid were being fed too quickly down a narrow opening into damaged pipes. The idea of "narrow" made me think of something Lady-Sidonie had said the day before, and days before that: "Remember, Viola, she has a narrow throat passage" and turning, I saw the baby, Julie, her face darkening, her eyes rolling like blue buttons inside a tilted cup. The terrible drowning sound was coming from her.

I had always thought that grown-ups moved too slowly; Viola lumbered, Lady-Sidonie strolled, Felicity even limped. But during those awful moments there in the kitchen, it was as if I were the only slow-moving person in the house, besides the baby, of course: Julie and I, powerless as always, frozen within the dangerous dependence of children's lives.

"Something's upsetted her stomach," Viola cried. "She can't have nothing stuck in her windpipe, I didn't give her nothing solid!" and she slapped the baby's back till I was afraid the small bones would crack under the force of the blows. Lady-Sidonie ran her finger down Julie's throat and brought up what looked like a ribbon of yellow jelly; the drowning sound went on, and now a sort of wheezing accompanied it, a strangled whine like wind howling through cracks in a flimsy wall. Then Felicity ran past me, so close her blond hair brushed the top of my head. The fearless spirit which governed most aspects of Felicity's life routinely deserted her when the well-being of her babies was at stake; she was notorious for "going to pieces" at such times. She looked at her child, dying there in Lady-Sidonie's arms, and she began to scream and to aimlessly circle the room, till Viola screamed back at her, "For Jesus' sake, take ahold of yourself—I can't hear the baby for all that racket!"

Suddenly Uncle Baby was there. He grabbed Julie out of Lady-Sidonie's arms and turned the child upside down, holding her by the ankles with one big hand, as a doctor would hold a newborn struggling for its first breath; with his other fist he struck her once, between the shoulder blades. A gurgling, free-flowing rush of vomit spurted from Julie's mouth onto the floor, and then she was still. Uncle Baby turned her right side up and looked at her. Her skin was pink for a few seconds, then it faded to greenish-white.

"Get my car keys," Uncle Baby told Viola. "I left them on the dining-room table. And bring me a small blanket of some kind. Felicity?" Felicity was one step ahead of him, at his side, her fur coat over her shoulders, Julie's black velvet dress in her hands. She began to fumble with the buttons of the baby's coveralls.

"What the hell are you doing?" Uncle Baby asked her.

"I'm dressing her," answered Felicity. Her voice sounded as though it were coming from inside an empty well. "She can't go to the doctor's office wearing coveralls."

"Jesus Christ, only in New Orleans," said Uncle Baby. He helped button the velvet dress and then wrapped Julie in the fringed afghan Viola handed to him.

"I'm taking her to Touro," he said to Lady-Sidonie. "We don't have time to drive all the way out to Ochsner. Contact her pediatrician and tell him to meet us there, in the Touro Emergency Room. And get hold of Airey, if you can find him."

"He's in surgery this morning," Felicity said.

"Well, get him anyway," Uncle Baby directed. "If he's already left the hospital, call the cathedral rectory, or Antoine's. He mentioned to me yesterday he'd be at both places sometime today."

He gave Julie to Felicity, and they were gone. Lady-Sidonie and Viola and I stood perfectly still there in the kitchen, listening to the expensive engine noises of Uncle Baby's foreign car as it backed out of the driveway and roared on down Philip Street.

I spent a second night at the de la Cordes'. Felicity was still at the hospital, and my mother had gone there to be with her and Airey, so my father telephoned Viola to tell her I should remain for the time being with Courtenay and Minette. That night I had a dream of waltzing in the dark with a top-hatted man, of becoming entangled in the folds of the cape he wore, and when fear finally shook me awake, I found little comfort in the snoring presence of Minette beside me. I left my bed and went along the hall to Lady-Sidonie's room, where a strip of yellow light shone beneath the door.

Lady-Sidonie was sitting up in bed, wearing a green velvet robe with a high collar of ivory-colored lace.

"What is it, Clay-Lee?" she said. "Are you thirsty?" I was ashamed to tell her that a dream had driven me in terror from my bed, when the reality of Julie's illness was weighing so heavily upon her, so I sat and watched her pour a glass of water for me from the thermos that stood on the oak nun's chest nearby.

"Do you know the story of the Star Dipper?" she asked. "Every time I give someone a drink, I remember my mother telling me that tale, of the little girl who was so loving and brave that the dipper she used for giving water to others was turned by God into diamonds, and then into stars." She tucked my hair behind my ears in a tense, distracted gesture. "It's a terrible thing, Clay-Lee, when a child dies."

"Julie isn't dead," I said. "Maybe she isn't going to die. Maybe Felicity will come home from the hospital and bring the baby back with her."

"Maybe she will. It's unlike me, you know, to feel so hopeless—despair is a grave sin. But this night, Clay-Lee . . . there's a coldness to it, an emptiness."

"It's because you loved her too much," I said unthinkingly. Quickly I amended, "Not *too* much; so much."

Lady-Sidonie smiled and took my hand, lacing her fingers with mine. Her hand was as soft as a young woman's, as firm and supple as my mother's hands. "No, Clay-Lee; you said it correctly the first time: I loved her too much. When I was younger than you are now, I had an Irish nurse named Siobhan who warned me against the dangers of loving too much. 'The Lord always finds out about it,' she told me, 'and then He takes away that person or that thing you love too much. He does it for the salvation of your immortal soul, to prevent you from having false gods before you.' Siobhan, I'm afraid, had a rather limited understanding of the mercy of God. But sometimes her words come back to me, and they stir in me some strange and sorrowful thoughts."

Outside Lady-Sidonie's windows, the night sky was fading to a dark blue. Morning was coming, Felicity had been gone almost twenty-four hours, and Airey with her. Courtenay and Minette had come white-faced and silent to the dinner table; Viola had promised us French toast for our next morning's breakfast, and still we had no word about Julie. As long as we don't know for certain, we can keep up hoping, Viola told us, and she spooned extra meunière sauce over Courtenay's trout. Courtenay had lifted her sad brown eyes to mine, then lowered them to her overflowing plate.

At last I fell asleep, and when I opened my eyes again, Lady-Sidonie's bedroom was gray with morning light. From downstairs came the ordinary smells of toast burning and coffee boiling over, the ordinary sounds of Viola bringing in the newspaper and slamming the leaded-glass front door with start-of-the-day disgust.

"You were crying in your sleep," Lady-Sidonie said to me. "Was it another bad dream?"

I couldn't answer her, because I wasn't certain why I cried.

Maybe my tears were for Lady-Sidonie, who had been kind to me always and who feared now the loss of another child whom she loved, or maybe it was, in fact, a bad dream that had saddened me. Lately I had had a recurrent nightmare in which my father, downcast, childlike, expected me to find for him something he had lost, but in the dream I could never seem to help him.

Lady-Sidonie laid her head close to mine.

"You're an imaginative child, Clay-Lee," she said, "but you must put your imagination to good use. Don't waste a lot of time fighting problems you only think you see."

Felicity came home that day at noon; my mother was with her. "Do I look a hundred years older? I feel it," said Felicity to the group of us she had surprised in the dining room—Courtenay, Minette, and me, with mustard on our faces, and Lady-Sidonie with apprehension on hers. Felicity dropped down heavily in the chair next to mine, and I could smell the lovely scent that clung to her fur coat. "Poor Julie," Felicity began, "at first they thought it was diphtheria and they wanted to put her in the contagious ward." Viola came in from the laundry room and stationed herself alongside Lady-Sidonie, ready to move into action should this prove to be the moment for Lady-Sidonie to slump to the floor. " 'Contagious ward'—my God, you should have heard Uncle Baby when old Weidner suggested that!" ("Old Weidner" was Dr. Sarah Weidner, a brilliant spinster pediatrician who annoyed Felicity by constantly referring to her during house calls to the de la Cordes as "the distraught mother.")

According to Felicity, the champion of the hour had turned out to be the dark horse, Uncle Baby Brother. He had galvanized the nurses into interrupting Dr. Weidner during surgery (she happened to be at Touro that morning, removing a pair of tiny tonsils from a welfare patient) and transporting the doctor over to the emergency room, where she looked at Julie and made a preliminary diagnosis of diphtheria. "Where's Dr. de la Corde?" whispered a shaken young nurse to Felicity, as Uncle Baby roared his refusal to allow Julie to be "offered up to the 'sacrificial ward—contagious.'" "We can't find him," Felicity wept to the nurse, while Julie vomited down the front of Sarah Weidner's surgical smock. Uncle Baby next threatened to tear apart the small, primitive-looking oxygen tent that was wheeled into Julie's private room on the pediatrics floor. "For Christ's sake!" shouted Dr. Weidner, still wearing her bile-smelling surgical greens. "Orderly! Bring in the biggest tent we've got, and then throw this overbearing son of a bitch out of here!"

By the time Airey arrived at the hospital an hour later, Uncle Baby was gone. He had driven over to Camp Street to get my mother, and then dropped her off at the hospital to sit with Felicity. When Airey finally saw his daughter, her illness had been correctly diagnosed as acute asthma complicated by bronchial pneumonia, and she was asleep within the vast plastic confines of the oxygen-tent-big-enough-for-two.

"Clay-Lee," Mama said, as soon as Felicity had finished speaking, "I'll bet Daddy and poor Mishka are frantic by now, wondering what's become of us. Let's go home."

"Without no lunch?" cried Viola in disbelief, staring after my mother's thin, retreating form. "The *dog* ain't going to be sittin' up waitin' for no news! Come on back and eat some sandwich!" I could hear her going on as we walked through the kitchen and out the back door. "Um, um," she was saying, "I can see it coming: that poor little thing going to be the next one to drop."

7

Clement "Baby Brother" Calvert had not returned to Louisiana because he missed grits and chitlins, nor because he'd been seized by a charitable whim to appoint his nephew, the artist, manager of a sugar mill. Months would go by after that Mardi Gras before we discovered his real reasons, months during which some predictable damage was done to my father's ego and, naturally, to Uncle Baby's profit margin.

Of course, it took considerable persuasion to get Rand Calvert to agree to go to work for Uncle Baby—but Uncle Baby's ally in the persuasion department turned out to be Constance, who, I suppose, was finally becoming disenchanted with Laudemeyer's bag-meat stew and with the chronic bronchitis she suffered each winter she spent at the drafty house on Camp Street. Uncle Baby did recruit her at a weak moment, though, and for that I will always feel partially responsible. The weak moment, which occurred a few days after Julie de la Corde was hospitalized, might never have come about had it not been for me and my wild Calvert hair.

Washing that hair had always been an ordeal. There was so much of it, and each strand seemed to grow in a slightly different direction, making for the kind of screams I didn't know I had in me till my mother attempted to comb out the wet, freshly shampooed snarls.

Finally, in order to make the torture sessions more bearable for both of us, Mama made up a game which she called, "Madame Loretta's Beauty Shop." She played the part of Madame Loretta, "the world's meanest beauty operator," while I took the roles of the various customers.

Because the water at our kitchen sink came out of the tap hotter and with greater force than it did out of the bathroom faucets, Madame Loretta's Beauty Shop was located in our kitchen. Mama made me promise not to tell anyone that, though; washing a child's hair in the kitchen sink, she explained, was the kind of thing people who were "the scum of the earth" might do.

That Saturday after Mardi Gras, Mama decided to shampoo my hair. She put on her Madame Loretta outfit, a tacky lilac housedress that Honey had found at McCrory's five-and-dime; the dress had a nylon collar upon which Honey had embroidered "Loretta." My costume consisted of my white slip, plus a bath towel which Mama pinned around my shoulders. Honey had the part of the surly receptionist who overcharged the customers and called them by the wrong names.

"Madame Loretta, report to Stall One, Madame Loretta," Honey began in a nasal whine, as if she were speaking into a microphone. "A Mrs. Moscowitz is here, for a blue rinse and a pin-curl permanent." I said, "Wait a minute. Where's Daddy?" (I had refused to let my father see me with my hair wet since the time he had looked at me, every strand standing out on my head, and asked if I had recently washed my hair, or if the governor had called in his pardon too late.) Honey said, "Mrs. Moscowitz, please contain yourself. I have no idea where your 'daddy' is. I *do* have a message for a Miss *Calvert*, when she arrives, that *her* father will be at his studio on Constantinople Street till about six P.M."

"What's the trouble here?" called Madame Loretta, from near the sink. "Mrs. Moscowitz, if you do not take your place at the shampoo basin immediately, I will be forced to shave your entire head. The Board of Health has recently cracked down on this place."

"Does that mean she gets her own rinse water, then?" said Honey. "You told me to save the water we rinsed the other customers' heads in to use later on Mrs. Moscowitz, Madame Loretta."

"Oh, Honey, that's disgusting," complained Mama, dropping out of character for a minute.

"What do you expect me to act like at these wages, in this dump?" said the receptionist. "The Queen of Comus? Oh, well, sorry, Constance."

"*You* are fired," said Madame Loretta, bending my head backward over the sink and brushing my hair. "Mrs. Moscowitz, how old are you now? Sixty-five, seventy?"

"I'm nine!"

"Then you definitely need a haircut. All this long hair is pulling your face down, making you look much older . . ."

The doorbell rang.

"Honey, will you run answer the door?" said Mama. "I'm just about to put Clay-Lee's head under the faucet."

Honey said, "But I'm barefoot! I came over here through the bedroom window, remember?" I supposed answering the door while barefoot must be another thing only the scum-of-the-earth people did.

"I'll get it," I said, glad to postpone the awful moment when the cold shampoo would creep over my scalp.

Through the front window I saw a shiny black car, a Negro wearing a uniform cap at the wheel. There was a funeral parlor nearby, on Magazine Street, and I thought as I opened the door that one of their hearses must have broken down in front of our house.

Uncle Baby Brother was standing on the front porch. He and his hair appeared to have grown several inches since Mardi Gras day. Uncle Baby said, "Hey, sugar. Where's your mama?"

"She's out in the kitchen," I said, trying to think what I should do next. Some instinct told me Mama would not care to have Uncle Baby Brother catch her dressed up as Madame Loretta, standing near the sink with the shampoo bottle.

"In the kitchen? You're not allowing her to wet her pretty hands, I hope."

You don't know the half of it, I thought.

"Clay-Lee, who is it?" called Constance. "If it's that Roman candy man again, you just tell him to go away, you hear?"

"Candy man!" yelled Uncle Baby. "Roman candy, two cents a stick!"

Constance rushed into the living room, ready to run the taffy merchant off the porch, and found herself face-to-face with Uncle Baby Brother.

He came closer to Mama and read again the name embroidered on the collar of her awful housedress. " 'Loretta?' " said Uncle Baby, sounding amused. "What the hell *is* your name? 'Lamb,' 'Loretta,' 'Constance,' what?"

"We were playing a *game*," I said rudely. I hated it when anybody, even Daddy, teased Mama; her eyes always turned so sad.

Mama said, "Clement, how nice to see you. Won't you sit down?" She was as dignified as if she were wearing a ball gown— my mother never made excuses for herself, even when she was embarrassed. She had told me excuse making was just as pointless as hanging back when someone asked you to play the piano or to otherwise perform.

"Thank you, no, I came by to ask you if you might consider coming downtown with me, to have lunch at Antoine's. There's something very important I'd like to discuss with you. It concerns a certain position in my sugar company that I think Rand might be interested in, and I wanted to run it by you, too." He grinned apologetically. "I spoke to Rand on Mardi Gras, so I happen to know he's away, working all day today."

"Well, maybe I could," said Mama, her cheeks reddening. I could tell by the tone of her voice how badly she wanted to go. She had never been to Antoine's for lunch before that I could remember. And I think she wanted to show Uncle Baby that she had a pretty dress to wear, after all.

"Clay-Lee, please go tell Honey that you're going to stay at her house this afternoon. I'm going to run upstairs for a minute."

"Take your time, 'Loretta,' " Uncle Baby called after her.

When I went out to the kitchen to speak to Honey, she told me to take off my towel, put on my dress, and go out to the parlor and entertain Uncle Baby while she sneaked up the stairs in her bare feet. (It never occurred to me, of course, to ask her how I was supposed to entertain him. "Entertaining" guests was a social duty Southern children were expected to carry out without ever being given specific directions, just like "minding your manners" was.)

Uncle Baby was squatting on the front porch, petting Mishka, by the time I put on my dress and rejoined him.

"This dog's a beauty," he said, running his hands over her coat. "Is she yours?"

"Oh, no, sir, she belongs to my mother," I said. Mishka, her tail perfectly still, the whites of her eyes showing, looked up at Uncle Baby as if she wished he'd leave her alone.

"You like cats?" I said conversationally.

"Can't stand the sonsabitches," replied Uncle Baby. "I wish somebody'd take and hang every goddamn last one of the creatures."

Out of the side of my eye, I saw two Negro boys about twelve years of age walking toward our house. They were the same boys who had laughed at me when they saw me on the porch Mardi Gras morning, dressed in my hooded monk's costume. One had hollered, "You a spook, or what you is?" and the other had yelled, "You *con*-fused, Spook! You dressed up for Halloween!"

"You want to go in now?" I suggested to Uncle Baby as we watched the two children run their hands over the fenders of his limousine, while the chauffeur motioned through the window for them to go away.

"Go in? Why?" said Uncle Baby. "What's the matter, you afraid of those two?"

"Not really. Well, yes, in a way. See, they'll sometimes yell things at you."

"They will, huh," said Uncle Baby.

He continued to stroke Mishka.

"Big *funny*-lookin' dog!" yelled one of the boys, pointing at Mishka.

"What you all call that crazy-lookin', skinny-leg dog?" called out the other boy.

Uncle Baby stood up and brought Mishka to her feet, along with him. "This dog? I call this dog, 'Nigger-Killer,' " said Uncle Baby.

"Go on in the house now, Clay-Lee," said Constance, appearing in the doorway just as the two black children took off across the front yard. She was wearing a plain black dress I didn't like, one that had come from Paris a long time ago, and she had on Grandmother Alexander's wedding pearls. "Honey's waiting upstairs for you. We won't be very long, will we, Clement?"

"I hope we will. Clay-Lee, you tell Miss Honey we're going to stay out just as long as your mother permits me the pleasure of her company," said Uncle Baby, escorting Constance down the steps.

I watched from the front window as the chauffeur helped them into the limousine, and they drove away.

It was after six o'clock that night when Constance returned. Daddy and I were upstairs, playing checkers in my bedroom, when we heard the front door slam, and then Mama's high-heeled footsteps clicked quickly up the wooden steps and along the upstairs hall.

"Well, look at you two," she said, speaking rapidly. She sounded out of breath, and she looked more beautiful, despite the black dress, than I had ever seen her; she looked like Rose Red, the girl in one of my storybooks who had tamed the fearsome bear with her loveliness. "Have you all eaten, or do you want me to fix you something? I think there're still some red beans in the refrigerator." She took her shoes off and lay back on my bed, on her elbows, her stockinged toes touching the floor.

"I thought we'd all go get something to eat at Camellia Grill," said Daddy, concentrating on the checkerboard.

Constance said, "Oh, Rand, I couldn't eat a thing. Clement took me to Antoine's. We had a private lunch in the Mystery Room, and I thought the courses would never stop coming. I ate enough soufflé potatoes alone to send my chair through the floor. Guess who our waiter was? Raymond! Remember Raymond? Or maybe you don't. He was Daddy's waiter, whenever Daddy took me there."

"I know Raymond. He's Airey's waiter, too. Maybe next Ash Wednesday, instead of having White Lunch with Airey and John, I'll take you to Antoine's instead."

"Rand, for heaven's sake, it's the one time in the whole year you can afford to eat there; go ahead and go with Airey, like you've been doing. You don't need me tagging along."

I said, "If we go to Camellia Grill, can I order ice cream in my orange freeze?"

"Sure," said Daddy. "What kept you downtown so long, Lamb? It's after six o'clock."

"We were at Antoine's till three-thirty; there were some Bordeaux on the wine list that Clement wanted me to try. Then the chauffeur, his name is Clarence, Clarence drove us to Solari's grocers on Royal Street so Clement could pick up some things he needed for the dinner party he's giving tomorrow. I didn't know you could buy smoked redfish at Solari's."

"You can buy anything you want at Solari's, if you can afford to give them what they ask for it. Where's Clement staying? For that matter, what's he doing in New Orleans? Did you get around to discussing that?"

"We did discuss that. He's in town to straighten up some mess at that sugarmill he owns, and he's staying in a suite at the Roosevelt Hotel till he decides whether or not to buy a house and live here permanently. By the way," she added, "he's going to call you. He wants to offer you an executive position plus an option to buy stock at La Dolce Vita Sugar Company."

"Me?" said Daddy as the telephone rang. "I don't even like sugar in my coffee."

"Why me?" poor Daddy kept asking, on and off, for days after Baby had offered him the job of manager at La Dolce Vita. "I'm working on an important canvas! I'm perfectly content! Isn't there anybody else he could pick on, some guy from Gravier Street in a pinstriped suit, who cares about whether the stock market closes down or blows up?"

"He wants a family member to take over," Constance told him. "He feels the manager he did have, the one who recently died, may not have been completely trustworthy. Hasn't all that been made clear to you by now?"

"A *family* member?" echoed Rand. "All right, Constance, now you tell me why this individual, this man who for the past ten years hasn't been completely sure he still *had* any family, why he would suddenly develop an attachment to the name 'Calvert'? And don't give me that pap about how he's heartbroken at never having had a son and heir." He shuddered. "Jesus Christ, what a bonus from the gods *that* was!"

"Oh, *I* see," said Constance. "It's 'pap' for a man to want a son. I'll remind you of that the next time you bring up the subject."

"If it's family he wants," shouted Daddy—he always shouted when he was embarrassed; maybe he thought his decibel level would obliterate the aural traces of whatever had been said to embarrass him—"why don't we propose Clay-Lee here for the job?" He looked at me. "Clay-Lee, what's interest?"

"Principal times rate times time."

"There you are," nodded Daddy. "Constance, pack her little briefcase. I guarantee you she knows as much about running a business as I do." But Constance would not be moved to laughter or indifference. I suppose she thought that here, at last, was a chance for her to make up for her loss of the Alexander treasure. Studying her face, I felt pity and concern. She looked the way Courtenay had looked the day Airey teasingly promised her a ride in a friend's private plane, provided she could think of a good opening line for a medical speech he was writing. My mother's face now held that same mixture of excitement and deliberate restraint, that fear-tinged eagerness to find exactly the words that would convince Rand to take her flying.

"Your mother has a childlike heart," Daddy said to me when Constance finally went off to bed, "and I mean that as a compliment. A childlike heart, and a soul that was taught by the Church to stay on the lookout for miracles." He shook his head. "And that, Clay-Lee, is one example of what is popularly known as a 'lethal combination.' "

Strangely enough, the person who indirectly settled matters concerning the job John McCaleb used to call "the sugarplum" turned out to be little Julie de la Corde. It finally occurred to my mother that Julie's near-miss at becoming an infant mortality statistic contained some elements that might be effective weapons against a sentimental man like my father. Thus, the illness of Felicity's youngest daughter had some surprising consequences for Constance and Rand and me.

The initial surprising consequence was first disclosed by Rand (although Uncle Baby had already been informed) during a Sunday brunch at our house. This one was held three weeks after Julie's asthma attack, when she was back home again, recovering. Daddy announced to the family and friends who were gathered "in honor of Clement Calvert's return to the States," that he would be "delighted to undertake the management" of his uncle's sugar business in the countryside of southwestern Louisiana. Rand's generally beaten-down appearance and weary tone suggested to the guests that here was a place—and an occupation—about which he knew little and cared nothing. "I can't imagine how you ever persuaded him," marveled Aunt Mathilde to Constance. I didn't have to imagine. For what seemed like hours a few nights before, my father and I had listened to Constance's "hero" speech. The gist of it was that like it or not, Uncle Baby was suddenly a hero, and now Rand owed him one. "Clement literally saved the life of my cousin's baby, and not once, but twice," she told Daddy. "God only knows what would have happened to the child at that hospital if your uncle hadn't been there to step in." While you and Airey were stepping out, her tone implied. I tried to picture them, my shy father and overly polite Airey, tap-dancing on tabletops at Antoine's, ashes on their foreheads and Baked Alaska on their chins, disgracing themselves downtown while Uncle Baby assumed the necessary burden of browbeating the medical staff at Touro. "I guess you're aware," Constance continued, "that Airey has decided to invest in Clement's new cement mixer company. He's counting on you to help out with the sugar business so Clement can give his full attention to this new venture. . . ."

"Airey's going into the *cement* business?" cried my father, completely astonished. (Poor Airey, whose "head for commerce" was indeed as useless as a sidewalk artist's, was being pressured by his own wife to repay Uncle Baby in some measure. "What a year that was," Uncle Baby reminisced to me shortly before he died. "I had an expert on women's bottoms holding the purse strings on my cement company, and a goddamn picture painter in charge of things in Houma. Thank God I'm a crook, or those two would have wiped me out completely.")

The next surprise came at the same dismal brunch, when Uncle Baby announced that he had arranged with Marguerite de Villeneuve, Mistress General of the prestigious Convent of the Sacred Heart on St. Charles Avenue, for me to be admitted to the school, right in the middle of the winter semester. "Admission effective immediately" was the unprecedented guarantee contained in the letter from which Uncle Baby was quoting. My mother looked properly stunned—such a bending of the rules was unheard of, especially since Sacred Heart had a long waiting list of girls who had been "registered at birth." (As I, too, had been registered, but when my father was notified of my acceptance to the kindergarten class, he couldn't afford to enroll me.) While everybody sat in my parents' tiny living room, wondering, probably, what on earth Clement Calvert "had" on Marguerite de Villeneuve, Uncle Baby declared he would like to make a further announcement: he had already paid my tuition through my senior year, as a gesture of his continuing goodwill to his newest employee, Rand Calvert. ("He must have sensed how badly Constance wanted Sacred Heart for Clay-Lee," Rand told John McCaleb a few days later. " 'Sensed' hell," answered John. "Lamb talked about it often enough to everyone else; it's a pretty good bet she mentioned it to your uncle, too. What he 'sensed' was that you'd never have agreed to let him pay the tuition. So he went ahead and made it a fait accompli. All of a sudden, Constance is repaid for whatever part she had in talking you into taking the job, and Uncle Baby gains a better position from which to call the shots. Now give me a while to think, boy, and maybe I can come up with why the hell he wants you for the position in the first place.")

The day dragged on tediously for me; I had no one near my own age to talk to. Courtenay and Minette had been sent home in disgrace twenty minutes after the party began, for what their father called "unfunny behavior." In an attempt to tease Rand about his well-known reticence concerning bodily functions and bathroom jokes, the two of them had lettered a sign which read RAND—WHAT ARE YOU DOING HERE? and placed it above the toilet.

By about two o'clock I was bored enough to wonder why Uncle Baby Brother was bothering to stick around. Most of the time he kept his face turned to the walls while he roamed back and forth between the parlor and the dining room, silently inspecting Rand's framed paintings and drawings. He seemed to have nothing to say to the other guests, although I overheard plenty of what they were muttering about him:

At fourteen years of age, he had sired an infant, but the mother, a devoutly Catholic Italian-American girl, had swallowed a bottle of lye a few months before the child was scheduled to be delivered.

He had some tie-in with the Klan over in Alabama, and he had been heard to use the term "nigger knocking."

He currently kept a gangster's daughter as his mistress, up in Chicago, Illinois, at the Palmer House Hotel.

He was seen cleaning his fingernails with a matchstick, nonchalant as you please, all during the ceremony joining him in marriage to Miss Ida Marie de Vries, a former Tulane homecoming queen, who later lost her marbles and died young.

He was the reason Ida Marie lost her marbles and died young.

He had returned to New Orleans after over ten years in London, with something crummy up his sleeve; nobody knew just what, as yet.

Finally, my brain overloaded with libel, I went out to the kitchen to see if the pineapple juice I had poured into one of the ice trays was completely frozen yet. On my way, I passed Uncle Baby Brother standing in a corner in the dining room, staring with murderous eyes at Griswald Harper, an aging artist who was making his usual kidding-on-the-level pitch to Constance to pose in the nude for him one day soon.

"You're married to an artist, my darling, there's no place in

your life now for reticence concerning the naked human form,"
shouted Griswald, who was deaf and always seemed delighted
about it, as if his handicap gave him a legitimate excuse for
shouting all his opinions.

"No place for you, either, Griswald," called out Uncle Baby
suddenly from his corner. "Go piss your platitudes someplace
else."

But Griswald ignored him, and so did Constance; from that
moment on, the murderous gleam never left Baby's eyes. Several
times I caught him staring at Constance as if the power of his
gaze, its angry intensity, could force her to look back at him, but
he kept his distance; he also kept drinking, with steady purpose,
as if he were revving himself into dangerously high gear for
something.

An hour or so after his remark to Mr. Harper, I saw Uncle
Baby collide with the wooden coal scuttle that stood near the
piano; Rand was seated at the piano, playing a Chopin étude for
Honey McCaleb.

"Why don't you cut out the classical crap, and play something
catchy?" Uncle Baby said. "Do you know 'We Ain't Got a Barrel
of Money'?"

There was a sudden silence at the keyboard, and then an expectant hush among the audience.

"Well, hell, I know you ain't got a barrel of money, everybody
here knows it. Felicity tells me this sort of gathering, where nobody gets anything but eggs and tomato juice, is the only kind of
party you can *afford* to give."

"Oh, Jesus," breathed somebody right behind me; Felicity
probably.

"Your uncle's drunk," murmured my mother from the floor
where she was sitting, her eyes cast down, her face near the top
of Mishka's silky head. Mishka did not appear surprised to
hear it.

"What the hell, though, all that's in the past, now that Rand's going to be working for me," continued Uncle Baby. "But now's as good a time as any to make something clear.

"I expect my manager to live out at the sugar plant. I've just bought myself a place here in the city on Audubon Boulevard, and I won't rest easy unless I know I've got a good man seeing to things out in the country."

"But what about the child's schooling?" inquired the intrepid Aunt Mathilde. "You've just finished telling us she'll be going to Sacred Heart!"

"Well, now, I thought of that," said Uncle Baby. "If Constance prefers to move out to Houma with Rand, we can board the little girl at the convent, and just run her out to the country on weekends." I wasn't sure whom he meant by "we," but in any case I knew I had nothing to worry about. I was looking at my father, and I read the message "Clay-Lee isn't going to any boarding school," very plainly in his eyes. I was right, too. What happened was that my mother and I stayed in New Orleans, where I attended Sacred Heart, and my father went to live in the country and came home only on the weekends. In effect, it was Rand who was boarded out.

The party ended abruptly for me. Shortly after the boarding school issue was raised, my mother told me I looked tired and sent me upstairs with two chocolate petits fours and a beaten biscuit. As the afternoon darkened and the smell of rain blew through my bedroom, I heard from downstairs the sad sound of Chopin on the piano; my father had resumed playing for Honey McCaleb. Under the notes I could hear the bass of Uncle Baby's voice, throbbing along in some Sunday-afternoon argument with whomever he was drunk enough to engage in conversation. The Chopin ended, and then my great-uncle's words boomed out clearly. "Goddamn liberals," he was saying. "Insanity's no defense! If the guy that did it's crazy, then, hell, that's two reasons to fry him."

8

The night before my first day at Sacred Heart, John McCaleb came to our house for after-dinner coffee. At my mother's insistence, Rand had asked John to draw up a will for him, and John brought it over that night to show to him.

"Fine," Daddy agreed when Constance first brought up the subject of a will. "Clayton Leland Calvert, I bequeath to you my entire supply of brushes, and you and your mother can fight over the paints."

"Oh, Rand, be serious," said Constance. "It's foolish not to have a will; even if you don't have a large estate now, you never know what might happen later. And besides, not leaving a will is . . . it's sloppy."

"God forbid I should die sloppy," said Rand. "All right. I'll talk to John about it." He sounded unconcerned but he looked worried; my father often had trouble matching up the words that came out of his mouth with the expression in his eyes.

While I was eating my dessert, Mama left the dining room and returned a few minutes later with a creased and yellowed newspaper clipping, which she placed on the table beside my plate. My father was finishing his coffee; he glanced at the piece of newspaper and then up at Constance. "What's that, sweetheart," he said, "an old news item about the Judge?"

"I want Clay-Lee to see it," Mama said. "It's about a Sacred

Heart school." The clipping was from the *New Orleans Times-Picayune* of August 18, 1946. It showed photographs of the crumbling facade of what had once been Saint Michael's in Convent, Louisiana, established and operated by the Society of the Sacred Heart a hundred years ago: CONVENT WHERE EARLY BELLES STUDIED IS BEING TORN DOWN ran the headline. "I want you to read it," Mama told me, "and to understand how lucky you are that Uncle Baby is doing this for you. You won't be going to Saint Michael's, of course, but all Sacred Heart schools are the same, wherever they are, and so are the girls who graduate from them." Felicity de la Corde had gone to Sacred Heart, and I couldn't imagine two more dissimilar products of the nuns' training program than my mother and her cousin, but naturally I didn't say so. "Just think," Constance was telling me, "Saint Madeleine Sophie Barat founded the Society of the Sacred Heart in France, in 1800, and here you are, almost two hundred years later, way over in Louisiana, about to share in all its history and tradition. The building you'll go to school in has been on St. Charles Avenue since the end of the nineteenth century." The building had been pointed out to me on frequent occasions. It was a beautiful three-storied brick structure, high-ceilinged, wide-galleried, and populated by the daughters of the city's oldest Catholic families. On the other hand, Saint Michael's Convent had been "doomed to destruction" more than ten years ago, according to the newspaper article, which was written by someone named Meigs O. Frost—this after "many a grande dame of those days before the War Between the States spent her girlhood there."

" 'The work of the nuns was at times very difficult,' " wrote Mr. Frost, quoting from a book called *The Society of the Sacred Heart in North America*, which had been written by a nun named Mother Louise Callan, A.M., Ph.D. " 'The maintenance of discipline was a problem among children who had been reared in plantation luxury, pampered, amused, and waited on by slaves.' "

"I'm afraid that means you," interrupted Daddy. "Clay-Lee, my dear, your days of being pampered and amused are numbered."

"Go on, Clay-Lee," said Mama.

" 'Yet they took the training well,' " I read, " 'and developed into those fine Southern women who bore with heroism the tragedies of the War Between the States.' "

"Right," said John, "so if New York drops an atomic bomb on Louisiana this time around, Clay-Lee will know exactly what to do."

The next section of the article dealt with how the students spent the Fourth of July, a holiday which took place during the course of the eleven-month school term, and with what the girls wore to classes. " 'Sound studies they pursued, for these girls soon would be mistresses of great plantations and city homes,' " I continued, " 'the arts and graces, music and dancing and drawing and the greatest literature of the world. Out of Saint Michael's they went, prepared to take their proud places in the proud world to which they had been born.' " (Out of the side of my eye I saw Daddy carefully arrange his coffee spoon on his saucer.) " 'And no man can measure how much through their daughters, granddaughters, great-granddaughters, even their great-great-granddaughters living today, they have given to the tradition of fine and gracious living, to the code of high courage and gentle dignity, of duties nobly met, that is the best of the South to this day.' "

Mishka sighed. She was the only dog I ever knew who sighed on command, and I have no doubt that Constance frequently gave the command, although I was never able to catch her at it. "Who wrote that?" asked Daddy, sliding the clipping over to his place. " 'Meigs O. Frost.' Well, old 'Meigs O.' was right about one thing. Clay-Lee and I have a good example of the 'best of the South' right here at the table with us, haven't we?"

"God, thanks, Rand. I don't know what to say," said John. Mama ignored them. "How would you like it," she was saying to me, "if you had to dress for school the way those girls did then? Embroidered white muslin for summer—imagine going to school almost all summer, too!—and red bombazine with a black velvet sash in the fall. . . ."

"What I like is that part about the Fourth of July celebration," said John, the practicing atheist. "Here, read it again, Clay-Lee, about how the nuns' slaves set off the firecrackers 'with the enchanted children at a safe distance.' I guess there's nothing like getting your thumbs blown off for the greater glory of God. Right, Lamb?"

That first morning, our neighbor, Mrs. Eigenbrod hurt my feelings by informing me, when she saw me leaving for school in my new uniform, that I looked just like Mickey Mouse. I suppose I did, too, although I was missing the mouse ears and the smile. Red bombazine and embroidered muslin had given way to a white blouse, a brown gabardine skirt with demoralizing straps buttoned onto the waist, and lace-up oxfords of the type to which old Mrs. Mococaux had been partial.

My teacher was Mother Suzette Maylie, whose last name sounded enough like my first ones to assure confused responses whenever anyone in the class called either one of us; this circumstance would eventually lead to a sort of sympathetic mutual awareness. Mother Maylie greeted me by announcing that I was certainly welcome, and that furthermore, I had a Guardian Angel. So what? I thought defensively; did Mother Maylie assume the faculty at Crown of Thorns had taught me nothing? I felt perversely rebellious amidst the studiedly decorous atmosphere. "This is your Guardian Angel," Mother Maylie said, gesturing "stand up" to a child in the front row, who looked like a small, dark-haired rabbit.

"Is that *gum* stuck to your hair, Sylvie?" Mother Maylie asked the celestial apparition.

"It's aspirin gum, *ma mère,*" said Sylvie, with dignity. She had what sounded to me like an authentic French accent.

"Oh it *is,*" said Mother Maylie. "Well, whatever it is, it doesn't belong in your hair, dear. Remove it, and kindly take Clay-Lee to a chair at the back of the room and explain to her the words I mentioned to you." She turned to me and smiled. "Sylvie will be your Guardian Angel all this week. She will show you around the house, and if you have any questions, address them to her. Sylvie will explain things to you nicely."

Sylvie was the child of an American mother and a French father; she had been born in Paris and, until recently, lived there with her parents. Then, the summer before, Sylvie had returned with her mother to the States. "My *grand-mère* is very ill," Sylvie explained, "and Maman helps to care for her. During the weeks, I must live here, and on the weekend I go to her at *Grand-mère's* house, where all is whispering, and the smell of medicines." She sighed. "It is a great bore, that; because I am the only child in the family. Do you have sisters?"

"No," I told her, "there's only my parents and me. And Mishka."

"Mishka? Is she a Russian child by any chance? Because if she is Russian, I will tell you right now to forget that the nuns will allow her to come to school here." She shook her head. "All this year they have been reading to us from a book entitled *Communism, the Evil Tree,* and they tell us that the Russian children give their parents to the Secret Police if they catch them listening to *The Voice of America* on the radio."

I assured Sylvie that it didn't matter to Mishka whether she was accepted at Sacred Heart or not.

"*Bon,*" said Sylvie. "I ask about the sisters only because there is the rule that if there are more than three daughters in your house, the others may come to school here without paying. The nuns, you see, want to encourage the families to have many children."

"I'll mention it to my mother," I lied. Sylvie then began her instruction. A *côngé*, she explained, was a holiday that was held at school, during which the children played *cache-cache*, a complicated version of hide-and-seek which involved the ringing of bells and fearful hiding places, such as the attic and the bell tower. ("The bell tower is a wreck," confided Sylvie. "Lots of loose boards everywhere. One false step and zut! a broken leg, and no more terrible gymnastics for the rest of the term.") *Goûter* was a treat to eat, such as pink cupcakes, served only on special occasions like "the Feast of Saint Madeleine Sophie." *Primes* was a weekly merit assembly for which I would need my white gloves ("There is also a completely white uniform, which you wear at the Christmas tableau"); and Mater Admirabilis was the Virgin Mother, whose pink-robed image I would see portrayed in paintings on the walls of the house. "Wait a minute," I said. "I thought the Virgin's name was Mary, and she wore blue." Sylvie stared at me for a minute. "At *other* schools, perhaps," she replied. "At Sacré Coeur she is Mater, and she prefers pink."

We moved on, to a more detailed explanation of *Primes*. "Each class stands by turn in a half-circle before Reverend Mother Shaw and Mother de Villeneuve, who sit on the stage in the assembly room. Then everyone together curtsies to the nuns."

"We curtsy?" I whispered, conscious of a sudden longing to be back among the roughnecks at Crown of Thorns.

"Mother de Villeneuve calls out the name of each girl, followed by 'Very Good,' 'Good,' or 'Indifferent,'" continued Sylvie. "What is called depends upon the child's behavior during the week that went before. *Par exemple*, Mother might call out 'Sylvie Despointes, Very Good'; 'Clay-Lee Calvert, Good for speaking in the locker room.'"

"I'm usually indifferent," I admitted.

"Oh, no, no!" cried Sylvie, horrified. "'Indifferent' is called only if you have done something truly bad, such as enter the Community where the nuns sleep."

"Then why don't they call out 'truly bad'?" I asked. I was becoming exhausted, as if I were attempting to master a foreign language in a single morning.

"Don't worry," Sylvie said, patting my hand. "You will soon understand. It was difficult for me too at first. And if you had to live here at school, as I do? *Quelle mauvaise chance!* Each day I must awaken while the sky is still black, to get up and go to the Mass in the morning."

"My mother told me the nuns let the boarders have coffee for breakfast here."

"That's true! They do. So you see, some of the ideas of this place *ne sont vraiment trop mal.*"

"Sylvie Despointes," called Mother Maylie. "Stand, please, and define the word 'dogmatic.'"

"*Ah bof! Ça commence,*" muttered Sylvie, about to forfeit her linguistic advantage. She stood. "'Dogmatic,'" she repeated uncertainly. "Would that be a place like the American washaterias, but where one washes dogs?"

Later that day, in the dining room, Sylvie brushed aside a thin blond child (whose mother had had the diplomacy to christen her "Barat" after Madeleine Sophie Barat, the school's foundress) and guided me firmly into what was apparently Barat's usual place at the table. "It is only for one week," Sylvie consoled the child, who stood uncertainly nearby, holding her tray of food. "After that I am no longer her Guardian Angel and she must find her own place to sit." This remark was followed by Sylvie's announcement that after lunch I was to go directly to Mother de Villeneuve's office on the second floor. "She has set aside a part of this afternoon to explain to you why you are here at Sacré Coeur."

"I already know," I said. "I'm here because my great-uncle paid my tuition through my senior year."

"No, no," protested Sylvie. "Mère de Villeneuve will explain to you the *real* reason." She leaned toward me, the light of her faith shining in her eyes. "The real reason is that from the beginning of time, our Lord Jesus Christ decided, up in heaven, that you, Clay-Lee Calvert, would be a child of His Sacred Heart."

I wondered why, if what Sylvie said were true, Jesus would pick somebody like Uncle Baby Brother to handle His arrangements for Him.

My mother and Honey and Mishka were waiting for me at the Carondelet Street entrance at dismissal time. Mishka had a new plaid collar and matching leash and she was showing her teeth in a sort of smile, as if to indicate her approval of the fact that I was finally doing something that pleased Constance. Constance looked very pretty and very young in her pleated skirt and a bright red sweater that Honey had knitted for her. "That's your *mother?*" breathed a little girl named Kerry who was in my class. "She's *beautiful.*" All the children within earshot looked at Mama then, and I could tell my own stock was rising because of her. I went over to Constance, who disliked public displays of affection, and hugged her in a frenzy of gratitude. She was carrying my canvas shoes from home and I felt them press against me as she hugged me back. "Did you find someone to sit with you at lunch?" she asked. "Look, I brought your tennis shoes. You can change into them after school and keep those terrible brown oxfords here, in your locker. That way you'll never have to wear them except during school hours." My mother had obviously forgotten nothing of her own days at Sacred Heart, and I felt quite blessed that she was one of the "old children," as the alumnae were called. I had heard the term for the first time that afternoon. It was spoken by Mother Marguerite de Villeneuve, as she walked with me along the dimly lit, pine-floored corridors, her remote Gallic eyes noting every detail of my appearance, her sharp mind taking in every nuance of my speech. Mother de Villeneuve exuded that uniquely French confidence in her ability to extract information from an individual without having to ask a direct question. On the stair landing, she stopped to straighten a framed reproduction of Gainsborough's *Blue Boy*. "I think you're going to be happy here, Clayton," she decided. She withdrew an immaculate white handkerchief from some hidden pocket within her skirts; the handkerchief fluttered briefly across a smudge on a lower corner of the picture frame, and was replaced. Marguerite de Villeneuve transferred her gaze from the Goya to me. "I feel that you will quickly acquire the basic elements of our Sacred Heart spirit: faith, simplicity, distinction, the love of Christ, and of course, great docility, so that the grace of our Lord may do its work within your spirit." Two steps above me on the landing, she stood looking down at me and I felt that she could see into all the unfinished rooms of my soul. "Your mother was Constance Alexander, I believe. She is one of our old children." The strange sound of it puzzled me for a minute, then I realized she meant that my mother had been at school here. I remembered my father's words concerning Constance's simple heart, her soul that still hoped for miracles, and I found myself in full agreement with Marguerite de Villeneuve's choice of words. "Yes, that's right," I said, as we resumed our journey together, "my mother is an old child."

At home, Daddy was transferring most of the meager contents of his closet and drawers into one of Judge Alexander's old Gladstones. Uncle Baby was coming at five o'clock to drive him to Houma, and my mother was in the kitchen, hurriedly smashing cooked sweet potatoes into a pie to be taken with them. Every few minutes a yelp from Mishka rang out, as a drop of hot flying yam landed on her nose or her paws. "Here she is!" Daddy said when he saw me at the bedroom door. "Well? How did it go? Did you duly impress the Madames of the Sacred Heart?"

"The who?" I said. I picked up one of his ruined neckties from off the floor and put it on the bed. My father always insisted on wearing a coat and tie whenever he went to a client's house to paint a portrait. He claimed he took off the tie when he started to work, but from the looks of them he must have forgotten to remove them at least half the time.

"Why don't you buy some new ties, Daddy?" I suggested. "I

heard Mama tell Honey she feels like she's out with a circus clown whenever you wear one of these ones with paint all over it, out in public."

"I'm waiting for a pattern to emerge," said Daddy, studying the striped and splattered length of silk in his hands. "Then maybe I'll sell them. Salvador Dali–style cravats. We'll make a killing, as your great-uncle would say."

"Mother de Villeneuve remembered who Mama was," I told him, sitting on the edge of the bed. "And they gave me a French girl, a real one, from Paris, to take me around and explain things to me. I told her about Uncle Baby paying my tuition."

"Well don't tell anybody else about it. Your mother and I have enough going against us as it is." He was folding his old green sweater, the one with the hole in the sleeve. I suddenly remembered him in that sweater, when it was newer and a deeper green; he had worn it the day Henry Kurtz moved out, and I had seen him in it that night, too, sitting up in bed with Constance, who had a cough. "Just wait," he was saying, "till Madame de Villeneuve remembers that Constance Alexander, class of whatever, was married without benefit of clergy. By a crooked judge, in fact, who jumped off the courthouse roof in Selma, Alabama, a few days after he performed the ceremony."

"Why do you call a nun 'Madame'? I thought Madame was what people called married ladies."

"Oh, I don't know, baby, I suppose because that's what my own mother called them, 'the Madames of the Sacred Heart.' Although my mother didn't go to school there. She was a Presbyterian—another strike against us." He closed the suitcase and stood it on the floor, then he went over to the mirror and began to knot his painted tie. "I'll tell you something, though. I don't think they like being referred to as 'Madames.' Your mother once told me that the last December she was in school, one of the top-brass nuns made a big announcement for the benefit of all those valiant souls who might be planning to send Christmas cards to the convent. 'The proper form of address,' said this nun, 'is Reverend Mother So-and-So and the Community. We are not *Madames* of the Sacred Heart. We are not *Mothers* of the Sacred Heart. We are not *Sisters*. And we are certainly not *Ladies*." He winked at me in the mirror, and the pain of his leaving hit me so suddenly and so hard that my knees buckled a little from the force of it. I went over and stood near him. His long-sleeved shirt was starched and creased and the scent of oil paints rose from his tie. "Why do you have to go?" I asked. "If it's because of money, then that's silly. Don't we already have everything we need to make us happy?"

"This whole thing is hard for you to understand, isn't it?" He had finished knotting his tie and was putting on his limp corduroy coat. "I'm not surprised you're confused. The trouble is, I don't know that *I* understand it well enough to explain it to you."

He gathered up off the bed a half-dozen socks whose mates he hadn't been able to locate, and replaced them in the sock drawer. "Do you know what a paradox is, Clay-Lee? A paradox is . . . it's something that seems contradictory or even ridiculous, but that's also got some truth to it. That's what we've got going in this family right now: a paradoxical situation." One of the straps of my uniform skirt had come unbuttoned and he reached down and fastened it. "You ask me if we already have everything we need to make us happy. I don't know about the 'everything,' but one thing we did have was freedom. Freedom to direct our own lives, which is something a lot of people spend money in order to acquire. What I'm getting ready to do now is to spend our freedom in order to acquire money. That's where the paradox comes in."

For the second time that day I had the feeling of being bested by a foreign language that happened to be my native tongue. One thing seemed clear, though. Whatever my mother's definition of freedom was, it was not the same as my father's.

"Where's Mr. Music?" yelled Uncle Baby suddenly, up the stairwell. "Come on down here and play 'Bye-Bye Blackbird.'

We're getting ready to blow this crummy neighborhood and head out for sugar country!" A minute later, John McCaleb appeared at the bedroom door. "I came over to help you with your luggage," he told Rand. He looked at the solitary Gladstone in the middle of the floor. "That's it? That's everything?"

"That's everything," said my father, picking up the suitcase himself. "McCaleb, while I'm gone I want you to get down on your knees every night and pray your baby will look like your wife."

"It worked pretty good for you, huh?" John said, following Daddy out into the hall.

Honey's baby was late. During the first week of April my mother would look at the kitchen calendar and say to Aunt Mathilde (who had come to stay, of course, while Daddy was away), "I have a feeling today's the day. That baby's going to be here before tomorrow." Every night she lay half-awake till dawn, part of her, I hoped, missing Rand, and part of her waiting for John's tap on her bedroom window, the prearranged signal that she was needed quickly next door. Finally Honey and Constance grew so puffy-eyed and grumpy from lack of sleep that I stayed out of their way as much as possible. Everybody on both sides of the house was short-tempered and overly sensitive from waiting; one night we even heard, through our dining-room wall, the unprecedented sound of Honey and John arguing.

"Why in God's name do you want to take flying lessons?" Honey cried. "We don't own an airplane!"

"Then I'll *buy* an airplane!" screamed John.

"For *what?*" Honey screamed back. "You'll buy an airplane for *what?*"

"So I can fly to my boat!" bellowed John, who didn't own one of those either.

"My word," remarked Aunt Mathilde. "I can tell the two of them aren't long for the neighborhood. Arguing about boats and airplanes while the rest of us are busy hunting up seven cents for streetcar fare."

The day after that, a Saturday, another unusual occurrence took place: Honey sat in her kitchen and cried for so long that Aunt Mathilde threatened to throw a glass of water in her face to make her stop—so much upset was bad for the baby, she declared. The scene was probably precipitated by John's perverse decision earlier that morning to go fishing in Empire, Louisiana, with Buddy Robilliard, but the direct cause of the trouble was Eddie Mae Albright. Eddie Mae had been hired sight unseen, through a domestic employment agency, to clean the McCalebs' house before the baby arrived; when she knocked on our kitchen door by mistake, Mama sent me to escort her to the proper place. As soon as Eddie Mae got a look at her new employer, she whistled once through her teeth. "Sweet Jesus, honey," she said, unknowingly hitting the name just right, "when's *your* party? It better be soon, cause I'm here to tell you your feet so swole up, they ain't going to be holding you up past another hour or two."

Aunt Mathilde heard the commotion all the way over in our front yard, where she was planting zinnias, and it took her and Eddie Mae Albright together to calm Honey. "Don't you worry! All this a good sign!" the cleaning woman called after Honey, who was being led up to bed by my aunt. "I got a sister works for a ladies' doctor, and she say whenever the examining rooms is full of hysterical ladies, they all have their babies by nighttime. She never seen it to fail." When there was no response from upstairs, Eddie Mae bumped past me in the hall, pushing a dust mop along in front of her like it was a shuffleboard stick. "Lucky for her she can take it; she still young," said Eddie Mae to me. "You remember what I'm telling you, little girl; you wait to have kids till you too old, and they all come out dumb and wearin' glasses."

As it turned out, Eddie Mae knew what she was talking about on at least one score: Honey's baby made known its imminent arrival before dark. John had not yet returned from Empire, but every other grown-up who lived in the house stood in the McCalebs' bedroom, quarreling over the privilege of carrying down Honey's suitcase.

"Why don't you just let me get my own suitcase?" said Honey, making an unsuccessful attempt to lift it. "I feel fine!"

"You're right out of your mind," observed Aunt Mathilde. "You'll rupture something! Give it to me." She lunged for it and bumped into Mishka, who was dodging warily from one end of the room to the other like a referee at a basketball game.

"You're sadly mistaken, Aunt Mathilde," said my mother, "if you think I'm just going to stand by and watch while you fracture your hip." Constance, easily the most determined of the three, picked up the suitcase and started for the stairs; she lost her balance on the top step and skidded to the landing, where she came to a stop with the suitcase handle still in her hand, extended out half a foot behind her.

"That's it! Tear your arm out of the socket!" screamed Aunt Mathilde from above her. Behind us, Honey moaned. I tried to think what the heroic women who had faced alone the tragedies of the War Between the States would have done, but my mother was already using her foot to nudge the suitcase down the remaining steps.

"Clay-Lee, you run down to the corner of Valmont and Magazine and get Deaf and Dumb William," said Honey. "He can put the stupid thing in the car for us, at least." Deaf and Dumb William was an elderly, down-and-out Negro who had been rendered speechless at the age of three, when, according to his sister Ernie, he had put his tongue to the screw-in part of a light bulb. Ernie said he was deaf from then on, too, but Aunt Mathilde maintained he was about as deaf as she was. "Maybe he'd rather not acknowledge he hears what's going on," my father told her once. "In his circumstances, who can blame him?"

Deaf and Dumb William, moving slowly half a block behind me, finally arrived on Camp Street, where he picked up Honey's suitcase and tossed it into the back seat of our Volkswagen. "Deaf, my hind foot," muttered Aunt Mathilde, glaring at him, "and about as feeble as Billy Cannon." Billy Cannon was a star running back for Louisiana State University.

"We'll call you as soon as there's any news," Mama said to the three of us on the sidewalk. Aunt Mathilde quickly made the sign of the cross and Deaf and Dumb William nodded vaguely.

"John and Buddy should be home any minute," Honey called to Aunt Mathilde as the car began to move. "You all tell him if he wants to get to the hospital before his baby's born to let Buddy clean the damn fish by himself."

Honey and her son, who was named David Robilliard Mc-Caleb for his late maternal grandfather, came home from the hospital the following weekend. After a two-week absence, my father was finally in from Houma for a few days, and our house came alive again. I spent that Saturday of Honey's and Rand's return running back and forth across the balcony from our side to the McCalebs'; from the scents of oil paints and turpentine and Constance's perfumed presence to those of baby powder, John's cigars, and the pastries and casseroles that Mrs. Robilliard's cook continually delivered to Honey's kitchen. On Sunday I went with Daddy and John to the Greyhound Terminal, where Sis Honorine was due in from Covington on the three o'clock bus. She would be staying with the McCalebs for two weeks to help out with the baby.

I picked out Sis right away among the travelers milling around the bus station. She was wearing her company wig and a party dress that showed the tops of her powdered, sienna-colored breasts. When she walked, the sides of her knees brushed silkily together, and the festive aroma of Evening in Paris perfume spun through the air around her.

That Sunday there was a minor disturbance in the passenger pickup section of the bus terminal when a short Negro with a freckled complexion attempted to come to Sis's aid by carrying her suitcase for her. "The day I require assistance from a midget I'll be too worn out to ask for it," Sis was telling him as Daddy,

John, and I came up. John introduced himself and took her suitcase, while the rebuffed midget moved on, complaining in a
startling baritone about the unpredictability of "the weaker sex."
"I'll weaken you," Sis called to him. "Cheeky, ain't he?" she said
to me, handing me her wig box. "Mr. Rand, you got a young
lady on your hands here. Clay-Lee, I think you big enough to
help out with the baby. How's your mama been feeling?"

As usual, when Sis Honorine was in residence on Camp Street,
a certain sense of well-being filled the house, even though with
my father away I had begun to sleep poorly, to awaken suddenly
at sounds that had always been the background music of my life:
the ghostly rattling of a streetcar somewhere on the avenue, the
funereal piping of a boat whistle out on the Mississippi.

Sometimes the telephone would ring late at night and I would
hear my mother talking for what seemed to me a long time, and
once I was sure I heard her say sharply, "Because it's not a good
idea, that's why," but at breakfast the next morning, when I
asked her if it had been Daddy who had called, she would just
look at me strangely and say no, Daddy hadn't called. Then I
would be afraid to ask her who it was who had called, afraid she
would tell me no one had, that I was once again confusing dreams
with reality, the way I used to when I was younger, and Mama
had finally had to ask Dr. Villere to give me medicine to make
me sleep.

Other nights were better; I woke and listened in the dark to
the sounds of Sis on the other side of my bedroom wall, to the
creak of her rocking chair as she gave the infant David his two
o'clock feeding, to the rumble of her voice as she spoke to him.
"No such thing as talking too much to a baby," Sis had told me.
"That's how they learn. And how they going to feel they part
of the family, if nobody talk to them?" I loved to visit the secure
little world Sis presided over in the McCalebs' nursery, where
David slept in Sis's arms, his body swaddled in a satin-bordered
blanket, his fists tight around her time-worn fingers.

My father had painted a small wooden stool for the baby's

room. It was blue with a green-jacketed rabbit on it, shown enjoying a vegetable lunch at the edge of a forest; my mother had
lettered on it THIS IS A NICE GENTLE RABBIT. HIS MOTHER HAS
GIVEN HIM A CARROT. At bedtime Sis allowed me to sit on the
stool and hold the baby while I gave him a little of his bottle. I
wanted time to stop then, I wanted to stay on in that room where
it seemed that a child could be nourished and sheltered forever
by Sis's comforting presence.

The Easter holidays arrived, and I spent the whole vacation
following Sis around. It never occurred to me that I might be in
the way, and I don't think it occurred to anybody else either. My
mother had taken a temporary job at the Tulane University library, and the library was open during spring vacation. With
both of my parents out of the house, and Aunt Mathilde off in
Florida visiting others among her coterie of defenseless relatives,
Honey and Sis took me in as naturally and willingly as if I were
little David's sister. "Oh, Clay-Lee," Sis would call, "come see
can you hold the baby's head up for me while I catches his arms
and legs," and together we would complete the mission of bath-
ing the infant without drowning him. Every morning, Honey
had her breakfast in bed, and after she finished it Sis and I
would present the freshly laundered David to her and descend
to the kitchen. Downstairs, baby clothes whirled in the washing
machine and bottles jumped in the hot water bubbling in the
sterilizing pot. While I folded sleep sacks and receiving blankets,
Sis chopped onions and green peppers, holding them in her big
palm, moving the knife as expertly as a surgeon. "I like to get my
dinner on in the early afternoon," she said, "before the ladies
start coming." And indeed the ladies came, old, middle-aged,
and young ladies, some of whom brought babies of their own to
show to Sis ("Let me see does he remember me," Sis would say,
taking from his mother a child she had once cared for. "Look, he
doesn't holler. What you think of that?") These ladies were
the contemporaries of Honey's late grandmother, or her mother,
or they were her own friends. Young or old, they fascinated me.

They were so self-assured that they bordered on arrogant, yet they exuded an aura of genuine, if deliberate, innocence, and they spoke as slowly as if they had all the time in the world to make themselves heard.

"Sis, how *are* you," they would say, hugging her; "what on earth went on at Tich Harper's, to make you leave her like that in the middle of the week?"

"Nobody had told me her mama-in-law was a sergeant," Sis replied. "I can't work with a elderly lady callin' orders over my shoulder."

"Are you going to Tina Wessel's in November?" asked somebody else.

"She had told me not to say nothing, on account of she made all those miscarriages last year," answered Sis, "but if she's telling you I guess it's not a secret no more."

The ladies gathered in the parlor, where David lay in the wicker bassinet that had been Honey's own, and they commented briefly on the fineness of the baby's complexion and the flatness of his ears against his head. Then their attention wandered to more interesting subjects.

"Honey, where's Lamb? Oh, is this Clay-Lee? Where's your mama, Clay-Lee?"

"Working," I said. "She has a job at a library."

"Well, what for? Somebody told me Rand went off to Houma to make a pile of money . . ."

". . . buzzing around Constance at that brunch, like I don't know what, like an old tomcat. You had to see it to believe it, although she of course appeared completely unaware—"

"She only has the one child," somebody else was saying, but the focus had shifted from Constance to another lady who wasn't present. "And now she's at Dabney Wessel's every day from dawn till dark, trying to have another one." Dabney Wessel was a locally famous fertility expert, not a stud bull, as might reasonably be inferred. The obstetrical discussions in which these women engaged were devoid of any mention of the male sex.

Listening to them, I would have thought the number of children a woman conceived was solely up to her and God, and in some cases to Dabney Wessel, the fertility expert, if I hadn't been informed of the truth a while back by Courtenay de la Corde, with the help of those illustrated medical texts.

"Clay-Lee, when's your mama going to give you a baby brother of your own to play with?" called a middle-aged woman from across the room. I pretended not to hear her, and went over to sit for a while near Sis, who was explaining to a hugely pregnant lady that she was too old now to care for twins.

"Clay-Lee," Honey called. "Come over here a minute. I want you to meet Mrs. Milne. She taught French to your mother a long time ago at the convent." Mrs. Milne belonged to my favorite category of visitors: the Elderly Ladies. The Elderly Ladies were ramrod straight, stringently well-groomed, and horribly outspoken: it was hard to believe they had once been so irresistibly lovely that men had lost their heads over them and made them into wives. They were good women, religious to the core, and noble in thought if not always in word. Most of them were deaf and would remain deaf; they had no intention, as Aunt Mathilde put it, of "announcing their infirmities to strangers by hanging contraptions off their ears."

"Where's that good-looking daddy of yours?" Mrs. Milne asked me. "He usually paints at home, doesn't he? Why isn't he around?"

"He's in Houma," I said. "He's working at my Uncle Baby's sugarmill." Mrs. Ferris looked at me as if I'd lost my mind. "Your uncle? What baby?" she said impatiently. She raised her hand halfway to her ear and then quickly lowered it again. "We're talking about your *father*, child. Where is he?"

"Go on, Clay-Lee, I'll explain to her," said Honey. "Will you take David upstairs now and put him in his crib? Sis is busy in the kitchen." As I lifted the baby out of the bassinet I heard Mrs. Ferris say, "You don't mean to tell me she's got him off on some farm out in Houma! That talented man. Why, Rand's an artist!"

"Artists have to eat, Lenore, same as the rest of us," murmured Mrs. Milne.

As I carried David up the stairs, the telephone began ringing. Answering the telephone during "visiting hours" was one of my household duties, but now, with the baby in my arms, I couldn't do it. So it was Honey who took Airey's call, and Honey who came upstairs a few minutes later to tell me that Lady-Sidonie was dead.

As Sis Honorine told me the day of Lady-Sidonie's funeral, it's the suddenness of things that knocks you down. "The truth is, you never ready for the bad news, not even if you see it coming awhile before it hits." She touched her left hand where a gold ring thin as sunshine encircled her finger. "When my husband, Lotus, finally lit out for California and took my little sister, Pretty Rosetta, along for the ride, I felt like a bucket of scalding water'd been poured on top my head. I crawled in the bed and got under the covers, and I didn't get up again for three days. Past three days my mama wouldn't stand for it no more. She said to me, 'Sis, why you laying there like you half-dead from the shock? You got the same look on your face you did when you'd been ailing three months straight and the doctor finally had to come tell you you wasn't going to keep your baby. Now this particular trouble been building up in Lotus and Pretty Rosetta a long while. You had to been expecting it.' 'Expecting it and ready for it's two different things,' I told her, like I'm telling you now. Clay-Lee, you never going to be ready to give up somebody who you loved. The best you can do is just be expecting the suddenness of the good-bye. The sad old suddenness of it . . . that's the one thing about it you can count on."

It was a Saturday noon. Twelve o'clock sunlight fell across

the crib where David lay sleeping and across the white uniforms in Sis's open suitcase. It was time for us to be down in the kitchen folding baby clothes out of the dryer and getting dinner on the stove before the ladies came to call. Sis slammed shut the suitcase and a gust of Evening in Paris perfume sailed toward me, masking the everyday scents of baby powder and freshly ironed bed linens.

"Clay-Lee, look up under the chair cushion there and give me my black book." Sis's book contained a record of her past and pending baby cases, as well as an account of the various farewell gifts she collected from her employers. "Mrs. Delphine Marigny, baby boy Edgar," she would write. "Four prs. stocking, Wild Chinchilla shade."

"I got the baby on a pretty good schedule," Sis said to Honey. "One more week, and he going to be sleeping through the night. If he gets the colic, offer him some sugar water, and don't forget you got Miss Lamb right next door; she knows about babies. You and Miss Lamb put me in mind of me and Lotus's sister Margie. Never a cross word pass between you." The doorbell rang. A Mr. Huddleson Brace had arrived to drive Sis over to his house on State Street, where Mrs. Brace and her new baby were waiting. Mr. Brace soon began to pound on the door as if the porch were on fire. "Clay-Lee, come give me a hug good-bye before he punch a hole in the wood," said Sis. "Why all the gentlemen has to get so beside theirselves is a mystery to me."

I allowed myself to be hugged, but I felt like an ice cube had been forced down my throat: unable to speak, and cold from the inside out. How could Sis stand there talking about colic and sugar water when such an awful change was about to go into effect? It was now horribly clear to me that once Sis left nobody in the house would be able to function any longer. And yet she stood there, expressing interest in David's feeding schedule and in the state of Mr. Huddleson Brace's nerves, at the same moment she was leaving David and me, leaving my mother too. I

hated all Change, but especially this one, this change superim-
posed over the unchanging background misery of Lady-Sidonie's
death.

"Tell your mama I said good-bye, Clay-Lee," Sis said, going
down the stairs. "Tell her Mrs. McCaleb's got my phone number on State Street, in case you need me for anything while
your daddy gone."

Constance didn't believe in children attending funerals, so
she had arranged for me to spend the afternoon of the Requiem
Mass for Lady-Sidonie with Courtenay and Minette. Viola would
drive us to Uncle Baby's house, where a houseman and a housekeeper were in residence, and then go on to attend the church
services with the rest of the de la Corde family. I asked my
mother if she thought Uncle Baby would be at home. "What
makes you think I keep up with Clement's comings and goings?"
she said. "By the way, his housekeeper's name is Regina. I don't
want you running in and out of the kitchen, asking Regina for
anything to eat. I know *you* wouldn't, but you can't ever tell
what Courtenay and Minette might do." She had fastened her
hair into a high knot and a few tendrils of it fell free and curved
against her pale cheeks. I thought she looked as bloodless and
lovely as the alabaster sculpture of her face my father had done
the summer before.

"Go wait downstairs," she told me, taking her gloves from her
dresser drawer. "Viola should be here by now. Daddy and I will
pick you up at Clement's after everything's over. Around five
o'clock, I guess."

"Can I bring my skates? Courtenay said he has a big curvy
driveway and I thought maybe I could skate on it."

"All right, then, bring them. Although I guess there'll be a
big fight over that, if Courtenay and Minette didn't think to
bring theirs."

I found the skates in the back of my closet, and as I carried
them down the stairs Rand passed me on his way up. He had

just returned from Houma, and was dressed for Lady-Sidonie's funeral. The darkness of his suit made his hair look lighter; his hair had grown fuller, longer; it gave him the European look of the young Viennese pianist he had taken Mama and me to hear, one Saturday afternoon at Dixon Hall, on the Tulane campus. Daddy patted the side of my face and walked on into the upstairs hall. "Lamb?" he called, and she came out of the bedroom, a small ivory figure dressed in mourning. "You're there," he said. He sounded as relieved to see her as if he'd spent the whole morning looking for her. "I'm always here," she answered, and going over to him she reached up and touched the windblown, dark-gold layers of his hair.

There was some part of my father that was unreachable, that he held carefully in reserve—I always thought of that unreachable aspect as his imagination, where visions stirred before he transferred them to his canvases. But that day of Lady-Sidonie's funeral he must have made a great effort to be completely with us; watching him from my position on the stairs I felt the warmth of his presence ease through me like the sip of fine sherry Lady-Sidonie had given me once, when I'd caught cold after swimming too late in the season at Summerhill. Maybe my father was like wine to Constance, too; a remedy for the chill that sometimes afflicted her spirit. The sound of someone leaning against an automobile horn announced Viola's arrival and I went down the rest of the steps and out the door.

Right after I got into the backseat of the yellow convertible I wished I hadn't. Viola, turned out in her churchgoing best, was engaged in a verbal brawl with Courtenay, whose general appearance suggested she had arranged her hair and put on her clothes while blindfolded. Next to her Minette sat staring silently out the window, while up in front little Julie was clapping in rhythm to the slurs. Maybe she thought their shrill voices were raised in song.

"Nobody has to tell me whose idea this whole thing is!"

Courtenay screamed. "You did it, Viola! You talked Mummy into making us go to this funeral at the last minute, because you want to see me cry!"

"If God Almighty'd set me on this earth to go puttin' ideas in white women's heads, you think I'd be doin' what I'm doin', chaufferin' around ingrates and losin' my mind while a baby clap in my ears?" yelled Viola, giving the accelerator another kick. Viola always drove the convertible with its top down, and she drove it like a demon, holding tightly with both hands to the top of the wheel, as if only her own weight kept it from jumping off the steering column and flying through the windshield. "If your mama don't want you and your sisters goin' through life stickin' your head in the sand every time trouble come along, then that's nothing to do with me! Felicity say you all going to stand up at your grandmother's funeral, and you going to do it, if I has to pull you by your hair to get you on your feet!"

"Then what about Clay-Lee?" cried Courtenay. "Why is it she gets to stick *her* head in the sand?"

"She's got her skates with her, too," put in Minette.

"That's *her* mama business, if she see fit to raise her child to duck misery, having her to skate up and down some fancy street while poor Mrs. de la Corde being laid six feet under."

I sat there, speechless from the impact of hearing myself described as a happy-go-lucky coward and from the awful realization that I was to be dropped off by myself at Uncle Baby's house. Courtenay suddenly flung herself back against the seat, then leaned forward again till her face was directly over Viola's shoulder. "You know what, Viola?" she hissed. "I just wish it had been you instead of Lady-Sidonie that excused herself from the dinner table and then dropped dead."

"The day I get the chance to excuse myself from a white lady's table, that's the day you going to get your wish, Miss Mouth. 'Cause I'd fall out on the floor, stone-dead from the shock."

The car screeched to a stop in front of Uncle Baby's big stone mansion. Dappled sunlight filtered through the moss-hung trees, and shone off the brilliant brass railing along the front steps. Inside the yellow convertible, silence fell as we sat staring out at the beauty of the place.

"Go on, get out and ring the bell," Viola told me, gunning the motor. "We ain't leaving you here till somebody come to the door." A certain Somebody coming to the door was just what I was afraid of. Halfway up the steps my hands started to shake and I dropped my skates; they hit the stone with a crash like cannonballs against marble. "Well, I guess you don't need to ring no doorbell now," Viola called out disgustedly from the car. "Everybody on both sides of the street know you here." The varnished oak door was then opened by an elderly Negro houseman who was dressed in black trousers and a starched white jacket. The houseman was also wearing a chauffeur's cap, and his white puffed hair showed beneath it in an even roll, as if it had been sewn on all along the cap's edges. "Good afternoon," said the Negro, watching the convertible peel away from the curb and roar down the street. "We was told to expect four children."

"The other three went to a funeral," I explained. "I'll only be here till five o'clock, myself. My father's coming to get me."

"Step right in," said the houseman, opening the door wider. "My name is Clarence, and Regina is out in the kitchen. She said for me to let the children know we got pink ice cream if you want any."

"Oh, no thank you," I said, "I won't even be coming in the house." I sniffed a little, in an attempt to detect the Uncle Baby smells of cigarette smoke and bourbon on the premises, but only the faint aroma of flour and onions cooking in oil came to my nose. Regina must have been making a roux. "I brought my skates," I went on quickly to Clarence, who was beginning to look puzzled, "and I'll just sit out here on the steps and put them on. I'll be right out in front, on the driveway, skating."

"Suit yourself," said Clarence. Suddenly a well-brushed wirehaired terrier shot out from the shadowy entrance hall. He was chasing a tennis ball and dragging a chain leash behind him; as his sharp little teeth fastened onto the ball, he came to a stop and looked up at me triumphantly, out of eyes like animated shoe buttons. "His name Jeb Stuart," said the houseman. "A genuine, one hundred percent, wirehaired fox-terrier. I wrapped his leash around a doorknob in the kitchen, but he done escape again." Jeb Stuart jumped forward, landed on his two front paws and stuck his tail in the air. "Say, little miss," said Clarence. "Why you don't let him stay outside by you? He about to run me crazy, dodgin' around and trippin' me up every time I tries to get out from under him." "Jeb Stuart!" I called as the terrier darted down the front steps. "Come here, Jeb Stuart!" "He don't know his name yet," said Clarence. "Or else he pretending he don't. Mr. Calvert just bought him last week. You want him, you got to catch him."

Jeb Stuart was temporarily worn out from his pursuit of the tennis ball and I caught him and sat him down next to me on the bottom step while I used my skate key to tighten my skates. Then I slipped the looped leather handle of his leash around my wrist and stood up. Clarence had gone inside and I started to skate around the circular drive with Jeb Stuart trotting along beside me. Suddenly the dog got his second wind and speeded up, pulling me behind him.

This is how it feels, I thought, to zoom in the wake of a power boat; the concrete under my wheels became white water and my skates water skis. All along the street, small children were out for their afternoon walks with their nurses, and Jeb Stuart, bolting beyond the boundaries of Uncle Baby's driveway, tore past them on the sidewalk, moving at a spectacular rate of speed, as if the weight at the end of his leash were no more substantial than a cloud. Then I became a cloud, a low-flying, astonishing cloud that awed the nurses as I blew by, leaving their little charges openmouthed in my trail. "Get out the way!" screamed one of the nurses to another nurse. "Here come that crazy animal who live down the street, and he draggin' a child with him!" Up ahead, just beyond the screaming nurse, was a steep rise in the sidewalk where an oak root had pushed up through the concrete. Jeb Stuart took it easily but the front end of my skate loosened as its wheels hit the top of the rise and my foot bent sideways and cracked loudly somewhere inside. I fell on my hands and knees and the loop handle of Jeb Stuart's leash slipped over my fingers. As I looked up from the sidewalk I saw his flying rump disappear down the block.

One of the nurses went over to Uncle Baby's house and brought back Clarence, who crouched down beside me and ran his fingers over my ankle bone. "Broke," he announced, while I sat there on somebody's lawn, trying not to faint. The sunlight darkened, then brightened, then darkened again and the pain ground down so hard it made my teeth chatter. "Um, um," said Clarence. He shook his head sadly, then he picked me up and began walking with me in his arms toward my great-uncle's house. "Too much foolin' winds up bad," he said, and he was right; I have remembered that wise statement during many a bad and foolish moment in my later years. Looking up into Clarence's kind, worried face that April afternoon, the realization that this was the hour of Lady-Sidonie's burial came to me fully for the first time and it was just as Sis Honorine had said it would be; the sad suddenness of the good-bye hit me so hard that I vomited on Clarence's white linen shoulder. "Hold on now," he said. "Don't worry about that. You go on and cry if you want to, too. You got something badly broke inside you, and you got a right to be sick over it."

At the house, Clarence placed me carefully on a wide four-poster bed in a musty-smelling bedroom. I looked up at the sunburst design in the canopy and tried to breathe more slowly. The window shutters had been closed against the sun but the air was hot and bright.

"Lay quiet while I go find Regina," Clarence said.

When he went out into the hall I heard a Negro woman's impatient voice. "I got old Dr. Ellis on the telephone now. Go talk to him and tell him what happened. Go on, hurry up! And then you can take off that dumb-ass cap and go hunt for the dog." I began to feel cooler, but my head hurt; when I put my hand to my forehead I felt wetness and then saw blood on my fingers. I must have broken the skin, I thought, when my forehead hit the sidewalk. After a while the yellow glow around the bed seemed to became gray, like early-morning light, and I imagined I was in Lady-Sidonie's bed that winter dawn we had lain awake worrying about the baby, Julie. Lady-Sidonie was always so brave that I had forgotten to worry about her. If I had worried about her like she had worried about Julie, Lady-Sidonie wouldn't have died. If you worried hard enough, it was almost as good as praying. I stared at the canopy to make the spinning stop, but its swirling design made the dizziness worse. I closed my eyes and spun out into blackness like a sea gull over night water, water as black as Jeb Stuart's eyes. . . .

When I opened my eyes again, I was lying in darkness, but after a minute or so my vision adjusted and I could make out two darker shapes across the room near the door. The door was open a crack, and in the light from the hallway my mother's profile and the familiar outline of her hair were visible. Someone with shaggy hair, like my father's, was standing close to her, facing her. Did he have his arms around her? I tried to call out, "Daddy," but no words came from my throat, and my head felt too heavy to lift. Then the bulkier form moved, and I could see that whoever it was, he was too big to be my father.

In the stillness, my hearing became as sharp as a lynx's.

The man's voice said, ". . . enough to knock out a horse. Don't worry about her."

Then Constance. "It's you I'm worried about. You've been drinking, and you're not making any sense. Go up to bed, why don't you, and forget about all this?"

"*Forget* about it? You're the one who isn't making sense. Maybe you should take up drinking, Lamb, you might see things more plainly if you were drunk from time to time."

"What am I supposed to see? That I belong with you? But I don't, I belong with Rand."

"For Christ's sake, cut your losses and get out of there! There's nothing I couldn't give you, Lamb; just *let* me, why won't you let me? You don't even have any respect left for him, how the hell could you?"

"I love him."

"You love him, my ass. Can't you see it was the timing, the goddamn timing of the thing? If you'd met Golden Boy at any other stage of your life, he'd never have been anything to you but a passing thing, a nice-looking kid who'd never amount to much, that you fooled around with to get back at your father, for God knows what."

"I was pregnant when I married Rand. There was quite a lot more to it than getting back at my father, as you put it."

"You always know just what to say, don't you? You said that because you know I'd sell my soul to have something of mine growing in you."

"I want you to shut your mouth, and I want to go home."

Then no more voices and then Constance, "You can't do that, I won't let you do that."

"I've been out of my mind with wanting to do it, ever since the afternoon I took you to Antoine's."

"I don't know what you mean, nothing happened that afternoon!"

"Nothing happened, but not because I didn't want it to, and you know exactly what I mean." He groaned softly. "I want it to happen now, I want to be in you, oh, Christ, I want—"

"You're drunk! You're drunk, and I want you to stop saying these things—"

Black pleats were gathering tighter and I couldn't see anything, then I couldn't hear the voices anymore either. I wasn't sure I'd really seen or heard anything; the voices, the shapes, filtered through the unlit places in my mind and lodged deep in my memory, among the half-familiar, half-forgotten dreams and visions that would float back, at odd moments, to the surface again, unasked for and unexpected.

The room smelled faintly of tobacco smoke and whiskey and strongly of peppermint. The peppermint scent came from a gray-haired man in a three-piece suit who stood near the bed, looking at me, in the lamplight.

"How are you feeling, little miss?" he said. "You're pretty badly bunged up. Are you finished sleeping? You've got a lot of medicine still in you." I couldn't answer him; my lips were as thick as if they had been coated with sealing wax. I thought I remembered hearing Mama's voice outside the bedroom door sometime earlier; I supposed she'd come to take me home. I would have to tell Mama how good to me Clarence had been; what had happened to me wasn't his fault, or Jeb Stuart's fault either.

"Clay-Lee!" said my father, and I came fully awake and felt his hand holding mine. He was sitting in a chair next to the bed, and he was wearing his old tan trench coat. Streaks of rainwater darkened the shoulders of his coat; diamond drops of it glistened in his hair. "If you can reach up and hold onto my neck, I'll carry you out to the car and take you home," he said.

"Jeb Stuart ran away," I told him.

"He came back too," said Daddy. "Of his own volition, which I'd say is a first in the history of wirehaired terriers. He must have been looking for you, and came back home to see if you were here."

"Who was the man with the gray hair?" I asked. "He smelled like whiskey and peppermints."

"That was old Dr. Ellis. He lives right down the street here. But you're mistaken about the whiskey—Hiram's a teetotaler.

This whole house is beginning to smell like its owner, that's all."
I looked down and became aware of something heavy on my
right leg. "You now own a fine but temporary plaster container
to carry your foot around in. The problem is, your foot is still
hooked onto your leg, so you're going to need some assistance
from a pair of crutches for a while." He smiled and touched the
bandaged place on my forehead.

"When the cast comes off, am I going to have a limp?"

"I don't think so. But even if you do, all is not lost. Look at
Felicity. Her limp is quite romantic, in my opinion. Romantic
in the literary sense."

On the way out we passed the dimly lit dining room. Its table
was set for one; a sweating silver pitcher dripped water onto a
white, cutwork cloth.

I said, "Who's that table for?"

"Uncle Baby. Clarence and Regina are waiting dinner for
him, but they might as well go to bed. It's after ten o'clock now,
and your mother told me she saw Uncle Baby go tearing out of
the driveway in his Mercedes just as she drove up here to take
you home, a few hours ago."

"Why didn't she? Take me home, I mean."

"You were sound asleep. Dr. Ellis had knocked you out so he
could go to work on your ankle and you hadn't awakened yet.
So Mama left, and came home again, and by that time I'd gotten
home, too."

"But where were you while Mama was over here?"

He hesitated. "I was with Felicity, honey, at her house. She's
very upset over Lady-Sidonie, and Airey couldn't be there with
her; he was called to the hospital right after the funeral. You
know what all this is beginning to sound like? It sounds like that
old rhyme I used to tell you when you were little; Patty was a
Welshman, Patty was a thief, Patty went to my house and stole
a piece of beef. I went to Patty's house, but Patty wasn't home,
Patty went to my house and stole a marrow bone. I went to

Patty's house and Patty was in bed, so I took the marrow bone and I hit him on the head."

He waited a few seconds and when I didn't respond, he said, "Not funny?"

"I don't know if I remember seeing Mama while she was here. My head feels dizzy, I can't remember right."

"You can't remember seeing Mama because you *didn't* see her, honey; she told me you were dead asleep when she looked in on you. If your head feels dizzy, then give it a rest, quit trying to think so hard."

Clarence appeared and opened the front door for us. A night breeze blew in, its damp scent mingled with the smell of over-browned pork that hung in the entrance hall.

"Good-bye, Clay-Lee," said Clarence. "You come back and play with Jeb Stuart after he get past the puppy stage. He too much for everybody just now."

"Good-bye, and thank you, Clarence," said Daddy. "I hope Jeb Stuart remembers Clay-Lee the next time he sees her."

"I don't doubt he will," said Clarence. "Be careful on the steps there, sir, the marble's slick with rain. This young lady can't afford to take no more tumbles. Not for a while, anyhow."

9

For the next two weeks I spent almost twenty-four hours a day in bed, working needlepoint on a beginner's canvas my mother had bought for me, or reading the books my father left on my night table before he returned to Houma. Sometimes Aunt Mathilde read to me from the *Lives of the Saints for Little People*. "What are you crying about now?" she greeted me one afternoon when the two weeks were almost up. "I don't remember," I said, drying my eyes with the completed half of my needlework. "If anybody in this house would listen to me for half a minute," said Aunt Mathilde, staring, "they'd get you off all that painkiller you're full of. Weepiness, nervousness . . . you'll be thinking you heard voices next. Hallucinating, they call it."

"*Confessions of an English Opium Eater*, by Thomas De Quincey," I said, holding up one of the books my father had left for me. "Daddy told me Thomas De Quincey was a dope fiend. So was Sherlock Holmes."

"Where do you get expressions like 'dope fiend,' if you don't mind my asking?"

"I don't remember."

" 'I don't remember.' That's your answer to everything since you cracked your head," said Aunt Mathilde. She picked up another book from my table; it was *Louisiana Hayride: The American Rehearsal for Dictatorship, 1928–1940,* by Harnett T. Kane. "What's the matter with your father, letting you read this kind of thing?"

"Aunt Mathilde, listen: what were the only words the mayor of New Orleans said to Franklin D. Roosevelt when the president visited the city in 1938?"

"I've no idea."

" 'How you like them ersters?' He meant oysters, but he had an Irish Channel accent."

"Is that from this book? I thought this book was about Huey Long."

"It is about Huey Long. Huey Long and his friends."

"Well *today* we're going to learn about some of *Jesus'* friends. The saints," she said, tapping the cover of *Saints for Little People*. "Much more suitable for a child to hear about than Huey Long." Then she began reading.

After a long time she said, "Are you awake, Clay-Lee?"

"Yes, ma'am."

"Then open your eyes. I don't like reading to people who keep their eyes shut, it reminds me of my late husband. Howard! The *pages* I wasted my breath on, with him asleep the whole time."

"Howard's dead?"

"I like to think he is. Better he's dead than living, breathing trash that's wandering around someplace, never bothering to contact me."

I laughed.

"Are you deliberately trying to annoy me? The trouble with you, young lady, is you've been getting too much attention. It's my opinion you should spend more of your time *praying* to the saints instead of making fun of them!"

"Maybe I'll pray to Huey Long instead." My head was beginning to ache again and I closed my eyes. "Daddy told me he used to see it in the newspapers all the time, in the Personals

column. There'd be something like, 'Thanks to Saint Jude and
the Virgin for helping to find lost brooch,' and then right under
that, 'Thanks to Huey P. Long for favors granted.' "

"Constance!" called Aunt Mathilde, slamming shut the book
and going out into the hall. "I wish you'd run up here a minute
and listen to what's coming out of your daughter's mouth!" She
came back into my room and yanked the window shades down
to the sill. "Go to sleep! Maybe when you wake up you'll be
making better sense. And you can scream and cry till your eyes
fall out, nobody's giving you one more drop of that pain-killer if
I have my way about it. You're acting like a completely different child!"

When I woke up again it was after five o'clock and Aunt
Mathilde was gone. My mother was standing near my bed; next
to her was Sylvie Despointes, from school. "You have a little
visitor," Mama said. "Sylvie's brought you the rest of your school-
books and a homework assignment."

"Forgive me," said Sylvie. "They have made me do it."

"Sylvie's been given permission to stay and have dinner with
us, too. I'll bring your dinner up to you on trays, how would
that be?"

"Ah, *bon*," said Sylvie.

"I'll be back in a little while," Mama said. "Be careful with
those crutches, Sylvie. You're too tall for them."

Sylvie put the crutches back against the wall and walked over
to my bulletin board. Thumbtacked in a lower corner of it was
an old photograph of Rand and Constance, taken at Summerhill
the first year of their marriage. They were both dressed in white;
my mother was holding a ribbon and frowning a little in the
bright sunlight. Rand was looking at her instead of at the cam-
era.

"They are very pretty, your mother and father," said Sylvie.
"They look here as if they had been chasing one another. You
see that your mother's hair is wild, blown from the wind? And

there is her hair ribbon in her hands; it has come loose while she was running."

"I never thought about it," I said. Actually I couldn't picture Constance allowing Rand to chase her around Summerhill. It seemed very unlikely. Sylvie had wandered over to my desk, where Aunt Mathilde had placed *Louisiana Hayride* out of my reach. She picked it up and opened it to the flyleaf. " 'To my friend, Rand, with best regards from Harnett T. Kane,' " she read. "Your papa, he is a writer, too, like his friend Mr. Kane?"

"He's an artist," I said. "Although right now he happens to be in the sugar business. My father doesn't even know Harnett T. Kane—he wrote that in the book himself. For a joke, I guess." Sylvie looked down at the book and said nothing. It was hard to tell with Sylvie whether she was being quiet because she was sad or just because she hadn't caught the meaning of all the words. My mother came to the doorway then with a tray in her hands, and Sylvie put down the book and went to help her settle it on my lap. "I'll be right back with yours," she told Sylvie, and I thought she sounded tired. She had quit her job at the library, but maybe having me at home, bedridden, was harder than working with books had been. There was a tremor to her voice.

We were having round steak with red gravy, and breaded mirlitons. The round steak was *bon*, according to Sylvie, but the mirlitons were dull. "Perhaps some pepper," Sylvie suggested. "Here it is," I said, handing her the shaker. "Or do you want Tabasco?" "What means 'Tabasco'?" "Red pepper, in a bottle. Liquid pepper." *"Tout à fait,"* cried Sylvie. "I had Tabasco once at the convent. Where is it?" "It's downstairs, I guess. In the kitchen." You stay here, and I will go and get it," said Sylvie. *"Comme je suis stupide!* I forgot, you must stay here; you are paralyzed."

Sylvie was gone for so long that I had finished everything on my plate by the time she returned.

"I am sorry I was gone for so long," she said, sitting down at my desk again. She sprinkled Tabasco all over her mirlitons and picked up her fork. "By the way, downstairs there is something afoot."

"What?" I said, confused. Sylvie had first learned formal English from an old Scottish nanny and sometimes the nanny's antiquated vocabulary cropped up in Sylvie's choice of words.

"Your maman is crying, and so is her sister. The sister was saying to your mother, 'Don't cry, don't cry,' while she herself was crying. Big tears, down her face. They are very close, these sisters, yes? I wish I had a sister."

"My mother doesn't have one either. That was Honey McCaleb you saw. They even have the same dreams sometimes. She looked like my mother and had a baby with her?"

"*Ça, c'est exact.* The baby was crying too, but loudly. He made it difficult to hear all of what was being said."

"Couldn't you hear *anything* they were saying, besides 'Don't cry, don't cry'?"

"Of course. I was in the dark passageway between the steps and the kitchen. They were sitting at the kitchen table.

"Your maman's friend said to her, 'You know you are all he wants from being alive, that is part of his problem.' Then your maman said, 'He is not like himself. When he is with me, he thinks always about something I do not know. And this afternoon, Aunt Mathilde told me that Felicity spends days with him at Home. She was at Home with him the day Lady-Sidonie died.' Who are these women, Felicity and the Lady-Sidonie?"

". . . days in *Houma*, not Home. Felicity's my mother's cousin."

"She is a beauty, this Felicity?"

"I don't know. I guess so. What else did you hear?"

"Nothing else. A big dog who was lying on the floor next to your maman looked up and saw me in the passageway. The dog barked and both the ladies turned their heads and saw me."

"I don't understand what's going on," I said. "What would Felicity be doing in Houma? And my father. I see my father every week. He's the same as he always is. What does she mean, he's not himself?"

After Sylvie had gone I sat alone in the dark. I remember wondering when my own life was going to begin and I could stop being an audience at other people's. So far it seemed as though I'd spent most of my time listening in on my parents' lives, watching their eyes, trying to figure out what they were going to do next. It was sure as rain neither of them ever wasted a second wondering what I was going to do next. I didn't blame them. Usually I was up to nothing; the only important things that had happened directly to me were going to a new school and fracturing my ankle, one about as much fun as the other. I was dull, as dull as a nun. Duller; nuns, at least, had the power to make people afraid. As it turned out, though, I was dangerous too in my way, a dangerous audience to have. I was the sort of spectator who gets caught up in a particular scene and steps up suddenly onstage from the dark, upsetting the progression of the plot. I wondered what kind of a plot was unfolding right now out at Uncle Baby's sugar mill. Whatever it was, it surely couldn't have anything to do with my father falling in love with Felicity, could it? He didn't have any room left inside him for anybody else, not after Constance got through taking up all her rightful space. For a paperweight on his desk my father kept a metal sculpture he'd done of one of Constance's little sandals; when he scribbled on a tablet to get the ink going in a pen, it wasn't wavy lines or circles he wrote, but her name, as if he took particular pleasure in the way the combination of the letters looked. Maybe if she believed he had somebody else on his mind, though, she'd be nicer to him than she had recently been. I remembered just a few days ago Daddy and me, coming to the dinner table, sitting down and waiting to begin. Let's wait for your mother, Clayton-Leland, he had said. But my mother decided not to come, to lie down in her bedroom and not have anything to eat at all. Daddy was making me laugh, smiling back at me across the meat and rice, although the gravy'd gotten cold.

"You are all he wants from being alive, that is part of his problem." That sounded like one of Sylvie's poor translations. What Honey'd meant to tell her was, He loves you too much. The words like an alarm tripped off a memory in my head, but I pushed my mind away from it and lay there in the dark, willing myself to become drowsy.

Later that same night, I heard my mother call to me. "Clay-Lee," she said, "are you still awake? Airey's here. He wants to tell you something." (I hadn't heard the doorbell but that was because it probably hadn't rung—it only rang when it felt like it. It was a trick to get that door to take its own key into the lock, too. "You ought to feel completely safe here by yourself," John McCaleb had told Mama when she'd told him she had become afraid to stay in the house at night without my father. "Even if a burglar had a key to this place, it wouldn't do him any good. It's as if this house doesn't want to let anybody in."

"Or let anybody out either," said Mama.)

Airey's blue seersucker suit was rumpled and in the overhead light I could see that his eyes had dark pouches under them. "Excuse me, Constance, for barging in on you all, unannounced, but I'd been over at my lawyer's, going over Mother's will, and I was driving home past your corner and I thought, well, why not stop by there and let Clay-Lee have the satisfaction before she goes to sleep." He reached into the breast pocket of his coat and took out a square of folded yellow paper. "I wrote down the exact wording of this, because I believe it was important to Mother that Clay-Lee hear it the way she put it. It's a codicil to her will; that means it's something she added on. Apparently she took the unnecessary step of bringing it to her lawyers' office, just two weeks before she passed away."

The bedroom window was open, and I could smell the sweet olive tree Daddy had planted on the side of the house; the scent of it seemed to promise that the last remains of winter had finally been laid to rest. Airey began to read. "To my good friend and valued confidante, Miss Clayton-Leland Calvert, I hereby give, devise, and bequeath Rosehue, the house and grounds which my own father once gave to me, on Three Rivers Road, in the Town of Covington, Louisiana, and all fixtures and furnishings belonging to said house, in the hope that she will find there, as I did for many years, the blessings of serenity and of joy."

Airey was looking at me as if he expected me to say something, but I couldn't talk. If I could have, I'd have gotten up and telephoned Sis Honorine over on State Street, like she'd told me to if I needed her. I needed to tell her something; I wanted to let her know that sometimes it's the suddenness of things that lifts you up, and that sometimes you can count on feelings way past the sadness in good-byes.

10

"Rosehue" became a magic word; the very mention of it could transform Constance Calvert into a wide-eyed girl again. She telephoned Felicity and told her all about "our inheritance," the "estate which, in all probability, closely resembles Summerhill." Felicity said she hadn't been to Rosehue in years and years, not since Lady-Sidonie had stopped spending summers there, but she thought the place might need a lot of work; she declined my mother's invitation to drive over with us to see the house and grounds. Then Felicity asked Mama if Courtenay and Minette could go instead; she said they would be delighted to make the trip.

"I wonder if Felicity's drinking again," said Constance to Honey, after she had hung up. "She sounded like she was about to cry. Brandy, I guess. Brandy always did make her weepy."

"Maybe she just misses seeing you as often as she did years ago," said Honey. "You two used to be so close; she told me that once, and she sounded sad."

"I don't know what you mean," said Constance. "She's still family, isn't she? Just because we're not sixteen years old together anymore. . . ."

A week or so later, Daddy borrowed the de la Cordes' station wagon and took all of us—Courtenay, Minette and me, Mama,

Mishka, and Honey and John—over to Covington. Aunt Mathilde wasn't asked, but she stopped by Camp Street that morning, just as we were getting ready to go out the front door. Mama
felt compelled to invite her to come along with us, to see "the
inheritance."

"I've already seen 'the inheritance,' thank you very much,"
said Aunt Mathilde. "I drove onto the property by accident one
time and I'll never forget it. It's my opinion Mrs. de la Corde
had it rented to Negroes. The whole place looked filthy dirty
from the outside, and badly in need of repairs."

"That's not true, Aunt Mathilde," said Mama. Mama's neck
was suddenly mottled red, as if somebody had splashed hot water
on her. "You know perfectly well Lady-Sidonie's rented that
house for the last twenty years to some German woman named
Anna Hoff. And if there's anybody more fastidious as a rule
than Germans are I haven't heard about it."

"Then maybe I'm mistaken. However, to be on the safe side,
I wouldn't wear a white dress if I were you, or put my full
weight on the porch steps either."

Rand was familiar with St. Tammany Parish because he'd
spent his summers there when he was a boy, at his Aunt Compton Calvert's house on Military Road. Aunt Compton Calvert
was now deceased, and her house had burned to the ground in
1945, but Daddy said he still felt he knew the town of Covington, and on our way across Lake Pontchartrain, he told us some
of what he knew.

For several centuries, said Daddy, Covington had been popu-
lar with consumptives and asthmatics nationwide, who traveled
to Louisiana to inhale the curative ozone St. Tammany's pine
trees secreted into the atmosphere. The visiting invalids were
welcomed by the townspeople, but Covington natives had a reputation for orneriness as well as for hospitality; they liked to argue
just for the pleasure of it. If one lady claimed Miss Sophie

Vardeman's fiancé was a falling-down drunk, that was the signal for another lady to speak right up and say, no, he wasn't, the man had diabetes, plain and simple, and suffered from insulin fits. Daddy said most of the arguers were the people whose ancestors, back in 1799, had taken it into their heads to swear an oath of allegiance to the United States just as they were being annexed to Spanish West Florida; they were descendants of the citizens who petitioned Congress in 1812 to allow them to join the Mississippi Territory at the same time Louisiana was being admitted as a state. St. Tammany people voted pro-Union in the 1860 presidential election, and against secession at the same year's state convention. Apparently, they did it just to be contrary, not from any moral conviction—in 1865, the townspeople reportedly still owned slaves, despite the realities of the Civil War and the Emancipation Proclamation.

"Is the lady who's been renting Lady-Sidonie's house from Covington?" I said, wondering if she would turn out to be hospitable or cranky.

"Anna Hoff? She was born in Germany," said Constance. "People as far away as New Orleans used to talk about her when I was growing up. Anna Hoff's been famous in Louisiana for years."

"Famous for what?" asked Courtenay.

"Oh, people out in the country started the rumor that she could see into the future, that she was a psychic," said Mama. "Anna Hoff had been involved in some tragic episode as a child, in which she was held indirectly responsible for another child's death, and she was supposed to have become psychic shortly after that. She was born in Germany, as I said, then lived in some small town upriver from New Orleans till she moved to Covington in the 1940s. I believe her family was practically run out of the town where they lived originally, and where the child's death had occurred. People there complained Anna had a direct line to Satan."

"Oh, Lord," whispered Minette next to me. "I'm going to dream about all this tonight, I know I am."

Honey said, "I remember hearing people say that Anna Hoff would know only sorrow in her own life, that she could predict only sorrow, because she'd caused sorrow as a child, when her soul was newly gone from heaven to earth."

"I wish I was deaf," said Minette. "Please, don't say anymore."

"This Hoff woman, she's still living in the late Mrs. de la Corde's house?" John McCaleb asked.

"As of last week, she was," said Constance. "I don't know what she's going to do now. I don't think she's even got any furniture of her own. All of it in the house was Lady-Sidonie's, and now it's ours."

"Clay-Lee's," said Daddy.

"Rand," said John, "what kind of a humor do you guess old evil-eyed Anna's going to be in when we show up on her doorstep to claim the roof over her head? I think I'll wait for you all out in the car."

"I'll wait with you," said Minette. "That'll be easier than keeping my eyes shut the whole time I'm in the house." She stared back at Courtenay. "I'm afraid of her, Courtenay! I'm afraid she's going to look into my eyes and see something there."

"If she does she'll be the first," said Courtenay.

I remember thinking, when I saw the house, that I'd like to be inside its screened porch during a rain. It was that kind of porch, wide and high, with fine screen like a veil protecting it. The house was set far back from the road; you wouldn't be able to see it in the dark, unless the lamps were lit. Behind the screened porch were long windows hung with white curtains, made of what looked like bed sheets. The whole place was a gray-brown color and the paint was peeling, but before I'd ever laid eyes on the house I'd got my father to promise he'd paint it snow white for me, and that's how I saw it from the start. The ground in back of the house tilted in a muddy slope to the Bogue

Falaya River; John and Rand headed off in that direction and took Minette with them. They'd be back up and join us in a while, they said; they weren't in the frame of mind right then for a bad-tidings fortune-teller. The other four of us, five counting Mishka, went up the wooden steps to the porch and my mother knocked on the screen door. Confederate jasmine was blooming all along the railing, a comforting smell, like sachet on a lady. The porch itself was dark with shade from the cypress trees that leaned against it, but I could see the door into the house was open, and a deeper darkness behind the opening. After a while somebody walked toward us out of the doorway and stood looking through the screen: a tall, ox-faced woman, middle-aged.

"I'm Constance Calvert from New Orleans," said my mother. "Are you Miss Anna Hoff?"

The ox-faced woman uttered a desperate, grunting sound as though she'd got some large object stuck in her mouth. She was wearing clean white cotton gloves.

"She sounds like a woman in childbirth," whispered Honey. "Do you suppose she's a mute?"

"If she is then you probably don't have to whisper," I said. "Remember Deaf and Dumb William. He doesn't hear a thing."

"Cottel!" cried a voice from the darkness. "What are you standing there for! Is it somebody come?" Cottel stepped back a little and then standing next to her was another middle-aged woman, as tall as Cottel was. The second woman had a worn-out fractious face and a mouth that bent down at the corners as though it were too tired to hold itself up any longer. Her hair was straw-colored, and like Cottel she wore it in a thick braid that twisted around her head. Their dresses were alike, too: seersucker housedresses, one blue, the other green; beltless, with zip-up fronts.

Anna Hoff pushed open the screen door and looked at us one by one, her nostrils flaring. "Thank God Minette's down at the river," whispered Courtenay. "She'd have dropped dead by this time."

Inside, the house was as dark as if a storm were coming; the shutters on all the windows had been pulled shut and the whole place smelled of pine-oil disinfectant. The rooms opened off along the sides of the wide, windowed hall. The kitchen was oddly placed; it was the first room behind the porch and had a long window in it. "This could be relocated," I heard Constance say to Honey. "But it costs a fortune to relocate a kitchen, Lamb," Honey told her.

"You go on and look in any room you want to!" called Anna Hoff, behind us. "You won't be able to find no dirt and clutter in none of 'em!" I turned to look at her, but she and Cottel were already gliding away into the gloom, in the direction of the porch.

"This is a big house," said Mama, excitement in her voice. "Heart pine, and beautifully built. Airey says it's over a hundred years old! It could be a showplace, Honey, like Summerhill. Rand's so good at fixing things; we could do a lot of the work ourselves."

"Look at those beautiful blue and white tiles around the fireplace," said Honey. "What is this room, the dining room? Why would they keep a cot in the dining room?"

"Maybe old Cottel has fits at dinnertime," said Courtenay to me. "I can't see my hand in front of my face. Was that your foot or the dog's paws I just stepped on?"

"Come here, Mishka, come here, girl," called Mama, up ahead of us. "Stay with me, I won't step on your feet."

"We've already been in this room," said Honey. "Constance, the ceilings are relatively high. I think this room would hold your big cypress bed."

Then we were back on the porch, where Anna Hoff and Cottel had propped themselves up like twin bolsters on either side of the glider. "You seen all you want to see?" said Anna.

"What do *you* see in my eyes?" said Courtenay, going over to stand in front of her. "Are there catastrophes in them?"

"Doubtless there is," said Anna Hoff, "but I won't be pointing 'em out to you. I don't fool with children. Children's souls is in turmoil." She looked over at Constance, and reaching out, she took her hand and turned it palm up. I could see that my mother was ill at ease but she left her hand in Anna's. "You come from a lot of sisters, a big family," said Anna. "And right after your papa died . . . an accident. A fire? Your mama, she was put away somewheres awhile—" She raised her eyes to my mother's face. "Have you lost a child as yet?" Mama took her hand away and glanced at Honey, who was standing next to me. Anna's blue-marble eyes interpreted the look, and she shrugged her shoulders. "I only done that one time before, picked up on the wrong life in somebody's hand. With a set of twins. It's blood relations alone that happens with."

"You got the particular life wrong, too," said Constance. "My friend didn't lose a child, she just had one. In April."

"She ain't your sister, then? Her face is like yours," said Anna. She leaned back on the glider and I can picture her still as she was that day, her own face an ugly duplicate of her wordless döppelganger's.

"What would you see, then, in *my* hand?" Honey asked her.

"Not again," protested Mama, but Honey already had her palm outstretched. Anna Hoff couldn't have spent more than two seconds on it, though. "I see a stone," she said, sounding bored. She let go of Honey's hand.

"What kind of a stone?" asked Honey. "Is it an emerald?" She turned her head and said to Constance, "Remember I told you John's mother might give me that heirloom emerald ring of hers, for having the baby?"

"I thought Anna Hoff was only supposed to tell bad things," complained Courtenay.

"Some things I choose to tell, and some things I don't choose," said Anna Hoff. She looked over at me and grinned suddenly, showing the dead teeth in her mouth. "Sometimes not telling, that can help the evil happen, too. The badness! That quiet child there, she knows what I'm saying."

I closed my eyes for a few seconds, to still a sudden surge of dizziness, and saw an unmarked stone, white and immovable, against a background of storm-blackened sky.

"There's Rand coming now across the yard," said Mama. I opened my eyes as she unlatched the screen door to the porch. "You won't mind, Miss Hoff, if I show my husband through the house?"

But that day my father wasn't as taken with Rosehue as I hoped he'd be. He just let Mama lead him from place to place while he walked along behind her, looking preoccupied, and he didn't remark on the hospital cot in the dining room or the framed magazine photograph of a little boy that was lying, wrapped in a blue blanket, on one of the beds. After he'd seen all the rooms once, we left—John and Minette had never even come in to look around. It was just as well, though, that we didn't stay any longer; I was beginning to get the feeling I sometimes got in the middle of watching pirate movies or horror shows, that desire to run out of the dark theater, to get away from the awful presences lit up on the screen and to see the real world again, out on the good old gray sidewalk in ordinary daylight.

"I'll say one thing for it, it's clean," declared Daddy, starting the car's engine. I looked back at the house as we drove away, and I saw Cottel, white-gloved, come out and open the door to the porch. With a white cloth she wiped off the doorknob where we had touched it.

11

In some ways that was a good summer. We had a country place
of our own to go to; it was no longer necessary for me to wait
around the Camp Street house for the telephone to ring, hoping
it would be one of the de la Corde children with an invitation
for me to spend a few days at Summerhill. Of course, Rosehue
would never be as grand a place as Summerhill, but I loved it
anyway, it had a kind of holiday air about it. The bad beginning
to the house, which Anna Hoff and Cottel had engineered,
faded from my mind as soon as I saw the sunlight on the newly
polished wood floors and breathed the scents of dried eucalyptus
and of bread baking that replaced the pine-oil smell. My mother
brought the eucalyptus, and her needlepointed pillows, and several of Rand's framed paintings; Sis Honorine, whom Mama had
hired to "help out" three days a week, baked the bread.

One rainy afternoon during the first week Mama and I were
in Covington, Sis's nephew turned up unexpectedly on our front
porch. He was a licorice-candy-smelling black boy whom Sis introduced to Mama and me as her nephew, Book of Knowledge
Thompson. "Go on, sit yourself on the swing there next to Clay-
Lee a minute. And quit your wriggling. You act like you got
worms!" Book of Knowledge obediently crawled up onto the
swing. Judging from the size of him he was a five-year-old, but

his front teeth were missing like they would be if he were closer to seven. "He already knock half his teeth out his head with his wildness," Sis explained to my mother. "I don't know why he can't sit still for three seconds running."

"Uh . . . oh," said Book of Knowledge, opening his mouth wide and jutting out his jaw to show me that his bottom teeth had pretty much completely disappeared, too.

Sis was shelling butter beans, and Constance picked up a handful and began shelling, too. "Guess what, Sis?" Mama said. "I'm buying a little sailboat, a Rainbow, to keep over here in Covington. I got it for a reasonable price, too, because I bought it secondhand from one of the girls who was in my class at school."

I was astonished—my mother had mentioned nothing to me about buying a boat.

"Mar-di Gras, chick-a-la-paw," chanted Book of Knowledge, swinging violently. I stuck out my feet and scraped them along the porch floor to slow us down. "Shee-it," hissed the black boy.

"What does Mr. Rand say about it?" asked Sis, shifting a little in her wicker chair. "He want you to buy a boat?"

"Oh, he doesn't know yet, this is going to be a surprise for him. He used to sail all the time before we were married, so having a boat of our own will be a special pleasure for him."

"Miss Lamb," said Sis, "from what I've seen, men don't much like surprises. When you going to let Mr. Rand in on all this?"

When it was too late to do anything about it was the answer to that question. Mama's school friend, Miss Pilsby Avery, reached Daddy by telephone in New Orleans the following weekend and told him she needed "the balance due" by the next Monday morning. The balance due on what? Daddy asked her, and was she sure it was J. Rand Calvert she wanted, not Mr. Clement D. Calvert?

"Is this Lamb Alexander's husband I'm talking to?" inquired the bill collector. "If it is, then you owe me the balance due on a twenty-foot sailboat." As soon as Daddy was able to speak again, he telephoned Constance in Covington and told her he was just leaving New Orleans to drive across the lake and by the time he arrived could she please come up with an explanation as to why somebody named Pilsby Avery thought the Rand Calverts had bought a sailboat from her? "And if you can also come up with what Miss Avery called 'the balance due,' that would be a big help, too," said Rand, talking so loud I could hear him two feet away from the phone, "because I just took out a second mortgage with the Whitney Bank on the Camp Street house, and according to my figures, the amount we've got left in our savings account will just about cover the price of a new inner tube."

Then, just before hanging up, Rand took Constance by surprise by telling her that in addition to refinancing the house, he'd wiped out his accumulated earnings from his job at the sugar company and "reinvested the money."

"What in God's name could he mean by that?" cried Constance, talking to herself, out loud, and darting like a frightened bird from the kitchen to the front porch and back again while we waited for Daddy to drive up. "Why would he have taken out a second mortgage on that albatross on Camp Street? I hate that house! It could burn to the ground tomorrow morning, and I'd get over it by noon!"

She flew past me into the hall, picked up the telephone, dropped it on the floor, and picked it up again. "I don't care if it *is* long-distance!" she said to me, her chin in the air, as if I'd forbidden her to dial anything but local calls. Then, "Honey?" she said. "That Pilsby Avery went and called Rand and asked him for the money for the sailboat before I even had a chance to tell him we'd bought one!"

I passed Mishka on the front steps where she'd taken up her post as lookout—was she planning to run inside and alert Constance the moment Rand, foaming at the mouth, sprang onto the premises?—and went down the road to visit the McQueen twins, a pair of mole-sprinkled ten-year-olds called Beeper and Booper.

That afternoon, Beeper and Booper had another visitor, a pushy little girl, my age, named Renée Ewin. Renée wore us all out by reenacting, while Beeper, Booper, and I were expected to continuously applaud, the movements of the skaters in something she called "The Ice Capades," which she had recently witnessed at the Municipal Auditorium in New Orleans. When I finally walked home at dusk, Renée walked along with me, reciting a garbled story of where babies come from, the more scientific version of which I had already heard from Courtenay.

"You mind if I come in?" Renée asked, when we reached my house.

"I don't think you'd better come in today," I said. "We're expecting company." That was true in a way; we saw my father so seldom he was beginning to take on company status.

"You're expecting company?" sneered Renée. "If that isn't the lousiest excuse I've ever heard." She ambled on without looking back, her hips as loosely jointed as a marionette's.

It was after dark when Rand finally came up the front steps that evening, but Constance didn't ask him where he'd been. That wouldn't have been her style. Instead she sat on the screened porch's glider, looking up at him, her little face half-shadowed in the light from the hallway, and she swung back and forth as belligerently as Book of Knowledge Thompson had the week before. The air all around Constance and Rand was charged that night with a kind of intermittent lightning, like the hot dark air of a screen box with fireflies inside.

"Had you told me of your grand financial dealings," I remember her saying to him, "then this whole mess would never have taken place! I'm not inclined to attempt to read a man's mind." A mild breeze blew over her, tumbling her hair around her cheeks that were stained pink from the June heat and from her own contentiousness. She looked the way she had in that photograph of herself at Summerhill; she looked like a woman chased. Rand was chasing her now, although he hadn't moved a step.

"It's true," he said, "that you've never shown any great interest in the workings of my mind." His face held a hurtful misery and the anticipation of more hurt to come. At the same time there was a deadly calm about him that reminded me of Mishka's calm before she lunged to tear apart a bluejay in the yard. "Would it interest you to know that up till now there's been nothing on the debit side of your ledger? Does that sound businesslike enough for you? I loved everything about you, even your spoiled foolishness."

"Rand!" she cried. The pain in her voice startled me and I could see it startled him. "It was either call on Clement for help or look like a perfect fool to Pilsby Avery!"

"A circumstance to be avoided at all cost," said Rand wearily. "Imagine, for a minute, what it costs me to spend all week at his command, dancing to whatever tune he cares to play, and now, God damn him, I've got to choke on his so-called charity every time I look at that sailboat you couldn't get along without. Why the hell did you have to drag Uncle Baby into this?" There was the real thorn—in her panic, Constance had telephoned to Uncle Baby while Rand was on his way to Covington, and gotten him to send a check by special messenger to Pilsby Avery. That was just after Honey'd told her Pilsby had another buyer waiting in the wings for the boat.

"I just *borrowed* the money from Clement!" said Mama. "You can pay him back right away, if you want to—take out a personal loan!"

"Why do you think I'm reacting to this the way I am?" Daddy asked. "I told you I've already taken out one loan, using the house as collateral. Because I needed a certain amount of cash to get in on a stock-market transaction John McCaleb's got me on to. A sure thing, involving the merger of two off-shore drilling equipment companies." He sounded as if he'd memorized the last half of what he'd said, but Constance suddenly looked wildly excited. She stared at Rand in a strange, dazzled way, as though she saw a genie's lamp reflected in his eyes. "Clay-Lee, go on in the house now," she said, without shifting her gaze from his face, and her soft voice caught on her words as if she were close to choking on pleasure and surprise.

Lying in bed, I spent some time before I fell asleep examining a toy my father had brought me that evening, from the cane farm near the sugar mill, in Houma. It was a little wooden toaster with wooden, toast-shaped pieces fitted into its slots; one of the toy pieces of toast had a bite-shaped wedge carved out of it. I imagined a sweet fragrance clung to my fingers where they'd touched the wood, and it came to me it wasn't wood at all but sugarcane, its ripe thickness hardened into a new shape and tempting enough to suck on. In the dark, I lay with the smooth sugar in my mouth, against my tongue, while the warm night wind teased my nightgown up over my legs, and from the porch came the sound of the swing, creaking and bumping in the sudden silence. Parts of that summer are mixed up in my mind with those of the summer that came after it, the final summer; my memories of both summers are caught up with that taste of sugarcane and the hot brightness of the water, and my mother in white dresses as clean and fine as the sail on the *Mishka,* the boat whose name she'd changed from *Precious Ridicule.* "Bad luck to change a boat's name," John McCaleb told her, but she didn't heed him, she heeded no one; she never had, except maybe her father for a time.

The McCalebs came to visit us in Covington that summer, and Sylvie Despointes a few times, and the de la Cordes, who were out at Summerhill for most of every summer anyway. Uncle Baby Brother drove over once or twice, and stayed right through dinner, even though his presence seemed to put a damper on the day. Felicity would glare at him while he stared at my mother, while my mother stared at Felicity, and then Daddy would begin to look as if he wished he were someplace else entirely. Many times we took the sailboat out and brought a picnic basket with us, packed with Sis's honey-glazed chicken, and little biscuits with sweet butter that Constance kept hard and cold in an old-fashioned wooden ice chest.

Autumn came, and with it came changes as inevitable and startling as the sudden darkness that fell across Camp Street at dinnertime in the cool, windy evenings. John McCaleb was asked to become a partner in his law firm, and right after that he and Honey moved into a pretty Creole cottage in the Garden District part of Chestnut Street; the house had originally been a camelback double, but its previous owners had torn down interior walls and left standing the brick-chimneyed fireplaces in the wide parlor and in the dining room. "This is the way your own house could look," Honey said to Mama. "When Rand's profits come in from this stock transaction, you can turn out your new tenant and remodel so that you have a single house all to yourselves." The new tenant was an aging bachelor whose belongings were few and whose very presence seemed to irritate my mother. "What does he need all this space for anyway?" she would wonder aloud, with a mean frown between her eyes, after Mr. Louvier had left his rent check in our mailbox. I guess she blamed him for not being Honey, but she wouldn't allow herself to grieve over Honey's being gone. It was just a temporary setback, after all, their no longer being neighbors. Mama had her heart set on a raised cottage two doors down from the McCalebs' new house; she told Honey that she was going to persuade Rand to sell the Camp Street house as soon as his projected windfall materialized. All that autumn, nothing seemed to faze my mother, she was as fired-up and superior as a city schoolteacher with a roomful of farm children. I heard her tell Honey she'd given up on picking apart every word and gesture of Rand's—"If he's more than usually preoccupied, it's because of business dealings on his mind, that's all"—and when John called and told us he might really buy an airplane, Constance just laughed and asked Daddy how was it John McCaleb hoped to fly a Piper Cub when he couldn't even manage the tiller of our sailboat?

Then one November night I was awakened by the sound of Rand and his Gladstone bumping up the stairs, and I knew as surely as if I'd heard him say so that he was home to stay. A while later I fell asleep again to the rhythm of my parents' voices down the hall, my mother's voice high and indignant, my father's going on steadily underneath her interruptions, and an irrational gladness came over me, like the feeling that comes to a child who's told he won't be obliged to attend school on a given day, as a killer hurricane is due to hit the town.

I was a grown woman before I fully understood what had happened to effect Rand's return that night. For the past several months there had been a criminal investigation, prolonged and hushed up, into Clement Calvert's various businesses within the State of Louisiana, an investigation prompted by certain recently discovered activities of a gentleman named Harry Acree. Mr. Harry Acree, who'd obligingly dropped dead before he could testify in court, had been the vice-president and general manager of, among other of Clement's enterprises, La Dolce Vita Sugar company; it was Acree whom Rand replaced. The trouble began when an overly zealous young investigator for the Justice Department's Racketeering Strike Force tumbled to the fact that Harry Acree, in his executive capacity at one of Clement Calvert's grain storage warehouses on the New Orleans wharves, had for several years been engaged in a profit-making venture with the owner of a grain-weighing service, involving the deliberate overweighing of stored grain and a subsequent inflated cost to buyers. Acree then laundered his portion of the illegal profits through the books of La Dolce Vita Sugar Company, of which he was a major stockholder. Whether or not my great-uncle was a knowledgeable party to all this is unclear; in any case, Acree's death and his own pending legal troubles had forced Clement Calvert to return to the States the previous winter.

According to what Rand had been able to piece together, one of my great-uncle's attorneys must have contacted Clement before he left London for Louisiana, to inform him that La Dolce Vita Sugar was among the companies slated for investigation by the Terrebone Parish district attorney's office. The attorney had some surprising advice to impart to his client: place James Rand Calvert in the vice-president, general manager slot at La Dolce Vita, and do it right away. The advantages to hiring Rand were his complete innocence of the matters at hand, his fine old Louisiana name and unsullied reputation, and most important, his relationship by marriage to the late Judge Thomas B. Alexander. A little investigating of his own had apprised Uncle Baby's attorney of the fact that the young Terrebone Parish DA owed a rather substantial debt to the memory of the Judge. It had been Judge Alexander, a generation or so ago, who'd overturned the conviction of the DA's own daddy on a bootlegging charge. A lot of men might have considered such a debt discharged, owing to the death of the Judge, the lawyer reasoned, but this boy out in Terrebone Parish, this young DA, his last name was Genella. Sicilian. It just might be that his Old World sense of honor would be offended should an investigation by his office drag Judge Alexander's son-in-law into the line of fire. Then, too, Mr. Genella's oldest boy had recently been accepted at some fancy Catholic prep school up East, and beyond that, this happened to be an election year. It sure would be a pity for all concerned if somebody at the newspapers took it into his head just now to remind the voters about Mr. Genella's daddy's unfortunate past, a natural enough consequence of Rand Calvert's being identified in any investigative account as Judge Alexander's son-in-law.

The attorney had been right, of course. After suffering through several months of uncertainty and suspense, Uncle Baby had it on good authority that the Terrebone Parish district attorney's office had decided to drop its investigation into the La Dolce Vita Sugar Company, and my father was allowed the privilege of resigning his position. By then, Felicity de la Corde had come to Rand with her own suspicions regarding certain curious elements present in the running of Uncle Baby's new cement company, in which Airey had heavily invested.

"Felicity drove out to Houma several times to go over the sugar books with me—she was afraid we'd all gotten in over our heads with Uncle Baby Brother, and might find ourselves criminally liable for some stunt he'd pulled. Then, surprisingly, Uncle Baby came to *me.* 'Good news, my boy,' he said. 'The time has come for you to go back to your finger paints.' He explained what he felt like explaining of this investigation mess, and then he told me, 'We're in the clear up to this point, but was I you, I'd get out while the getting's good. If this Genella boy should suddenly get to feeling Sicilian, he'll hang me and take you along for the ride.'" Uncle Baby then offered Rand a respectable sum as "severance pay," which Rand had grandly refused to take, calling it "tainted money."

"What's the matter, sweetheart?" Constance teased him. "Did you think they might have been marked bills, planted on Clement by that Mediterranean district attorney? What could he have charged you with, blackmail?" Her equanimity seemed to astonish Rand, who must have returned home expecting her tears and protests. Instead, Constance said she'd never liked the idea of Rand's being in debt to Clement for his livelihood, it was simply that financial considerations had made it necessary. "Now that you've got all this money going to be coming in from John Mc-Caleb's venture, what do we need your uncle for?" she said.

12

On a gray day in December, the month after Daddy's permanent return from Houma, I was home from school because of a sore throat, and Constance was wheezing through another attack of bronchitis. Around noon, we went down to the kitchen together, dressed in our robes and slippers, to have lunch. While we ate our soup, Mama and I looked through the Sears catalog for pictures of things I might want for Christmas, and we were so absorbed in the big book that neither of us heard Airey de la Corde come into the room. When I looked up and saw him standing in front of us, my first thought was that he had heard I was ill and had come to look down my throat or to bring medicine, although I knew he was a ladies' doctor.

"Your front door was open, Constance," he said. "Not just open, ajar. You've got to be more careful in a neighborhood like this one." He looked pale and his voice was shaking. I stared down into the vegetable-strewn depths of my bowl of soup for a few seconds, and then up at Airey again. My eyes were level with his shirt front, yellow stripes on a white background, like a sugar candy called Fruit Bubblets that was sold in tins at McQueen's Drugs in Covington. I recollected eating a whole tinful of Fruit Bubblets once, in the backseat of the de la Cordes' station wagon, on the way to the Annunciation Parish Fair. Right before I vomited up the candy I felt like I did now, filled with fear and sick anticipation.

Constance said, "What's happened, what's the matter?" and stood up so quickly that her legs bumped against the edge of the table. I watched soup slosh over the rim of my bowl in a greasy wave.

"Is Rand here, Constance?" said Airey. "I stopped by his studio over on Calhoun Street and saw it was locked up, and I thought he might be here." He looked at me. "Clay-Lee, sugar, why don't you run upstairs and ask your daddy to come down here a minute?"

"He's not upstairs, he's gone down to the Quarter, to some gallery meeting," said Constance. Her voice was wary, and she was very still, the way I'd seen cats grow still, as if they were making sure of the presence and the location of danger before running from it.

"Constance, let's go sit down in the parlor, dear, and we—"

Constance said, "I don't want to go-sit-down-in-the-parlor-dear."

Airey looked at her.

"I had a call at the clinic this morning, from a friend of mine who also knows John McCaleb. As a matter of fact, this friend happens to be a newspaper reporter."

Mama and I waited.

Airey went on: "John's Piper Cub went down over Lake Pontchartrain at seven o'clock this morning, on the return trip he and Honey were making from Key West."

Mama sat down again. "He's dead? John died?"

Then, without waiting for Airey to answer, she asked him, "Can you drive me to the hospital? What hospital did they take Honey to? I have to go to the hospital now, and be with Honey."

She didn't move from where she was sitting though.

"Honey's gone, too, Lamb. I'm sorry, dear, I'm more sorry than I can say."

Airey reminded us that there had been a bad thunderstorm

just after dawn, and he said the officials at Lakefront Airport were blaming the crash on the storm and on pilot error; John had apparently decided it was unnecessary to read the wind indicator on his approach to the runway, and had attempted to land downwind.

Airey wanted to take us both to his house for a while or send Felicity to stay with us, but Mama said, Thank you, no, I wouldn't dream of exposing everybody in your family to these colds of ours. Then she told Airey she appreciated his coming, and she went upstairs and lay on her side, on top of her bed. She was still dressed in her robe, and when I talked to her she looked right at me but she wouldn't answer me. I gave up after a while, went on into my own room, and tried to make some sense out of *L'Histoire de Pierre Lapin,* a storybook about Peter Rabbit that Aunt Mathilde had given me, that was all in French.

"Flopsaut, Mopsaut, Queue-de-Coton, et Pierre," I read aloud, trying to concentrate on pronunciation.

I felt that if I let myself start worrying, I might not be able to stop.

For weeks after the accident I dreamed every night of Honey; I saw her seated, smiling, next to Mama at our table on a Sunday afternoon, or holding the baby David for the ladies to admire; I heard her knock on our window, seeking shelter from some other, lesser storm. My mother grew suddenly, dramatically paler, as if Honey's death had drained some of the life-force from her own body.

Some nights I heard Mama wake, screaming, from nightmares. The first time that happened, I ran into my parents' bedroom and stood by the bed while Rand held her and she cried out to him what she had dreamed: Honey was frozen, she had been placed in a big rubber bag and locked away in a freezer, but her eyes were open, she could see, and she was in agony, she was crying for help because her soul was trapped there inside her body. Because nobody buried her, Mama wept, nobody even buried her.

That was the first I knew that Honey's body had never been found, that she was still down there somewhere, in the frigid depths of the lake.

Ten days before Christmas, further tragic news was delivered to us.

The stock-market transaction which John McCaleb had let Rand in on, the "sure thing" involving the imminent merger of two off-shore drilling equipment companies, proved to be a bust, a dead end reached via an erroneous insider's information tip that cost John's broker his license and cost everyone else involved their total investments. For a time there was wild speculation concerning the filing of lawsuits against the stockbroker; then somebody's lawyer explained what it meant to enter a courtroom, as a plaintiff, with unclean hands, and the speculation ended.

When Rand told Constance there would be no lawsuit after all, no chance of recouping any of the money he had lost, and we would be lucky not to lose our house, too, she just stared at him, her eyes shadowy, as if she were trying to make some sense of the awful things he was saying to her. We were at the dinner table, but none of us was eating what Mama had cooked: fried corned beef hash and broiled tomatoes.

"What you're telling me, then, is that we have nothing at all to fall back on. We're out of money completely now, is that it?"

"I haven't lost my talent along with my bank account, have I?" said Rand. "I'm still working, darling. I won't let us starve. But yes, you're right, we have nothing to fall back on, as you put it." He smiled at her. "Maybe you'd better get Aunt Mathilde to say a couple of novenas that I stay in good health."

Constance said, "I don't know how to do anything; nobody taught me how to do anything that pays any money. If I had even a little money, I could take one of those typing courses. Can we afford for me to take a typing course?"

"Sell Rosehue," I heard myself saying. "It's mine, Lady-Sidonie gave it to me, and I can give it to you to sell; I want you to sell it. It's got some loose boards and some cracks, but Felicity told me I'd have a good sum of money someday, if I sold it. I don't care about the summers and everything, go ahead and sell it now."

"Thank you, sweetheart," said Daddy, reaching over to pat my hand. "I thought about selling Rosehue, but I didn't want to upset you."

Constance said, "You sicken me."

Startled, I looked over at her, afraid she was talking to me, more afraid she was talking to Rand.

She was talking to Rand.

"And you know what else? You've sickened me before now. The day Courtenay was over here, for instance, playing with Clay-Lee, and they asked you to take them to that hobby shop on Carrollton Avenue? Courtenay came to me later and told me that when she and Clay-Lee asked you for money to buy some things at the shop, you said you didn't have any, and drove them home again." Constance laughed. "She thought you were just being mean; I guess she thought that because you didn't even have the sense to be embarrassed."

"Mama, that day was my fault," I said quickly. "See, Daddy had given me my allowance, and he thought I still had it, but I had already spent it on—"

"On what? Some two-cent stamps? What *is* your allowance, by the way, a nickel a week? Just think, Clay-Lee, if you saved it all up, at the end of a year you'd have, let's see, you'd have a cool two-fifty."

Daddy got up from the table and started for the front door. His face looked slack and gray, and there was gray in his hair, too. I'd never noticed that before.

"The child isn't giving up Rosehue, I don't care if we have to double Mr. Louvier's rent," Constance screamed after him. She had started to cry, though. She was so thin in the face that her tears fell straight down without curving, the way raindrops do on glass.

Rand stopped and looked back at her.

" 'The child isn't giving up Rosehue.' Who are you referring to, Constance? Clay-Lee? Or yourself?"

"She meant me, Daddy," I started to explain, but he was already gone.

The Christmas that followed the double tragedy of the McCalebs' loss and the loss of Rand's investment was a tragedy in itself. Constance not up to opening her presents or trimming the tree; Constance crying out in her sleep for her daddy on Christmas Eve, waking the whole house; Constance leaving the dinner table Christmas Day to lock herself in her bedroom and weep for all the irretrievable opportunities of her life; Aunt Mathilde crying outside the bedroom door, "Now it's Christmas, Constance! Remember how the Judge loved Christmas Day? Seeing you all smiles over your presents? Honey, your daddy'd die all over again to see you so beside yourself!"

Daddy leading me back to the dinner table, his hands as cold as mine.

After Christmas came a series of Mama's intermittent angry silences, lasting for days at a time, during which I tried to guess which one of us, Daddy or me, Constance was holding some old grudge against. My mother looked as pale and distracted as she had during those weeks after she had smashed in the skull of the Negro intruder on Camp Street.

When I try now to place events in their proper sequence, it seems to me that it was then, shortly after that awful Christmas, that Constance began to drive alone to Covington, to spend days and nights there in the house on the Bogue Falaya, taking only Mishka for company, although I asked more than once to accompany her. One afternoon I came home from school and found my father, drinking alone, in their bedroom.

For the first time, his speech was slurred when he spoke to me, and I became so frightened, so anxious to make him feel better, that I suggested the two of us take the next bus to Covington and surprise Mama.

"Your mother's had enough surprises," he told me. "That's just the trouble." He poured more whiskey into his glass. "Lower the window shade there when you go out, will you, Clay-Lee?"

After that, I was particularly careful of what I said to Daddy. I was afraid to tell him things I didn't completely understand, fearful that I would unintentionally give him something more to worry about. That was why I never mentioned to him Felicity's visit to our house on Camp Street, one afternoon that same winter.

I didn't know Felicity was in the house at all that afternoon till I looked out my mother's bedroom window and saw the yellow convertible parked in front. Felicity had left the top down, and some of the Irish children who lived at the corner were climbing all over the upholstery and violently twisting the steering wheel, as if they were wrestling a wild animal to the floor.

I debated for a minute on whether I should go downstairs and tell Felicity what was going on, but that seemed an Aunt Mathildeish thing to do, so I opened the window and shouted to them to leave my father's car alone.

"Yer father's car, me sweet arse," one of them yelled back at me. "Yer father drives a goddamned Kraut tricycle."

I slammed down the bedroom window and was trying to decide what to do next when I heard the sound of angry voices from downstairs. I walked as far as the top of the stairs and sat down to listen. Eavesdropping had become such a regular diversion in my life that I didn't even feel guilty about it anymore.

"Somebody ought to lock you up every Mardi Gras! That's two separate Mardi Gras's now you've managed to get your ass in a sling!"

That had to be Felicity speaking. My mother would never mention anybody's ass.

"Why don't you just come right out and tell me what you mean, Felicity? What is this veiled reference to Mardi Gras?"

"Oh, I'll be happy to unveil it. I'm talking about Rand Calvert, and I'm talking about Clement Calvert. Both of whom you met on Mardi Gras, although several years apart, and I'll let you fill in the rest. Just answer me this: on your little jaunts to Covington with this individual, do you feel 'completely safe, completely protected' like you once told me you used to feel with Rand?"

"Who told *you* about the so-called jaunts to Covington?"

"Apparently Uncle Baby Brother's got the town crier working for him, posing as a chauffeur. Every Negro from the Garden District in New Orleans to Three Rivers Road over in St. Tammany Parish knows you've been out there with Baby; it's only a matter of time before it's leaked to the local Ku Klux Klan, and on up from there."

"He likes to drive out to the country for lunch, Felicity. So what?"

"What is it that pulls you to him, Lamb? The money? The ruthlessness of the man, his power? The fact that he's night-and-day different from Rand? Or is it just that he reminds you of your father? I'll bet he loves making you feel like Daddy's little girl again."

Silence.

"Lamb? You don't need me to tell you what you're doing, do you?"

"No, but I have a feeling you're going to tell me anyway. Felicity, please, please, spare me the latest diagnosis you've picked up from your psychiatrist."

"You know what I told Airey once? I forget when it was, what made me finally see it, but I told him, 'Constance is an extremist. If she liked the taste of alcohol, she'd be a drunk.' And he agreed with me!"

"What a shock, Airey agreeing with you! When *hasn't* Airey agreed with you?"

"There's something peculiar about this conversation, and now I know what it is: you haven't gotten angry. Why hasn't what I said to you made you angry?"

"I don't allow myself to get angry with an illusion. That's all you are, Felicity, you're just a figment of your own imagination, and so is all this about my 'jaunts' with Clement Calvert."

"You don't deny you've been seeing him, though. Are you aware, at all, of the way he looks at you? Sometime before I die, I'd like to have a man look at me like that, I admit it, but not a man like *him*. And what about Rand, what if this got back to Rand?"

"Believe it or not, Rand's a big boy, he can rise above petty gossip. And you can believe this or not, too: I love Rand. I'm still *in* love with him, in spite of everything that's gone wrong for us. I'd never do anything that would hurt Rand, in the end."

"Wait a minute. This is beginning to make a little more sense. Now don't tell me, let me guess: Uncle Baby has another financial 'proposition' for you! Am I right?"

"Well . . . yes, in a way. You know how Rand's been talking about selling Rosehue, ever since he lost all that money on John McCaleb's big scheme? I don't want that to happen, Felicity; Rosehue's the only thing we've got left! And Clement can help me save it, he—"

"Holy shit. This is a whole lot worse than I first suspected, than the idea of you giving the rotten bastard a little thrill, out there on the back porch overlooking the Bogue Falaya. Remember Baby's last 'proposition,' the one that almost got Rand sent up the river to Sing Sing? You'd better be careful, you can't afford—"

"He's dying, Felicity! Clement's dying!"

There was a brief silence. Then Felicity said, "I don't believe you. I don't believe *you* believe *him*! How old are you now, twelve? He's just trying to get you to feel sorry for him, which leads me back to my first theory: he's after your little twat, plain and simple."

"I'm not even sure what that word means. I don't want to know what it means! I want you to stop all this! And I want you to *swear* to me you won't tell anybody Clement's ill."

"Don't worry, I don't like making people laugh at me. Constance, I know I sound like I'm being hard on you, but it's only because I love you! I know our friendship isn't what it used to be, and I know my drinking and my big mouth are mostly responsible for that. But just listen to me one more time: why don't you have a baby, you and Rand? Give him a son. He loves you so much, Lamb, and he looks half the time, now, like's he's grieving over something; he's grieving over *you*, and the way you've been ignoring him. Give him a little boy."

"But plan to nurse it, right, Felicity? You told me once, a long time ago, that Rand Calvert wouldn't have any spare change lying around to buy steak for a baby and me, and it was true then, and it's still true."

"You'll manage, you always have. My advice stands—give him a son."

"Why don't *you* offer to give him a son? You've been dying to start that fire up again for years, haven't you? I'm not even sure you haven't already done it."

Loud, limping footsteps across the wood floor, and then the front door slamming. By running on my toes, I managed to get to the upstairs front window again in time to witness Felicity throwing the Irish rats out of her convertible and spraying gravel in their faces as she zoomed down the street.

A child's mind has a selective, protective memory. For a long time, the only things I allowed myself to consciously recall about my mother's argument with Felicity were that she was still in love with my father, and that Uncle Baby's "proposition," whatever it was, was going to save Rosehue before he died.

A little later, though, it appeared that my mother had taken to heart a different segment of that conversation.

13

Spring came, and suddenly Constance began to take new interest in the Camp Street house. One afternoon, I returned home from school and there was Shine, Deaf and Dumb William's nephew, busy with a paintbrush and a bucket of white paint, touching up the woodwork in our downstairs rooms. Another day, a wizened varnisher came to polish the wood floors; that same evening Constance cooked a lamb roast with exotic spices and served it to Daddy and me by candlelight.

She took to sitting on Rand's lap while he drank his coffee after dinner; once I heard her teasing him about Molly Luce, his model at that time. Mama wanted to know if Rand was in a Rubens phase, was that the reason he'd picked a girl with all that puppy fat on her? Rand seemed cautiously delighted with this new Constance, but it seemed to me he was afraid to break some mysterious, fragile spell by hugging her too hard or laughing without restraint.

One night, later that same spring, Constance placed a little beribboned box beside my father's dinner plate.

"What's this?" he said.

"You'll have to open it and see," Mama told him. She put one of her hands on top of his for a minute. "I warn you though; if you don't like it, I can't take it back."

230

Inside the box was a small, sterling silver napkin ring, newly polished, its edges delicately beaded. Engraved on it in a fine script was the word "Baby."

"It belonged to my mother," Constance said. "I found it in a box of old keepsakes I was going through last Christmas. Isn't it a pity it was lost the whole time Clay-Lee was little?" Rand was smiling so wide his teeth seemed to have suddenly multiplied. He stood up, the silver trinket in one hand, and with his other hand he pulled her close and hugged her. "When?" he said. "Sometime in October," she told him; at Mama's feet Mishka sighed on cue.

At the beginning of the summer, my parents announced another surprise: we would be moving to Covington to live there year round, and return to the house on Camp Street only for certain special weekends or when Daddy had to come to New Orleans on gallery business. Mama seemed anxious now to leave the city. She said Dr. Villere had told her the clean pine air in Covington would help to ease the added strain, brought on by the pregnancy, on her lungs. Daddy obligingly decided he could paint better out in the country.

"Better for Baby, better for Papa the artist," explained Mama to Aunt Mathilde, who sat, horrified, in Mama's bedroom one night just before we moved, watching her fold my grandmother's wedding linens into wicker trunks. "For once I hope you're being sarcastic, sugarplum," remarked Aunt Mathilde. "One too many trips to idiotic Ben Crowell's General Store and you'll be hopping the night train for New Orleans, if there is a night train. And what's going to happen to all the things you have to leave here, your rugs and draperies, for example? Dry rot and vandals, wait and see!" To Aunt Mathilde's apparent disappointment, the bachelor gentleman, Mr. Ronald Louvier, who rented out the other side, had already told Mama he would be glad to keep an eye on things in our half.

"Don't give it thought one," he reiterated on moving day, watching from the porch with appraising eyes as the moving men carried past our furniture and Daddy's artwork. My mother was displaying a certain cold dignity that seemed to intimidate the workers, and they paused almost patiently at the front door as she examined each piece of furniture to be sure it was properly wrapped in quilted bunting. I decided she looked too queenly for our tiny wooden porch; Uncle Baby's showplace on Audubon Boulevard was more her style. Standing quietly nearby, as always, was Mishka, as dignified as Mama was.

Daddy and I drove to Covington together, ahead of the moving van, leaving my mother in New Orleans to finish closing up the house. "Mishka and I will drive over in a day or so," she told my father. "There're a lot of little details still to see to, and Clement said he'd let me use his Renault." It occurred to me then that she was the only person I'd ever heard call Uncle Baby Brother by his given name.

All the ride across the lake, I thought about how wonderfully my luck had changed—my mother seemed finally happy. We should have moved to Covington long before now; Sis Honorine always had said that New Orleans damp could chill anybody's soul after a while. The whole world looked different now, Constance told my father. Maybe that was because of the new baby coming. "This baby's going to be a boy," she said to him. "And he'll have everything on earth he wants. I'm going to name him after Daddy." I thought she meant my daddy, till I found scraps of paper on her desk with "Thomas Benedict Alexander Calvert" written on them.

Daddy and I reached St. Tammany Parish just after noon. I was glad to see Rosehue again, glad to stand on its back porch, which was only fifty yards away from the Bogue Falaya River. I had a vivid memory of a water-skiing accident one night the previous summer, on that river; of my mother running with me by the hand to the water's edge and of a blond girl screaming, surrounded by noisy people and holding onto her twisted and bloodied arm. Most of the time, though, the back porch was as still as midnight, and it was easy to forget that a dusty road with other houses, other children, on it ran in front of the place.

By sundown of the day Daddy and I moved in, my hands were stained black from unpacking newspaper-wrapped glasses and china. But the knotty-pine kitchen was ready for Sis Honorine, and my own room, off the pine-floored center hall, kept calling me in to look at it one more time, like a long-awaited letter from a secret love. My mother's Louisiana four-poster had been placed in the biggest bedroom, up the hall from mine, the room with cross ventilation. In the gray light of twilight the bed seemed to rise and fall with the currents of wind, its down comforter billowing over the sheets like a satin sail. My father had spent weeks repainting and polishing the house, and the smell of varnish was in the air, as compelling as the scent of sweet olive near the back porch. There were new screen doors, front and back, and I liked the sound they made slamming, a magic summer sound.

That night we were too tired to cook, and had our dinner outside, sitting on the porch steps and eating fat black olives from the can, and Creole tomatoes. The tomatoes we ate like apples, salting them at every bite and feeling the juice on our chins. Daddy was drinking beer from a green bottle; I pretended my own green one, full of ginger ale, was the same as his. It was easy to feel grown-up around my father; he asked a lot of questions, not dull ones like what was I learning in school, but good questions, like which of the legendarily dumb McQueen twins did I think had better sense, and why; or how did I think he'd look with a full-grown beard? When we finished the olives and tomatoes I picked up the olive cans and threw the juice on the grass. Some of it splashed on the newly painted steps. That was one of the last sloppy things I did all summer.

Early the next morning, Sis Honorine called me into the kitchen for breakfast, and I sat at the white wooden table and watched Sis make *pain perdu,* lost bread—stale French bread

slices dipped in egg and milk and fried in butter. Puffs of powdered sugar sailed over the stove top, driven by Sis's firm hand
on the shaker.

"Thank God you all back in Covington again," she said, leaning against a counter and watching me eat. "No more mean
wolves walkin' the streets instead of human people, like in New
Orleans. You can't open your door without letting in ax murderers."

I had the same feeling of safety, not from ax murderers, exactly, but from all the trouble that haunted our Camp Street
house. It was hard to believe, here in the simple country sunlight, that only a short time ago, I had been afraid of awakening
in the night to find my mother gone. The truth was that she
was so aloof at times, so sadly beautiful, that her continued presence never seemed guaranteed. At times I even feared the loss of
both of them, Mama, and Daddy with her; at any moment they
might start off on some private journey together, leaving me behind.

I went over to Sis and hugged her wide waist, my cheek
against her apron that smelled of detergent and laundry starch.
"I'm glad we're back in the country, too," I told her. "Any time
you want, I'll take you and your brother Orville sailing. We can
go way out on Lake Pontchartrain if you want. Daddy taught me
how to sail last summer."

"Catch me on a boat with a baby at the wheels," said Sis.
"How old your daddy thinks you is? Or were you born old, Clay-
Lee?" She tilted my face up and rested her other big hand on
my head. Whatever remained of the specters of Camp Street
vanished from my soul.

Sundays were Sis's day off. I went into the silent kitchen at
eight o'clock and fixed a breakfast tray for my parents; prize
oranges from Plaquemine and English tea in the thin china tea-
pot Uncle Baby had brought Mama from his trip to Paris the

summer before. The cups and saucers were pink and blue, painted with a white cloud design. English muffins and Sis Honorine's lemon-rind marmalade.

"Clay-Lee? Just leave it in the hall there for a minute," came my father's voice through their bedroom door. "Mama and I are discussing something now, but you get yourself some toast and milk and run over to the Jumonvilles' to play." Confused, I stood there a minute in front of the closed door. It was a Sunday, wasn't it? My mother had always told me Sunday was a family day; you didn't just show up in somebody's yard on a Sunday. I went back to the kitchen and ate an orange, and then went down to Sis Honorine's house and swung on the tire in her yard for a while.

At noon Sis called me into the gloomy room off her kitchen that she and Orville referred to as "the refectory." It had an oak plank table in it, with benches along both sides, and was as dark as the rest of their little house. Sis had gone temporarily blind when she was fifteen, following an attack of measles, and her eyes had been sensitive to sunlight ever since.

"Is your mama feeling well, Clay-Lee?" said Sis. She was in her white church dress, and she had on a high-swirled wig that made it hard to remember what she looked like weekdays, when she wore her hair tucked into a knot at the nape of her neck. "You said she hadn't been out the bed all day?" She put in front of me a plate that had a piece of bread with a hot meatball on top of it, and green pepper gravy dark as coffee.

"I hadn't seen her up yet when I left," I told Sis, watching smoke rise from the meatball.

"Soon as you finish, run on home and check on her. I know your daddy is with her, but you come get me all the same, if she says she needs me."

When I walked into the hall at home, Mishka was stationed in front of my parents' closed bedroom door. From behind the door came their voices, sounding faraway, like voices on a next-door neighbor's radio.

"Just what the hell is it you're afraid of, Lamb? No, don't shake your head at me, I know when you're afraid. Fear's the only thing that could have generated this monologue you've been performing for me. Why on earth do you want to move out of Louisiana?"

"I *told* you, living in Boston or New York, where everything is, could mean your painting would—"

"I can paint just as well in Louisiana, where, incidentally, I don't have to worry about losing you to pneumonia during the first blizzard. We'd have to uproot Clay-Lee from school, and she's happy here; I thought we'd all be happy here!" There was a silence, and then Daddy went on.

"Why do I detect the heavy hand of Uncle Baby somewhere in all this? Has another opening for the position of lackey opened up somewhere in his financial empire? I have to admit the idea of moving East appeals to me for *one* reason: We'd be rid of Uncle Baby—his lungs are shot from smoking too many Picayunes and living in London all those years. He's come South for life, or whatever's left of his life. If you ask me, Uncle Baby's ill; he looks like devils are chasing him all the time." Mama said nothing. Apparently Uncle Baby's secret was still safe; Constance hadn't told Rand that Clement was dying, and neither had Felicity.

"There are people with a lot of money up East, Rand."

"But I've got a new backer *here* now; I've got an influential backer from North Louisiana, who's extremely interested in this next gallery show. . . ."

"And you've got me carrying a child I wish was dead!"

"Jesus Christ, you know how to go for the jugular, don't you?"

The breakfast tray sat, undisturbed, in the hall; Mishka was too well-bred to touch a crumb. I went out to the screened porch and climbed onto the glider, swinging till the creak and the motion made me sick. Then I walked back to my room and sat at my pine desk, drawing dogs' faces till darkness came. The voices from my parents' bedroom had stopped.

As if the day hadn't gone on long enough, Uncle Baby Brother drove up in his blue Mercedes just at dinnertime. My mother had by then come into the kitchen in her wedding-present white satin robe from Aunt Mathilde. She was heating Sis's she-crab gumbo; she looked as pretty as if she'd spent the day on a sailboat, with her pink and white face tilted toward the sun. The heaviness of her gold-threaded brown hair was held back from her face with a violet ribbon.

"Oh, Lord, Clay-Lee," she said to me. We watched from the kitchen window as Uncle Baby came toward the porch, his new, brass-tipped cane clacking against the wooden steps. What's he need that silly cane for, I thought, even if he *is* twenty years older than Daddy? I knew why he needed a cane, though. I'd heard Mama say he had recently developed circulatory problems in the veins of his legs from too much drinking. "Be polite now," said Mama. "Clement's driven all the way from New Orleans." She sounded as though she were talking more to herself than to me. Mishka rose from her place near the stove and stalked away into the hall; she usually avoided Uncle Baby.

My mother took an aluminum colander of washed and cut strawberries from the refrigerator. Uncle Baby had a passion for Louisiana strawberries, and for George Dickel Sour Mash, and for making people feel uncomfortable. He certainly made *me* uncomfortable. Recently, he had taken to patting my hair whenever he first saw me, and then pulling back his hand as if my head were a hot stove.

I could hear my father moving around in his bedroom down the hall; a drawer slammed, the closet door creaked open. He must have heard the car and was getting dressed.

"Go get the little pink silk-shaded lamp out of your bedroom, and bring it out to the back porch, please, Clay-Lee," said Mama. She was holding a folded tablecloth in her arms. "I'm going to set the table out there, and that lamp casts such a nice light." She and I were united in our hatred of the yellow bug lamp Sis had installed on the porch ceiling.

By the time I got back out to the porch, having taken as much time as I reasonably could, Uncle Baby was helping Mama set the table. The white cloth looked blue in the thin summer darkness. On my way out, I'd passed Daddy in the kitchen, where he was ladling gumbo into the soup tureen. It struck me then how hungry he must've been, rushing dinner onto the table like that without even asking my uncle to sit for a while and have a drink. On the porch, I got down on my knees and plugged in the lamp, and centered it on the cloth. Its pink shade made a sudden rosy island of the table.

"Here's Clay-Lee!" shouted Uncle Baby. "You going to greet your favorite uncle on your knees? Where're those fancy convent-school manners of yours?" Another humorous reference to the fact that he paid my tuition at Sacred Heart. I hoped I was around to see his face when he found out Daddy had enrolled me for the fall term at Covington Elementary. From the kitchen came the sound of breaking china, and a loud "God DAMN it!"

As soon as we were seated and I got a good look at Uncle Baby's face, I could see he was either sick or deathly afraid of something.

"You use the filé powder in the gumbo, Lamb, or just okra?" said Uncle Baby, sounding as if he couldn't care less what was in the soup. He was just putting off whatever it was he really had to say.

"I'm not sure," said Mama, trying to signal Daddy with her eyes not to drink his dinner so fast. Daddy pretended not to understand and kept right on like somebody eating between buses at the Greyhound Terminal. "Sis Honorine made the gumbo."

"That's right!" said Uncle Baby. "I forgot. You all have a girl working for you. You people over here pay the Negroes next to nothing, don't you? Or does yours come just for the privilege of doing for the late Judge Thomas Alexander's only daughter?" Under the sarcasm, the heavy humor, I picked up something else. Sis Honorine said I was an old soul, that I could read people's hearts by the light in their eyes. I read urgency in Uncle

Baby's now, a fearful urgency, as if he had a matter of importance to see to, and was afraid of running out of time. His big hands fisted and flexed against the tablecloth. The thought came to me that maybe he'd had some more bad news from the doctor.

"If you'll excuse me, I've got a business matter to attend to on the telephone," said Daddy suddenly, balling up his napkin and leaving the table.

"A 'business matter'?" yelled Uncle Baby after him. "You're passin' up Louisiana strawberries, son! Come on back! The people who buy those cartoons of yours can wait till morning." Mama gave a sort of nervous laugh, and Daddy kept on going along the hall. As soon as I finished my strawberries, I asked to be excused. Mama got up when I did, and began to clear the table and to tell Uncle Baby in a hurried voice about the half-blind Negro woman down the road from Sis's house, who'd caught fire the day before while stirring a tub of laundry over an open flame. Constance half-turned and put one hand lightly on my arm, as if she didn't want me to leave her there on the porch with my uncle. Uncle Baby's face looked puzzled for a minute, then he stood up too.

"Airey de la Corde repeated a disturbing rumor to me at the Louisiana Club the other night," he said. "He had a few bourbons and got to talking about something his wife had told him. According to Felicity, you've been trying to talk Rand into leaving Louisiana, into going up East."

Constance froze for a few seconds. Then she said, "I just thought a city like Boston or New York might be the best place for him as an artist, for him and Clay-Lee and me, that it would help Rand's chances for—"

"What are you talking about? I'll help you, Lamb," said Uncle Baby quietly. He picked up an empty soup bowl, then another. "I've always said I would, remember? We help one another, you and I." The sound of a child crying somewhere along the riverbank was carried in on the warm air. I made a long production of unplugging the pink-shaded lamp and carrying it carefully back to my bedroom. I hated that lamp, and the whole strawberry-smelling night. There was a rosy glow to it that failed to disguise several kinds of dying.

Parts of that final family summer remain clearly in my memory. Even now I see the sailboat, *Mishka,* riding high above the waves of Lake Pontchartrain on sunny afternoons, I look back on warm windy nights when Sis Honorine served my parents dinner, just the two of them, on the hurricane-lamplit porch, while Sis's brother Orville taught me how to tap dance, our shoe soles clicking on the cracked stones near the river's edge, the sunshine burning low, like footlights, through the cypress trees.

There were, of course, a few bad days that summer. The Sunday I'd listened to Mama and Daddy discussing her strange urge to move us all up North was one bad time, and the other bad times almost always coincided with Uncle Baby's increasingly frequent visits. For some unclear reason he would quiz Rand about his career plans for the future, just as if he had always cared what my father was going to do next, and he would take it upon himself to see that Constance didn't sit in a draft, that she wasn't on her feet too long, that she didn't stay up too late at night. ("Now I know he's sick," said Rand, after Uncle Baby had driven away following an extended luncheon visit. "Only the fear of approaching death could make that guy act like St. Francis of Assisi.")

Sometimes, too, I would feel miserable whenever I thought of Honey and John, and their surviving child. Poor baby David, lost in the shuffle of Robilliard grandchildren, slated to be raised by Honey's mother, whose recurring emotional "states" had worsened after Honey's death. Neither Rand nor Constance ever talked of the McCalebs in my presence, and I believe that even when they were alone together the painful mention of John and Honey must have been avoided. The night she died, my mother called out Honey McCaleb's name. Other than on that occasion,

I heard Constance speak of her friend only once that entire summer, and that was to, of all people, Anna Hoff.

It was the night before the Fourth of July. Mama and I had walked to McQueen's Drugstore on Lee Road, to buy pineapple ice cream and cherries for our sailboat picnic the next day, and as we stood in the checkout line we saw Anna Hoff and her roommate, Cottel, the mute, waiting just ahead of us. Anna was holding an odd assortment of items: a box of Ace bandages, a tin of sugar wafers, two red candles and a blue one. I wondered idly what kind of holiday celebration they were planning. Maybe a sack race by candlelight, with the sugar wafers for the winner and an Ace bandage for the loser? Anna suddenly lost control of the cookie tin and it fell onto Cottel's foot; Cottel emitted a loud, enraged grunt, the sound of which caused an elderly lady at the prescription counter to place her hand over her heart. As Anna rose from retrieving the tin, her narrow eyes met mine and her nostrils flared.

"Good evening," said Constance, behind me. "How have you been, Miss Hoff?" Anna shrugged. Mama put her hands on my shoulders and I could feel the tenseness in her arms. "You know you did that friend of mine a rotten turn," she said teasingly to Anna. Her voice sounded high and falsely gay. "Remember how you told her last summer, when you read her palm, that you saw a stone? But she never got that emerald she'd been wanting, after all. She's quite upset with you, Miss Hoff; she wants me to ask you what you meant!"

The German woman took a carefully folded five-dollar bill from the pocket of her seersucker dress and handed it to the checkout clerk. Then she motioned to Cottel to pick up their bagful of purchases from the counter, and just before the two of them went out the door, she turned and spoke to Mama.

"Don't play games with me," said Anna Hoff. "I know she's dead." Mama and I stood there watching through the glass storefront till Anna and Cottel disappeared from view, walking along single file into the darkness.

The next morning, Constance wasn't feeling well, so Daddy and I went sailing by ourselves; we took the *Mishka* out over the lake for most of the day. With her red and white sail, her yellow-striped hull, she was the sportiest of the smaller boats, and my father the blondest, the best-looking, of the sailors. Women with sunburnt shoulders and sky-blue eyes smiled at him as they glided past on other boats. At the tiller of the *Mishka* he was anyone they took him for: a golden-haired banker, a lawyer trained in the Napoleonic Code, a cotton broker on holiday from the Exchange. *Mishka* had come, inevitably, from Uncle Baby; her name had come from Judge Alexander's last gift to his daughter. Still, my father loved the little boat; I liked to watch his face as he scoured her deck or raised the jib or just stood on the smooth, wooden pier, looking at her in the fading daylight. That Fourth of July I asked him why Mama had named the boat after a dog, instead of "Windswept" or "Lamb Chop" or even "Sweet Clay-Lee." "I guess the name reminds her of something, honey, just as Mishka herself does," he told me. Then he sighed, and looked away. "Something rich and simple and impossible to find again. It reminds her of her life before she married me."

"Daddy," I said. I wished, sometimes, he would remember I was a child, that there were things I shouldn't have to hear. I whistled all the way home so he wouldn't try to speak to me again.

14

That last weekend of August, hurricane warnings had been issued by the National Weather Service for the entire Gulf Coast, from Galveston, Texas, to Apalachicola, Florida. I spent Friday morning in my bedroom, switching my flashlight on and off and checking my supply of Lorna Doone cookies. The kitchen had been stocked with candles and canned goods, bottled water and radio batteries. The next morning I awoke to a green-smelling breeze blowing through my bedroom window. The sky was light gray, a winter sky, mismatched with the warm wind that lifted my hair as I walked along the hallway to the kitchen.

"Clay-Lee, your feet are going to be wide as bed slats, you keep running around without shoes on," said Sis. She poured a half-second's worth of coffee into a cup of hot milk and gave it to me. "Your mama would as soon walk on hot coals as set foot on a floor without her slippers on."

"Where is Mama? Still in bed?" How could she lie there in her room, when the smell of coffee and biscuits had pulled in even a few of the mean tomcats from across the road, two of whom were at that moment staring at me through the open window?

"Your mama's awake, but resting," said Sis. "Your daddy called early this morning and said it don't look like he'll get here till tomorrow." My father had been in New Orleans all week, arranging details for his show at the Cooper Gallery on Royal Street. The show was scheduled to open the Saturday after Labor Day. I wished he was back in Covington. My fascination with hurricane weather was touched with fear; something in the smell of blown-apart leaves and in the look of the dark mornings reminded me of a picture book Uncle Baby had given me. It was about a little boy who didn't "appreciate" the things he had, and so he awakened one day to a cold and empty house, a backyard dark and windswept. One by one, all the living things he had failed to love for what they gave him appeared and took away their gifts: his lamb's-wool slippers, his goose-down pillow, his milk, his eggs; even his wooden bed. Hurricane weather looked to me just like the drawings in that awful book.

Sis sat down heavily in the chair across from mine, a mug of coffee in her hand. "Just between you and me, I'm worried about your mama," she said. Her eyelids fluttered rapidly behind her glasses, like they always did when Sis was angry or upset. "She doesn't look right to me. White-faced, like there's something on her mind." I tapped my coffee spoon against my cup to drown her out. Sis Honorine was another one. I was a child! It was true that I eavesdropped a lot, but, still, why did grown-ups expect me to listen to things that made me afraid? People went out of their way to protect other children from the truth. Jimmy Leche, a second-grader who lived down the road, had a mother who'd never even told Jimmy that his father had fallen into a paper mill last Holy Thursday. Jimmy still thought his daddy was on a holiday at Six Flags Over Texas, out in Dallas–Fort Worth. Born old, Sis Honorine said I was. I was sick of feeling old as a grandmother and powerless as an infant at the same time.

"Weola Wiggins said to me last Friday night, 'Why your Miss Constance went and got herself having another child after her baby all grown and out the way?' I said to her, Weola, sometime the Lord send what He choose, when He choose. 'Suffer the little children to come unto Me.' "

Usually I got a good silent laugh out of Sis's twisted interpretations of the Gospels, a laugh sweet with all my convent-school superior scriptural knowledge. I didn't feel like laughing that morning. Maybe that was what Jesus had meant, anyway. Maybe He was thinking of Mama, pale, and moving heavily, when He said that about suffering, and little children.

Sis's face brightened, and I turned around to see Weola Wiggins herself, standing in the kitchen door.

"Miss Weola, what's that you got on?" called out Sis. "What you wearing a foxtail stole around your neck for, the end of August!"

Weola strolled in and leaned against the sink. "Mornin', Clay-Lee," she said to me, flinging the scrawny tail of the unfortunate fox over one skinny shoulder. "What I'm wearing it for?" she said to Sis. "This the fur Miss Bonnie Snowden give me on her deathbed, and if I drown in this hurricane, he drownin' with me. I won't be floatin' facedown twenty seconds before one of those young girls in my church circle be ransackin' my chest of drawers for this animal."

I wrapped my buttered apple square in a paper napkin and went out on the porch steps to sit. For some reason, I didn't want to be in the kitchen, should Weola and Sis begin discussing my mother's health.

After a while, the screen door creaked open, banged shut, and Weola departed. "How long you been sitting out here, watching the wind blow?" came Sis's voice behind me. "I thought you'd be under the bed by now, with your scariness." I tilted back my head and looked at her, upside down. "You want to carry in your mama's breakfast tray?" I went in and took a silver tray from the kitchen table. Strong coffee, and Sis's tiny biscuits and a china pot of strawberry jam.

Mama was sitting up in bed, a thin lacy bed jacket around her shoulders. At the foot of the bed lay Mishka, who lifted her long head in disapproval at my intrusion, then put it down again on her paws. Wind buffeted the pink down comforter, and lifted the white gauze curtains like confetti. I put the breakfast tray carefully across my mother's legs, and sat cross-legged on the little slipper chair pulled up near her bed.

"Clay-Lee, I've been listening to the radio," said Mama. "The weatherman says the storm is heading for Brownsville, Texas. Just the same, I'd feel better if your father were here. We still might get the tail end of the wind and rain." She picked up a biscuit and broke it in half, then put it down again. The veins in her hands stood out, blue as the china coffee cup. "I don't feel I can ride out a bad windstorm all by myself."

I wanted to ask, "Why not?" but the words sounded sassy in my mind. After all, it was no secret that Mama managed most things very well all by herself. She was so sure of her ability to decide things. "The inability to make decisions is a form of insanity," she used to say to Daddy, as he stood immobilized over a choice of neckties.

"I thought Daddy said, when he left, that he was driving back across the lake tonight," I said.

"I wasn't listening. He kept going on about his art show, his 'hanging.' One more word on that, and I might've hanged myself. Except I can't hoist myself up onto a chair anymore."

"Who's talking about gettin' up on chairs?" said Sis, coming in and standing near the side of the bed.

"We were just talking about the hurricane. Hurricane Greta, isn't it, Clay-Lee? I hate to say thank God it looks like it's turning toward Brownsville, but thank God. We can't stand another one like Gussie, remember, Sis?" Hurricane Gussie had ripped up the whole town of Covington in 1954, knocking over trees and houses, and even vacuuming up dead bodies from recently dug graves and scattering them in people's yards.

"Lord," said Sis. "I don't want no more days like that one! Be just my luck to have Weola Wiggins' grandpaw blown up onto my porch." Mr. Wiggins had taken a great fancy to Sis in the last years of his life, and Sis had admitted to me she had been less than sorry to see him pass on.

"Can I ask a friend over today?" I said. I missed Courtenay and Minette already, though they'd only been gone three days. All the de la Cordes were in New York City, where Courtenay was entering the eighth grade of the Sacred Heart boarding and day school at Ninety-first Street.

Mama moved restlessly in her bed.

"Oh, Clay-Lee, no, I don't feel like having children around to-day. Why don't you run over to the Scotts? Patricia Scott told me at church last Sunday she'd give you lunch anytime you care to come and play with Woodrow the Fourth."

Woodrow the Fourth was Mrs. Scott's beetle-browed eight-year-old. He was fat, smelled like old butter, and had been dig-ging the same hole to China in his backyard since the previous summer. You couldn't even go swing on his gate a minute with-out Woodrow the Fourth shoving a splintery shovel at you and telling you to dig.

"I guess I don't feel much like digging," I muttered. I lowered my voice another decibel. "Maybe I'll walk down to Renée Ewin's?" Sis was clattering the breakfast tray and Mama had her eyes closed and didn't hear me. That's how I found myself in Renée Ewin's orange bedroom, with its smell of drugstore dust-ing powder, and a green taffeta bedspread no one was allowed to sit on. "That little Renée Ewin was born with her ears pierced," I once heard Mama say to Daddy. For my mother, pierced ears carried the same social stigma as ankle bracelets and rhinestone-studded evening shawls. "I don't care if Jack Ewin's your sailing pal or not, he's married to trash," she told him, "and Clay-Lee's not going to play with her child." Ever since Mama had said that, Renée had had for me all the allure of a forbidden book.

When I arrived at her bedroom door, Renée was lying on the rug, listening to Freddy Fender sing "Holy One" on her Cisco Kid record player. She ignored me while she mouthed some of the words to the music, then she sat up to flip over the stack of 45s.

"When's your baby brother or sister coming?" she asked. It took me a minute to understand the question; Renée's mouth was coated with what I recognized, from a previous afternoon with her, as Mrs. Ewin's Talk About Red lipstick, and Renée was talking in a stiff-lipped monotone as if more vigorous speech would cause the waxy coloring to crack off and crash to the floor.

"Six weeks. The beginning of October," I said, trying to sound nonchalant. I had just recalled that Renée had last seen me at a birthday party two weeks earlier, to which I had been forced by Sis to wear black patent leather pumps. Renée's own feet had been dazzling, in pink vinyl sandals with a plastic daisy between her big toe and her second.

"Six weeks," said Renée. "God, she's big! My mama said she looks like she's going to drop it in the road any second!"

I tried to think of some remark devastating enough to counteract this slur. Meanwhile, Irma Thomas, on the *New Orleans, Home of the Blues* album, began to sing "It's Raining." I half-closed my eyes and dropped my head back, propping myself up, stiff-armed, on my palms, while Renée sang along: "I got the blues so bad, I can hardly catch my breath / The harder it rains, the worse it gets."

Renée said suddenly, "Are you sure you know why your mother's going to have a baby? Remember what I told you grown-ups *do?*"

She reached out and pulled me down beside her, whispering in my ear, familiar words in a new, personalized context. The anonymous bodies in Airey's medical text suddenly took on my parents' identities.

"What are you little people up to?" called Renée's mother up the stairwell. "I've got grilled cheeses and grape juice down here!"

The square orange toast, the squat, purple-filled glasses, looked like puzzle pieces on the table, tasted as papery as photographs of food in a ladies' magazine. Odd sounds and pictures tilted against one another in my memory; closed bedroom doors and soft laughter, bedspring noises and my mother's stomach bulging against the satin of her robe. The crash of my father's shoes landing on their bedroom floor. Eavesdropping's a sin, Sis Honorine says. "Carrying a child I wish was dead." I asked Mrs. Ewin for some plain dry toast and a glass of water.

It was late afternoon before my stomach felt a little calmer. I left Renée slow-dancing with a foam rubber pillow in her bedroom, thanked Mrs. Ewin for lunch, and started toward home, and toward disaster.

15

I had stayed at the Ewins' house too long; daylight was fading as I walked home along the side of the road. As I crossed our front yard, I saw that the screen door to the porch was banging in the rising wind, opening wide enough for me to slip inside. There was a feeling of emptiness to the house. The shutters of the windows along the hall had been pulled closed and fastened; gray light, like cigarette smoke, seeped through their narrow wooden slats. The breeze flattened the low-hanging branches of the cypress trees against the gabled roof, and their leaves made a shushing sound, whispered like a worn-out mother to a restless child.

The kitchen was shadowy and forlorn without Sis Honorine in it. The table was set for one; next to a white cloth napkin lay a note for me, from Sis: "Clay-Lee your mother resting. If need be call Orville friend Ducky down at the Reinfirmary or get Miss Nora Nagnes. Oysters in oven are for you." Sis, whose tendency to expect the worst had intensified during the hurricane watch, must have had some premonition of danger, and had gone to the trouble of suggesting means of transportation and assistance for Mama and me, should the need arise. Duckworth ("Ducky"), a friend of Sis's brother Orville, owned a pickup truck, which he parked each Saturday night at the nearby St. Stephen Infirmary emergency room. Ducky worked there on weekends, mopping up blood leaked onto the floors by accident victims.

Second in rescue power only to a front-wheel-drive truck was "Miss Nora Nagnes," a being born of Sis's combining of the first names of the Misses Nora and Agnes Hall, elderly spinster sisters who lived just down the road from us, were rumored to be immortal, and were always referred to as a set, like Ham Neggs.

I opened the oven door and lifted a tinfoil bonnet from the plate inside. Spaghetti and oysters, the edges of each hardening beneath an overheated cream sauce. My hand held the oven's chrome handle too lightly; the door's springs snapped suddenly into action, and it banged shut. I left my dinner in the oven and went across the hall to Mama's room. There was no response to my knock, so I turned the knob and went in.

Her room was full of light. After the dimness of the rest of the house, the brightness was as startling as a flashlight shone upon a sleeping face in the dark. My mother was standing in front of the cheval mirror, twisting a strand of her hair around one finger, tilting her head as she watched her reflection in the glass. It was a habit she had, caressing her hair like that, but every time I saw her doing it I felt as uncomfortable as if I'd suddenly come upon her sucking her thumb. She saw me come into the room, and her hand dropped to her hip.

She was wearing a blue sundress that fell into gathered folds from the high waist. It was like an angel's gown, and her bare white arms like wings as she raised the heavy silver brush and brought it down through her hair. Her face had a high color to it, across the cheeks, an unnatural glow like the light cast by my pink-shaded lamp across a white tablecloth. Her glossy mouth smiled at me in the mirror.

"Clay-Lee, can you keep a secret?" she said, and she turned and put her hands on my shoulders. I could feel the coldness of her fingers through my shirt. "Your Uncle Clement's driving over here from New Orleans tonight," she said, "and he's bringing some good news for us." Her teeth were chattering a little. I wondered if I were about to be let in on Uncle Baby Brother's famous "proposition" to save Rosehue. "You're aware your uncle's not been well, aren't you, Clay-Lee? You're big enough for me to tell you right out that he says he's spent the last seven years drinking himself to death, and he can't possibly have much time left to him. Nothing to live for, he told me a few months ago, never had a real family, outside of poor Ida Marie who couldn't even have babies." She wheeled back toward the mirror and leaned close to it, examining her face, her aqua eyes, in the lamplight. When she spoke again, a few seconds later, her voice was different, slower, an offhand monotone, as if she were talking to herself. From atop the slipper chair, Mishka watched her with grave, sad eyes.

". . . taken a lot of abuse from your daddy for being nice to Clement," Mama was saying. "But now he's going to die, and he's going to fix it so that he takes care of me, of all of us, in his will. Did you know up to now he's never even made out a will? A businessman like that. It's remarkable the things men will let slide if you don't urge them along. . . ."

Something twisted deep inside me. Combination, long unthought of, an old memory, safe's door grinding open, forbidden photographs inside.

I stepped outside myself then, and I saw my own still body as it had been, lying in the dark, in Uncle Baby's bedroom, my ankle broken open and the pain up my leg to my heart. I watched the shadowy forms of Constance and Uncle Baby, outlined in black, standing close together. I heard their voices saying words which were lost somewhere nearby, just beyond the reach of my memory.

A cat screamed somewhere in the yard outside the window. The storm had come, no hurricane, just heavy wind and rain. I heard hail against the glass, a gentle cracking sound like the splintering of tiny bones.

"Mama!" I didn't realize I had shouted her name till I saw her jump. "Mama, it's hailing." I went over to the window and pressed my hands against the chilled glass. "He won't come out in this if he's sick."

"It's only a little hailstorm, Clay-Lee. He's coming. He'll be with his lawyer; they're bringing papers for Clement to sign. He wants me to see the papers, too. See, Clay-Lee, here's where the secret part comes in." She knelt suddenly and took the trembling Mishka's head and held it gently against her breast, stroking the dog's laid-back ears. I'd never before seen Mishka frightened of a storm. For the first time, I realized that Mishka was growing old. Mama looked up at me. Her face had lost its color; she was so suddenly pale a scattering of tiny golden freckles was visible across her cheeks. "Clement and I, we want this to be a surprise for your daddy. You know how he is, honey, so proud, so hardheaded, about what he calls your uncle's charity. And this is probably the last time before the baby's born your daddy won't be with me every second! Clement's making us a present in his will, Clay-Lee, a gift, in honor of the baby's birth. He's going to die very soon, and when he does, he wants to leave a family. All he wants is to be the child's godfather, and have the satisfaction of knowing the baby's provided for, the best of everything. He's leaving everything to me, and to the baby, Clay-Lee, in his new will."

"If he's coming, I don't want to see him," I said. "I'm too tired to see him." My body felt as much like a dead weight as my mind; I had had enough of the endless analyzing the day's events had forced me into doing.

"That's not such a problem," said Mama. She pushed Mishka's head gently away from her and stood up.

"You can visit with us for a while and then have your dinner out on the porch, or you can eat in your room and go to bed early." She looked closely at me. "You look as worn out as if you'd been all afternoon picking blackberries."

"I'm sleepy," I said quickly, to forestall any questions about where I'd spent the day. "I'll eat in my room, and then go straight to bed."

"Be careful, then, not to spill anything," said Mama. "Roaches, remember." She walked over and picked up the silver hairbrush, then put it down again, too heavily. It clattered against the rosewood surface of the dresser. The little enamel clock on the bedside table said 7:30.

All I could taste was shallots. The cream sauce was studded with them; they bit into my tongue like shards of glass. I pushed the plate aside and put my forehead down on my writing desk. The wood felt cool against my skin. Every time I closed my eyes I saw something I didn't want to see: my mother's pale face, her nervous, darting hands; Mrs. Ewin's sickening lunch; Uncle Baby's brass-tipped cane; Weola Wiggins' foxtail stole drowning in the Bogue Falaya. I undressed, found a batiste nightgown in my dresser drawer and slipped it over my head. One of its tiny buttons at the neck popped off and threw itself somewhere against the floor. As I lay in bed, in the dark, I heard the sound of a car door slamming. Just beneath the surface of a dream about white beaches and pearl-studded oyster shells, I heard my mother's voice, in high, polite greeting, then the words "—the lawyer?" and the dream shifted. Renée Ewin and I spun round and round on a carousel fashioned from a powder box, while from the sidelines Irma Thomas, black-faced, white-toothed, laughed at us and sang the blues.

I awoke with a sense of something wrong, a feeling as tangible as a hot hand on the back of my neck. As my eyes became accustomed to the blackness of my bedroom, I looked toward the window and heard, rather than saw, that the hailstorm had ended. Only a heavy wind rattled the glass. The wind was strong enough to have knocked down a power line; my bathroom light was out, and the hallway outside my door was as dark as a train tunnel. The wrongness named itself: *Mishka*. With my father away, I hadn't thought to have the boat battened down against the storm. Unless she were anchored in the lake and moored with a long swing, her towline would sink under propeller and rudder, her hull would smash against some poorly tethered craft nearby. Worse than the conjuring up of the wreckage of the *Mishka* was the knowledge that it was too late to make amends. Even if the little craft was as yet intact, I was physically unable, by myself, to rig her for what remained of the windstorm. Jack Ewin, Daddy's red-faced sailing pal, would gladly have spent part of the afternoon making *Mishka* reasonably safe from ruin. Instead of asking him to, I had hung around his daughter's bedroom, sampling Mrs. Ewin's makeup and listening to disturbing information.

Suddenly it was important for me to know the boat was still whole. If I could get down to the water and see that by a miracle she'd been spared, I would feel that things were righted, leveled off, on this night that seemed somehow tilted toward disaster. As I groped in my closet for my slicker and a flashlight, my mind was as clear as if I had never been asleep. I felt my way along the dark hall—my mother was a light sleeper and I didn't want to risk awakening her with the beam from a flashlight—and passed her open bedroom door. Next to it, the door to my parents' bathroom was closed. I could hear Mishka, shut in, whimpering from fear of the storm just past or with desire to escape. I walked on. As I walked, I had the sensation of having done this before. When had I moved noiselessly through blackness, along a familiar hall, afraid of whatever presence waited for me at the other end? The wind blew a stronger gust, rattled the windows, and then I remembered: it was Mama, not I, who had made a nighttime journey, years ago, through our house on Camp Street. At the end of that hall a man had waited, someone whose face she couldn't see, who whispered "whore," and talked to her of death while he held its instrument against her skin. I was flesh of her flesh, my body had once been contained by hers; wasn't it fitting, then, that I should find myself reenacting a fragment of my mother's life? Her life was bound up, now and always, with mine. A little farther along, candlelight from the living room cast moving shadows on the doorframe. I looked in; a half-dozen low-burning candles stood on the mahogany chest. The room smelled not of candle wax but of tobacco, heavily of tobacco. Uncle Baby Brother must have spent the evening smoking Picayunes, and had left one lit somewhere close by. In the flame-shot darkness the high-backed Victorian settee looked to me like a deserted Mardi Gras float in a flambeaux-lit, silent parade. My mother's shoes, little silk and straw espadrilles, were on the floor; I almost tripped over them as I backed out of the room. Mama was so careful always about extinguishing candles before she went to sleep. I thought she must still be up, watching the storm from the front porch, from which direction I saw the faint light of more candles. In my bare feet I stepped over the threshold of the porch and found my mother in Uncle Baby's embrace. She was half hidden by his bulk there on the sagging glider, her legs, golden in the candlelight, flung out like a rag doll's. Then the position of their bodies shifted and her dark head was down over his stomach, as if she were sucking the venom from a snake bite. I stepped back, just beyond the doorway, into the hall. After a while I heard her voice.

"Please," she said, so much weariness compressed into one small word. "Please. I've kept my promises. Keep yours. Please! Keep yours." There was a high edge to her voice. It held a warning, a frantic note, like the voice of a teased and thwarted child a moment away from hysteria.

"You know what a 'renegade' is, Lamb?" His voice sounded thick, as if his lips were moving against flesh. "Basically, it's somebody who reneges. That's what I'm going to have to do here, honey. Not on everything; you'll still get what I said you would, only you won't have to wait till I die before you get it, because I'm not going to die.

"I didn't set out to lie to you, but I couldn't get you to see that there's more to your feelings about me than just being excited by the money. You were excited the first time you saw me, weren't you?"

The direction of the voice changed; he was sitting up, looking at her. "You know so much, Lamb. Didn't you know I wouldn't give up the two of you? Did you think I'd stand off to one side and watch Rand with you, just do nothing but rewrite my will, while he claimed my child?" Uncle Baby gave a short, deep laugh. "I took one look at you tonight in your pretty blue party dress, and I thought, She's all done up to celebrate my funeral. Well, we'll just change the celebration from funeral to wedding; you just claim your rightful position, the one you carved out for yourself when you agreed to this thing in the first place." The voice dropped a notch. "I promise you you won't be able to count all the money. That's one I won't renege on." My mother was standing suddenly. Her hair was a darker shadow among the others, obscuring the outline of her profile. "You told me he would never have to know," she said. "You promised just knowing it was yours would be enough." She began to cry, a keening sound from some empty place in her soul, bled dry of free will and of guile. . . .

I was sick and sweating; under the yellow slicker, my nightgown was sticking to my stomach. I turned and felt my way along the hall, my right foot almost sliding out from under me as it made contact with the slippery edge of a throw rug. In the darkness sudden visions came to me: a vision of Lady-Sidonie, cautioning me against the dangers of wild imaginings; of Anna Hoff with nostrils flaring, smiling as if she recognized in me a kindred soul, destined for early sorrow and disaster; of Clarence, Uncle Baby's houseman, his sad black face above me on a pain-filled afternoon: "You got something badly broke inside you, and you got a right to be sick over it . . ." I had just pulled off my slicker when the vomit came up and onto the floor. I switched on my flashlight and cleaned the floor using a big monogrammed towel from the top shelf of my closet, a towel my mother had told me not to touch. By the time I finished, I was cold with an anger so overwhelming that something within me shut down against it; it was as if an inner clamp shut off the power from my limbs, and I was only just able to move to the bed and lie on it, on top of the blankets. The heat began again behind my eyes.

I dreamed of Rumpelstiltskin. His wooden leg was brass-tipped; it clattered against the stone floor of the queen's chamber. In a rage he reached out for what she had promised him, but the queen was only a reflection in a looking glass, smiling at him, holding out her empty hands for him to see. In a shadowy corner my father sat, rocking a cradle with a yellow-striped hull. Inside it, gold coins glinted beside a silver napkin ring marked "Baby," next to a cracked oil portrait of the judge.

After so many years, how can I be sure about the hours? It must have been toward morning I heard her call for the first time. I remember my room was black with the special blackness that comes before the blue light of four A.M., and there was a dog howling. The howling was what awakened me first. I thought some terrified mongrel from the road had taken refuge under the house, then I realized it was Mishka. She had broken her rule of never entering my room, and she was standing just inside the door, crying. Interspersed with the dog crying was the sound of a distant call, my name, repeated over and over, with a questioning inflection at the end, "Clay-Lee? Clay-Lee?" I responded to it with the automatic obedience that was part of the pattern of years of life as her daughter.

She was lying in their bed in the dark. By the illumination from my flashlight, I could see her knees were up, high, comforter-covered mounds. The room was hot, hotter than the hall, hotter than my own room, as if a heated battle of some kind had recently taken place within its walls. I walked over to the bed and looked down at Mama. Her face was shining white with a disturbing inner luminosity; to avoid seeing it I switched off my flashlight and we were there in the darkness together, Mama and I.

"Go get somebody for me," she said. She was breathless, like a person struggling to speak during an attack of croup. "If the telephone's out, run down to the Scotts', or to the Jumonvilles'."

I stood there motionless, and silent.

"Clay-Lee? Hurry up! For God's sake, go on! Something's wrong, it feels like the baby's coming, but there's too much pain—"

She cried out then, a high, agonized wail, and behind me Mishka began to howl again and to nudge me hard with her head. I lost my balance, and as I put out one hand to steady myself, my palm touched a thick wetness on the bed sheet. Instinctively, I drew back my hand and wiped it clean against my nightgown. The room grew still again, except for the sound of the wind and the noises coming from my mother's throat as she tried to speak. . . .

Other words she had spoken came back to me. "You've got me carrying a child I wish was dead." She had said that to Daddy, though. I had heard her through their bedroom door, that Sunday morning, months ago. "You've got me carrying a child I wish was dead. . . ." Blaming Daddy for a monstrous child, born wooden-legged and grinning, the image of Uncle Baby with his cane. Daddy would rock the child against him, he would teach it how to sail. . . .

In the dark, Mama was calling Honey McCaleb's name, as if she could see her somewhere nearby. "Honey?" she said. "That bedroom window's locked! Run open it for her, Clay-Lee; she'll catch cold standing out there on the balcony in all this rain. . . ."

I remember thinking, This could be a dream, a dream brought on by fever. I am hot and sick, I've been sick since afternoon, and it's so hot now in this airless room.

The best thing for a fever is bed rest, hadn't Mama often told me that? I turned and walked out, and went down the hall to my own bedroom. What with Mishka's endless howling, I can't remember falling asleep at all.

My room was full of sunlight by seven o'clock. I lay and watched the pink and white clock on my night table, my head heavy and sore. I felt so ill that I was almost unable to move, while a current of panic beat against my stomach so violently that I felt as if I were going to wet the bed at any moment. The sense of wrongness was as heavy upon me now as the wind had been upon the roof the night before. At seven-thirty I heard Sis in the kitchen, clattering my mother's breakfast tray, then opening her bedroom door. In the seconds of silence that followed that opening sound, I heard my father's footsteps in the hall, heard him call, "Where's everybody? Still asleep?" Then Sis screamed out, "Mr. Rand!" and the nightmare images in my mind became daytime things.

The bedroom door was wide open. My father was almost on top of Constance on the bed, half-kneeling, holding her up against him. I could see the bed was full of blood, it was on the sheets, the comforter, on my father, too, reddening the knees of his wheat-colored trousers.

"Sh," he was saying. "Don't try to talk, Lamb. Don't try to say anything."

I looked past Mishka, who was lying like a failed guardian, a beaten sentinel, near the bed. Sis was standing, half-crouched, against the far wall. "Miss Lamb," she was crying, "Miss Lamb." Agnus Dei, Lamb of God, I remember thinking, words from the Canon of the Holy Sacrifice of the Mass. I looked at Mama, but her panicky eyes, huge in her gray face, were on my father's face. She seemed to be struggling to tell him something, an urgent message, a secret born of delirium and pain, that only he could understand.

"Mishka's dying," she said. She reached out and touched my father's face, his hair. With white hands she held onto the matching white of his shirt front. "There's nothing we can do! Mishka's dying. . . ."

I don't remember how long I stood there. The next thing I recall clearly is being hurried out of my mother's bedroom by either Miss Nora or Miss Agnes, who, along with several of our other neighbors, had suddenly stormed the porch and converged in the dining room, called together by whatever mysterious communication system had telegraphed approaching death up and down the road. What a thing for a child to see, someone murmured, a child should be protected from such sights. The red light spinning like a kaleidoscope atop the mud-splattered ambulance; Ducky, his eyes fixed on his shoes, his black hands trembling as he helped carry the laden stretcher across the porch; somebody's little boy, dressed in a Superman costume, running into the kitchen and demanding orange juice. I sat at the table in the sunny dining room, surrounded by women who spoke in hushed tones of childbirth and of the weather. "To look outside now, you'd never know there was a storm last night, but for the leaves everywhere," remarked Miss Corrine Saucier to me, patting my arm as she set a mug of cold chocolate in front of me. The base of the mug was wet; I wiped it carefully with my napkin and set it down again. My mother was very careful always about wet marks on the wood.

As I replaced my napkin on my lap, I saw on my white nightgown the stain of my own handprint, red with my mother's blood. I looked up suddenly, renewed panic pulsing in my throat, but none of the ladies was looking at me. They were all of them preoccupied with waiting.

The hall telephone finally rang at about ten o'clock. Miss Agnes answered it. "Well," we heard her say, "no one really expected they'd be able to save the child." Miss Agnes was deaf. She was shouting into the receiver the way deaf people do. "Well. God bless her," she said. "God bless them both."

The circle of listening faces in the dining room turned painfully toward me. "Poor lamb," someone said, a woman whose name I couldn't remember. She meant me, I felt sure. She was just a casual acquaintance, she couldn't have known my mother well enough to call her by her nickname. Across the table from me, Sis Honorine bent her face into her outstretched hands. "Suffer the little children to come unto Me," she said.

That same afternoon Aunt Mathilde arrived to drive me back

to her house in New Orleans. I sat in the rear seat of her immaculate little Chrysler and talked on and on, about the odd ensemble, taffeta and lace, that Miss Nora had been wearing when she'd burst upon the scene with Miss Agnes; about the kindness of the young vet who'd come to take Mishka for boarding; about the fact that the Causeway over Lake Pontchartrain was the longest bridge in the world. I talked about anything because talking kept me from screaming. Finally I saw, in the rearview mirror, Aunt Mathilde's horrified eyes upon my face, and after a while I became aware we were driving along Prytania Street, in the opposite direction from her house. "I'm taking you to Dr. Villere's," she snapped. "You don't look just right to me!" Aunt Mathilde belonged to that school of order-crazed women who despise victims, victims who by their clumsiness, their vulnerability, contribute to the wreckage of things.

When his receptionist told the doctor we had arrived, Dr. Villere himself came out into the waiting room, striding toward us, his white coat flapping, his arms extended, his tragic demeanor eliciting jealous stares from all the less important patients. He took me into his examining room, alone, and listened to me for twenty minutes or more, to my endless voice, confessing, self-accusing, admitting I had heard her in the night, heard my mother cry, and then killed her by lying in my bed while she bled to death, lay there waiting while it happened, until dawn. At the end of it he placed his hands on both sides of my head and looked at me as if the fever in my brain were some simple physical complaint.

"She has a slight elevation in temperature," he told Aunt Mathilde. "Events of the night too much for her, and she needs to blame somebody, so she blames herself." He touched my cheek with his soap-scented hands, and shook his head. "Not even God Himself should have to take the blame for this one."

Daddy had arranged for a private burial the day before Mama's, for James Rand Calvert, Jr. So it was just Mama there in the shiny mahogany coffin in the center aisle of Louisiana Avenue

Presbyterian Church. There had been no wake. Daddy always has had a horror of funeral homes and wakes; he says the mourners remind him of children at some unwholesome game. But there was no way he could prevent the gathering of the crowd of people who appeared at the church thirty minutes before the services began. After a hurried consultation with Aunt Mathilde, the funeral director obligingly opened the coffin.

For many years afterward, I heard people in Covington and New Orleans speak of how beautiful Constance Blaise Alexander Calvert looked at her funeral. Dressed all in white, her nails perfectly polished by Sis Honorine's loving hands, her hair caught back from her face with a wide, blue satin ribbon. Tiny golden freckles, souvenirs of days spent in the sunshine, across her sculpted cheeks, her perfect nose. "Come see!" Miss Nora, by the coffin, called to her sister in a heartfelt half-whisper. "She looks like a pretty little broken doll!"

I remember hearing the words "placenta previa" murmured, like an unfavorable verdict, by women among the mourners. Aunt Mathilde had already told me what it meant: a misplacement of certain blood vessels, a fairly rare condition whose symptoms usually occurred earlier in a pregnancy, so that the woman and her physician were warned and could avert such a tragedy as had befallen Mama. ("She must have been having signs of trouble, and couldn't decide whether they were serious or not," Aunt Mathilde had said to me while we were dressing for the funeral. "Imagine! Your mama, always so decisive, usually so sensible about everything!" She reached out and buttoned my collar, patted it distractedly. "My guess is she wanted to have this baby so badly she couldn't bear to admit, even to herself, that something might've gone wrong." She paused for a second. Was she waiting for me to add my obstetrical opinion? "And then, of course, it was too late, there was no help for her. . . . Now don't slump like that, Clay-Lee! . . . It's time for us to get into the car.")

A door near a side altar opened, and Felicity de la Corde entered the church. Earlier, she had sent a telegram to Daddy saying she was on her way. She had flown to New Orleans from New York that same morning, and she must have come directly from the airport to the funeral, because her black silk dress was rumpled, and there was a windblown look to her bright hair. I watched an usher guide Felicity to a front pew. She was limping more noticeably than usual. From exhaustion, I supposed, and from the effects of her legendary, long-ago car crash. . . .

I smelled Uncle Baby before I saw him; whiskey-scented sweat rose off him like incense at a Satanic Mass. He came up to me where I was standing with Miss Agnes, near a spray of carnations and Easter lilies sent by the choir ladies of Sis's church. Aunt Mathilde and most of the others had drifted toward pews near the altar; Aunt Mathilde was gesturing to me to join her—there were only a few minutes left before the services began.

"Hello there, Clay-Lee," Uncle Baby greeted me crazily, as if we'd bumped into one another unexpectedly at a church fair. I could tell Miss Agnes was trying to read his lips; she was too proud to have worn her hearing aid. "You're looking surprisingly well," he said. "Catch up on your sleep last night? With all the nocturnal tiptoeing around you've been doing, I thought you might've taken to your bed this afternoon." I had a sudden, awful urge to laugh at him. He stood there, watching my face, hoping for what? For me to look guilty, for my eyes to show fear? Then a sad thought came to me: Uncle Baby and I were alike; we were both of us good at playing deadly pranks, at making fatal moves. What could it matter to me, though, that he'd heard, above the noises of the wind that night, my stumbling footsteps, that he'd guessed the truth about my fall into madness that had ended in the tragedy of the morning? The only person he could afford to tell was forever beyond the range of his voice. Uncle Baby stepped closer, causing Miss Agnes to draw away. He was sickly pale and red-eyed. "Tell me something. How long was it after I left she started hemorrhaging?

Twenty minutes? An hour? I didn't want to leave her there, the state she was in. But she made me go! 'Clay-Lee's with me,' she said. 'She's as good as having a grown person in the house.' " His lips bobbed up and down at the corners; he couldn't keep them still. I wanted to get away; there was a sense of a breakdown coming, of some intolerable scene. I looked past Uncle Baby and saw my father, standing near the coffin. He sagged against Jack Ewin's supporting arm, then steadied himself again.

"Mr. Calvert, the service is starting." Sis had come up behind us, a comforting presence in her mourning clothes that were scented with mothballs and Evening in Paris perfume. She put her arm around my waist and guided me away from him, toward the front of the church. I looked back at Uncle Baby once. He had started to cry, his cheeks squeezed upward to his overflowing eyes. I turned away and bumped into Renée Ewin, who stood staring at me with awe: I was the first motherless child she'd ever known. As we passed her on the way to our pew she leaned toward me. A shaft of sunlight shone through a stained-glass window, glinted off the golden, cross-shaped earrings that she wore. "Your sailboat's smashed to pieces on the Jumonvilles' pier," she said.

EPILOGUE

My father and I, at Galatoire's . . . was it one night we had
dinner there together, or many nights, many hours I spent watching his face, calling back the past? These days, I find I am mistaken in my mind about a variety of things, and sometimes I
tend to confuse the Galatoire's dinners I had with Daddy with
the ones Felicity and I shared on Harmony Street. The endings
I have kept straight, though. I clearly recall helping Felicity up
to her bed our last Friday together, and of leaving my father in
front of Galatoire's, in the early evening lull before the nightly
tourist and college crowds converged on Bourbon Street. A wide-
hipped, blond policeman was leaning against one of the green
metal traffic barricades that transform Bourbon Street into a pe-
destrian mall after eleven o'clock. Around us the voices of the
night had begun.

"Does I have any MONEY?" shrieked a yellow-haired, orange-
lipped Negro to a beaten-looking black man walking beside her.
"Shit! Now I KNOW you crazy!" "You know what? You *mean*,"
marveled the man, as if he had just discovered it. "Get that glass
off the street! No glass allowed on the street!" the policeman
shouted to a startled-looking, bespectacled man who was pushing
a bottle-drinking baby in a stroller. "That's right!" came a drunken
female voice behind the baby pusher. "Roll the kid over to Pat

O'Brien's! They'll sell him a carton to put his curds and whey in!"

"You see what you miss by not visiting me in the Quarter more often?" said Daddy. He bent down and kissed my cheek. "Get home safely, baby. God bless." "Which one of you faggot Frogs threw the condom?" the cop was screaming to a band of nonchalant French sailors in tilted caps; the *Jeanne d'Arc* must have been in port. Daddy edged past the sailors and walked on.

He walks now with a slight stoop to his shoulders, but in spite of that I sense in him a hopeful expectation, a refusal to admit his own life ended when my mother's did, on a sad Sunday morning more than twenty years ago. Why has he never learned that the healing of a soul is not guaranteed in return for fees paid with sorrow and with time?

For a long time after my mother died, I vacillated between fear of the questions I expected him to ask me, and a perverse desire to tell him every detail of that terrible night, just for the comfort of seeing the desolation in his eyes turn to anger. But he asked nothing of me; as time went by, I realized that the revelation would only punish him, and he'd been punished enough: by my mother, for having taken her like some dazzled, amateur art thief takes a fine painting for which he hasn't the proper niche; by Uncle Baby, who denied him a king's-ransom legacy because Rand Calvert's daughter once helped Death snatch a treasure from his grasp. Besides, he hasn't the kind of soul, my father, that's properly rigged for risky voyages into the past.

Not long ago I came upon him going through a photograph album of pictures from a thousand summers ago, sitting crosslegged and hypnotized by his faulty memories of love. "You know how I like to remember her best?" he said to me, indicating some glossy, forever-frozen scene. "Dressed for sailing, for a day on the *Mishka*. Her hair down her back and her skin turning gold in the sunshine. Laughing. Remember that laugh she had, like a child's?" He looked down at the photograph he held in his hands. "Maybe that was the trouble, Clay-Lee; I married a child, and I couldn't comprehend the woman she'd become."

I thought then that he knew; I searched his face for bitterness beneath the pain. But I saw there only the old longing for continuance of the dream, his eyes fixed forever on an unattainable horizon. He looked the way he had when I was a child, the way I want always to remember him: my father, ageless and undefeated, as if he still were standing on that smooth pier near the water, in the wind that lifted sailboats to the sky.

*V*OICES OF THE *S*OUTH

Doris Betts, *The Astronomer and Other Stories*

Sheila Bosworth, *Almost Innocent*

Erskine Caldwell, *Poor Fool*

Fred Chappell, *The Gaudy Place*

Ellen Douglas, *A Lifetime Burning*

Ellen Douglas, *The Rock Cried Out*

George Garrett, *Do, Lord, Remember Me*

Shirley Ann Grau, *The Keepers of the House*

Barry Hannah, *The Tennis Handsome*

William Humphrey, *Home from the Hill*

Mac Hyman, *No Time For Sergeants*

Madison Jones, *A Cry of Absence*

Willie Morris, *The Last of the Southern Girls*

Louis D. Rubin, Jr., *The Golden Weather*

Evelyn Scott, *The Wave*

Lee Smith, *The Last Day the Dogbushes Bloomed*

Elizabeth Spencer, *The Salt Line*

Elizabeth Spencer, *The Voice at the Back Door*

Allen Tate, *The Fathers*

Peter Taylor, *The Widows of Thornton*

Robert Penn Warren, *Band of Angels*

Joan Williams, *The Morning and the Evening*